CHERYL A. HEAD

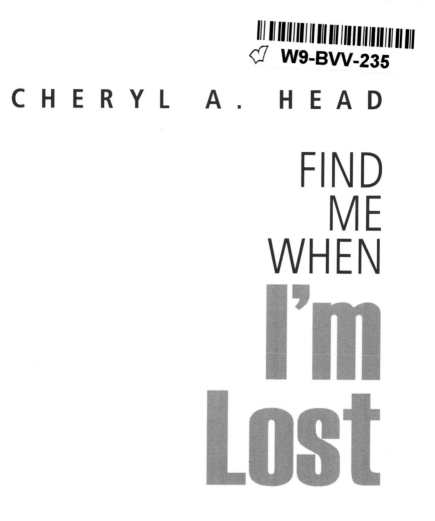

FIND
ME
WHEN
I'm
Lost

A CHARLIE MACK MOTOWN MYSTERY

Bywater
BOOKS

Ann Arbor
2020

Bywater Books

Copyright © 2020 Cheryl A. Head

Print ISBN: 978-1-61294-175-2

Bywater Books First Edition: July 2020

Printed in the United States of America on acid-free paper.

Cover designer: Ann McMan, TreeHouse Studio

Author Photo by: Leigh H. Mosley

Bywater Books
PO Box 3671
Ann Arbor MI 48106-3671
www.bywaterbooks.com

"It takes a fool to learn that love don't love nobody."

"Love Don't Love Nobody"
Written by Charles Simmons and Joseph Jefferson
Performed by The Spinners, *Mighty Love*, 1974

Acknowledgments

Thanks to my Bywater Books family:

Marianne K. Martin, Salem West, Ann McMan, Kelly Smith, Nancy Squires—and to Fay Jacobs and Elizabeth Andersen for all the heavy lifting.

Gratitude to my beta readers: AJ Head, Lynne Blinkenberg, Veronica Flaggs, and the Writers Writing Group.

Thanks to Teresa Scott Rankin for love, support, and encouragement.

Thanks also to these book reviewers, bloggers, interviewers, and podcasters who have supported the Charlie Mack Motown Mystery series: Angel Adams, MB Austin, Ed Aymar, Black Lesbian Literary Collective, Bolo Books, BookPeople's Mystery Bookstore, Book Riot, Scott Butki, Matt Coleman, John Copenhaver, Dru's Book Musings, Grady Harp, Greg Herren, Michele Karlsberg, Amos Lassen, Kristen Lepionka, Greg Levin, the *Lesbian Reading Room*, *The Lesbian Review*, *Lez Talk About Books, Baby!*, *Mystery Tribune*, *Monlatable Book Reviews*, *OjO*, Oline Cogdill, *Out in Print: Queer Book Reviews, Queer Words Podcast, San Francisco Review of Books, Washington City Paper*, and Jerry Wheeler.

And thanks always to Detroit for my roots, tenacity, and swagger.

Cast of Characters

Charlene "Charlie" Mack
Mack Investigations Principal;
former Homeland Security Agent

Don Rutkowski
Mack Investigations Partner; former police officer
and Homeland Security Trainer

Judy Novak
Mack Investigations Associate Partner

Mandy Porter
Grosse Pointe Park police officer; Charlie's girlfriend

Franklin Rogers
Chief of Staff, Wayne County Executive Office;
Charlie's ex-husband

Pamela Fairchild Rogers
Wife of Franklin Rogers

Stanford Fairchild
Millionaire businessman;
father of Pamela Rogers and Peter Fairchild

Sharon Fairchild
Wife of Stanford Fairchild;
mother of Pamela Rogers and Peter Fairchild

Detective Maynard Wallace
Detroit Police Department

Percy and Sylvia Rogers
Franklin's parents

Karen Scanlon
Interior Decorator

Caesar Sturdivant
Hit man

Serena Carruthers
Defense Attorney

Chapter 1

Charlie didn't recognize the number. *Telemarketers wouldn't call this late, would they?* She eyed her phone. *What if someone's calling about mom?* Shit!

"Hello?" she answered. Her voice a cross between annoyed and cautious.

"Hello. Is this Charlie?" It was a woman.

Charlie hesitated. Most people answered this question straight out. Asking it was a common technique for a private investigator.

"Who's calling?" Charlie was now completely annoyed.

"Oh, I'm sorry. I know it's late. This is Pamela. Uh, Pamela Rogers."

"*Who* is this?" Charlie asked.

"Franklin's wife," the caller said.

Charlie hadn't met her ex-husband's new wife. Franklin had mailed a pro forma wedding invitation to her mom eighteen months ago, enclosing an extra invitation for Charlie. Both Ernestine and Charlie had graciously RSVP'd their regrets.

"Charlie? Are you still there?" Pamela asked.

"Oh. Yes, I'm here. I'm just surprised to hear from you. We've never officially met."

"I know. I'm sorry."

"How is Franklin? Is anything wrong?"

"Things are terribly wrong." Pamela's controlled voice faltered. She began to sob. "Everything is such a mess. I didn't know who else to call."

1

"What's happened?" Charlie hoped her forcefully asked, direct question would calm the flustered woman.

"Franklin has been charged with first-degree murder. The police think he killed my brother, Peter."

"*What?*"

"Last night."

"No. That can't be right," Charlie almost shouted.

Mandy came into the bedroom and stood beside Charlie. "Is it your mom?" Mandy whispered with a worried face.

"No. Franklin is in trouble."

"Are you speaking to me?" Pamela asked.

"No. Sorry. I was talking to my partner. Do you need me to do something, Mrs. uh, Pamela? Did Franklin ask you to call me?"

"No. In fact, he'd be angry if he knew I called."

"I see. Okay. Is Franklin being held downtown?"

"The police say he fled the crime scene. They can't find him."

"Have you spoken to him?"

"No. Charlie, I hope it's okay to call you that, my father thinks I need some outside help. He doesn't particularly care for Franklin, and he long ago gave up on my brother, but he doesn't trust the police. My mother is terribly distraught. Daddy is bringing her back to Michigan in a couple of days to . . . to make preparations for Peter. Daddy wants answers when he gets here."

"Pamela, slow down. I need to ask you something. Do you believe Franklin killed your brother?" Charlie continued her direct questions. Mandy gripped her arm.

Pamela sobbed. "No. He could never do such a thing."

"Franklin couldn't do such a thing," Charlie announced to a skeptical Don and Judy.

"But his fingerprints are all over the place," Don argued.

Judy nodded her agreement. She didn't want to get off to a bad start in her probationary role as an investigator, but the facts were the facts.

"I know, I know," Charlie said, pacing the conference room.

"And the police report is pretty clear, Mack," Don added. "The evidence shows there was some kind of a scuffle, and your ex's gun was found on the floor."

"I don't care what the police report says. Franklin did *not* kill that man."

"Well then, where is he? And why is he running?" Judy asked.

Charlie didn't have an answer to the first question. It made the second bother her even more. She grabbed a red Post-it, wrote quickly, and pressed it firmly onto the whiteboard. *Is Franklin still alive?*

The room was quiet until Don spoke up. "You don't really think he's dead, do you?"

Charlie held her palms to her eyes for a few seconds. Her head had been throbbing off and on since she'd received the call from Pamela ten hours before.

Charlie hadn't been in contact with Franklin for almost two years. Following the invitation to the wedding, he'd sent a "happy birthday" text last July. He'd moved on with his life, and so had she. Still, there was a sense of loyalty. Franklin knew her better perhaps than even Mandy, and he was a decent man. Looking back on their few years of marriage, she realized she had never loved him, not the way he wanted, but even now she felt she had to protect him, and the thought he might be dead made her insides fold into a tight knot.

"I pray he's alive," Charlie said. "But it's unlike him not to call anyone."

"And the new wife, what's her name . . . Pamela. She hasn't heard from him?" Judy asked.

Charlie shook her head.

"Who would the guy turn to?" Don asked.

"His parents. His boss. Me, maybe," Charlie responded. "Although Pamela said he'd be angry to know she'd called me."

"What's she like?" Judy asked.

"I've never met her. But I checked her out online when I heard he was marrying her. She's a socialite, the only daughter in the Fairchild empire, with deep roots in the moneyed old families here.

3

Stanford Fairchild is not just well-to-do, like Judge Ferry, but a multimillionaire from the Northeast who moved to Michigan to keep an eye on his auto company investments back in the day."

"So her parents don't live here?" Don asked.

"No. They live year-round in a gated community in Florida. They also have a home on Lake Michigan. Pamela and Franklin live in the original family home in Indian Village. The parents are due to arrive in Detroit in a few days."

"Where does . . . did . . . the brother live?" Judy asked.

Don looked at the police report. "It says here it's one of those loft apartments downtown. That's where the body was found. In the bathroom."

"Nobody heard a gunshot?" Charlie asked.

"It doesn't say there were any witnesses. We'll need to talk to the police. Since Daddy Fairchild is willing to pay us big money to get some answers about who killed his kid, we should lay out a plan," Don said, moving to the whiteboard where the lone question clung to the middle.

Charlie realized she'd been standing this whole time, so she gathered her sticky notes—red for questions, green for facts—and took a seat across from the board. Sometimes she used blue notes for out-of-the-box conjectures. Those were the ideas their former business partner, Gil, had been so good at proposing.

"Okay, Don. Draw a four-cell matrix. For questions, facts, and big ideas," Charlie directed.

"What's in the fourth box?" Don asked.

"I don't know yet," Charlie said. "Let's be surprised."

Don rolled his eyes, but drew the box. He'd seen Charlie's technique work so many times that he'd stopped thinking of it as new-age weirdness. He put the "Is Franklin still alive?" note in the questions grid.

Charlie furiously wrote on more red notes, passing them to Judy who helped Don to organize them on the board. After a dozen, she picked up the green sticky notes.

"Now help me think through the facts we currently know," Charlie said.

Judy rattled off a few: "Franklin is charged with murder. He's the deputy to the Wayne County Executive. He's missing. His gun was found at the victim's apartment. What's the brother-in-law's name again?"

"Peter Fairchild," Charlie responded, and finished the four notes.

"I have a fact to add," Don said. "This Fairchild guy was in a fight at a bar the night he died."

"Good, Don. We need to get the name of that bar," Charlie said, nodding to Judy who started a list of to-do's.

"Do you have Franklin's cell number?" Judy asked.

"Yeah. I do. I didn't even think to call it." Charlie reached for her phone.

"You think he'll talk to you?" Judy asked.

"I don't know. He might."

The Mack Partners paused their brainstorming while Charlie punched in the number. The call immediately went to voicemail. "Franklin, this is Charlie. I know you're in trouble. Pamela told me. I want to help you. Please, call me."

Don and Judy watched Charlie try to regain her composure. She finally looked up. "Damn. I don't know why I'm so emotional."

"Because he's someone you care about. You were married to him," Judy said.

"He put up with a lot from me. I didn't make things easy," Charlie said, wiping at her eyes.

Don restored order. "You know the police are probably monitoring his cell phone."

"They probably are," Charlie said. "Franklin may be aware of that. What else will the police be up to?"

"The detective who faxed the official report says DPD is getting pressure from the chief, who is getting pressure from the county executive. They've had a call from the governor's office, too. They have four detectives assigned to the case—all veterans."

"Given the rich victim, his influential family, and the politically connected suspect, I'm not surprised the police are being squeezed from all sides," Charlie said. "Okay, let's look at our open questions and make assignments."

Tamela appeared at the conference room door. "There's a call for you, Ms. Mack. From the police." Her brows were at full attention. "They're holding on line two."

Don offered an "I told you so" look and took a seat at the table. He pushed the tabletop speakerphone toward Charlie who pushed the call button.

"This is Charlene Mack."

"Ms. Mack, Detective Wallace at police headquarters. I'm the lead detective on the Peter Fairchild murder. You've heard about it?"

"Yes. Of course I have. How can I help?"

"Our primary suspect is Franklin Rogers. Your ex-husband."

"I know."

"May I ask *how* you know?"

"I received a call last night from his wife, Pamela Rogers."

"I see." The pause on the other end was long enough for a passed note or two, or a whispered conversation.

"I wonder if you wouldn't mind coming in to answer a few questions for us. You're probably also aware that Rogers is missing?"

"Yes. His wife told me that, too. I might as well tell you now, detective, that Pamela Rogers has hired the Mack Agency to look into the murder of her brother."

There was an even longer pause. Charlie, Don, and Judy sat quietly. After almost a minute, Detective Wallace's voice boomed through the speaker. "Can you come in this afternoon?"

"I can. May I bring my partner, Don Rutkowski?"

"Yes. We know Don. See you at 2 p.m.?"

Charlie lifted her eyes to Don for an okay. "Yes. We'll be there."

"They're pissed," Don said when Charlie disconnected the call.

"Can you blame them? Let's finish up and pass out assignments. I assume we'll have a lot more questions and maybe a few more facts after our sit-down with Detroit's finest."

Chapter 2

Charlie never felt comfortable at Detroit police headquarters. The grand old building with its marble floors, wood paneling, and wrought-iron staircases was a neglected throwback to Detroit's glory days. Recently, it had been added to the city's condemned properties list. Given the economy, even if the city could sell the building, it was unlikely a developer would be willing to bring the old girl back to her original splendor.

Charlie and Don sat at a conference table in Captain Travers's office. Detective Wallace and two other detectives were also seated. Travers was a bureaucrat. Charlie had met him on an earlier case, and they had a mutual dislike for each other. Don, on the other hand, had worn the blue uniform for fifteen years, so the atmosphere and bureaucracy at headquarters was fondly familiar to him.

Charlie sat, unspeaking, for almost five minutes, watching the men joke with each other. Travers was also assessing the group. They locked eyes.

"Shall we get down to business?" Travers ordered. "Thank you for coming in, Ms. Mack. I know this must be an awkward situation for you. Your ex-husband is missing, charged with murder, and his new wife hires you to find him. That seems like a healthy amount of complexity." Travers managed a smile of fake sympathy.

"It might even be a conflict of interest," Detective Wallace interrupted, receiving glowering disapproval from Travers.

Charlie didn't take the bait. "It's not against the law for me to take this case, is it?"

"No, Ms. Mack," Travers responded. "But it is a felony to harbor a criminal. I know you're already aware of that."

Here it comes, Charlie thought.

Travers's comment was an overt reference to their Cass Corridor case, where the Mack Agency had neglected to reveal the whereabouts of a person-of-interest in the murder of a drug kingpin. Charlie and Don glanced at each other, but said nothing. With a nod Travers gave Wallace permission to speak.

"We've subpoenaed the cell phone records of Rogers. Uh, Franklin Rogers. We're aware you called him earlier today, Ms. Mack."

"Then you are also aware that I didn't speak to him. Of course I called Franklin. His wife wants us to find him."

"Then you've had no contact with him?" Wallace asked.

"None."

The meeting lasted less than an hour. The police spelled out their case against Franklin, and revealed they had a witness who saw him leave Peter Fairchild's apartment. The gun on scene was registered to Franklin, and his fingerprints were found in Peter's apartment. The bartender at Club Lenore said both Rogers and Fairchild had had a few drinks before Fairchild got into an altercation with another patron. That's when Franklin had led him from the bar.

"The bartender said the conversation between your ex-husband and the deceased wasn't friendly when they left the bar," Wallace said.

"Look, let's get something clear," Charlie said, noting Don's warning of a raised eyebrow. "Franklin Rogers and I have a personal history, but I haven't seen or talked to him in a long time. So you don't have to keep referring to him as my ex-husband, detective."

Detective Maynard Wallace shifted in his chair. He was a seasoned law enforcement officer. Like Travers, he hadn't been caught up in the pervasive corruption infecting the department. He was a second-generation officer from Atlanta who had witnessed the culture shifts in policing during his decade of service. Travers signaled Wallace that he'd respond.

"This is a high-profile case, as you know. Our goal is to work cooperatively with you and Mr. Rutkowski. We have the same interest. We just want to locate Rogers."

"I want that too. I don't know why he ran, but whatever his reason I know he didn't commit this crime. That's where our interests diverge."

"We understand," Travers said. "But Fairchild's father has strong political connections in Detroit. I've heard from the chief, and he's heard from the mayor and the governor. We're following the evidence. If you bring us new leads, we'll investigate them. Isn't that correct, Wallace?"

"Yes sir," Wallace said dutifully.

They departed police headquarters after Charlie promised to call if she heard from Franklin.

Charlie and Judy sat for a moment in the deep circular driveway of the home of Pamela Fairchild Rogers. Or, rather, small brick mansion. There had been snow earlier in the week, but there was no sign of it on the landscaping. The lawn was dormant but still well maintained, and the house was surrounded by mature trees. Judy identified them as evergreens, flowering trees, plus maple and oak. Charlie counted six large windows across the front divided by a massive space for what might be a two-level fireplace. Unlike other homes on the block, the Fairchilds' entrance was behind a wrought-iron fence leading to the side of the residence. Charlie rang the bell. A buzzer sounded, and the gate disengaged from the lock.

"Nice place," Judy whispered as they walked a cobbled path to an eight-foot portico.

A gray-haired butler opened the door. Standing next to him was a thin blonde with a worried face. She looked about thirty.

Maybe younger. She wore turquoise lounging pants under a matching silk tunic. She would not have been out of place in *Vogue*. Charlie's three-hundred-dollar business suit suddenly felt like an outfit for grocery shopping.

"You must be Charlie," Pamela said with a half-smile and an extension of her hand. Her flawless makeup couldn't cover her stress or the redness in her eyes. Charlie shook Pamela's hand and introduced Judy.

The butler took their coats. He was old. The weight of their outer garments made him slouch more than he already did. Pamela led them into a sitting room at the front of the house where the six draped windows—three on each side—flanked the fireplace Charlie had noticed from outside. Pamela pointed to a sofa, then took a seat in a modern cushioned chair with a tall back. "Would you like a fire? This room can get very cold."

"That would be nice," Charlie said, scanning the room. "You have a beautiful place."

"Thank you. I grew up in this house," Pamela said, aiming a remote at the fireplace, which with a flick of a button set the hearth ablaze.

She noticed Charlie's puzzled look and explained. "I had the fireplaces converted to gas before Franklin and I moved in." Remembering her situation, a shadow touched her face.

"I'm very sorry we have to meet under these circumstances," Charlie said. "First of all, have you heard from Franklin?"

"No, I haven't. He always checks in with me. Always. I'm so worried."

Judy took out a notebook. "I hope you don't mind my taking notes."

Pamela's quizzical look at Judy was the kind she might give a maître d' who was taking too long to escort her to a table. "You're Charlie's assistant?"

"Actually, she's a new partner in my firm," Charlie intercepted.

Both Pamela and Judy looked at Charlie with surprised faces.

The ancient butler entered the room, struggling to balance a tray of tea. Pamela gave a disapproving scowl when, without permission, Judy pounced from the couch to help him pour and serve the tea. Charlie used the opportunity to take a long look around the parlor, and was aware of Pamela eyeing her.

The wallpaper, oak wainscoting, and leaded windows were blue blood, but the room had been updated with other modern touches besides the gas fireplace. Recessed lights nestled in the ceiling, the rugs sported contemporary designs, and the furnishings had clean lines. It was a bright, cheery room. Charlie could see Franklin's touches in the artwork and plants.

"Is there anything else, ma'am?" the butler asked.

"No, thank you, Case. You can go," Pamela answered without looking up at the man.

Charlie glanced at Judy who stared at Pamela with a grimace and wide-eyed judgment. Charlie dropped a cube of sugar into her tea and stirred. Judy finally followed suit.

"The tea is delicious," Charlie said, meaning it, but ready to get back to the work. "Pamela, please take me through Wednesday. Tell me everything that happened."

"What do you want to know?"

"Start with the morning. How was Franklin when he got up?"

Pamela looked confused, which quickly changed to annoyed. "How will knowing that help you find Franklin?"

Charlie gently placed her teacup into the saucer and took a deep breath. She tried to remember Pamela was grieving and probably in shock.

"Sometimes there are small details, things that don't seem important at all that can help. The police will probably ask you the same questions at some point. Have they asked to meet with you yet?"

"They called this morning."

Pamela sighed, and began to talk. Wednesday had been an average day. Franklin had gone to work early. She had a hair appointment, and then a meeting with the executives of one of the charities she sponsored. Franklin had come home at five and changed clothes before going out an hour later to meet Peter. She'd invited a couple of college roommates in for a dinner of salads and wine and gossip. Her friends left about nine o'clock. When she hadn't heard from Franklin by ten, she'd called his mobile phone. When he didn't answer she called her brother. She'd asked the attendant at the front desk to check Peter's apartment, and he'd discovered the murder scene and called police.

"The police say a witness saw Franklin leave the apartment. Is that the front-desk security guard?" Judy asked.

"I believe so," Pamela responded.

"Did Franklin and Peter normally go out for drinks?"

"No. They didn't. Franklin called me here around 3 p.m. to say Peter wanted to meet him to discuss a business opportunity. I guess Peter knew better than to call me again with one of his fast-talking schemes."

"Oh?" Charlie raised an eyebrow.

"You might as well know my brother was . . . he was never able to make anything of himself. He had all the opportunities one could have," Pamela made a slight gesture to take in their surroundings, "but he failed at everything—school, a job abroad Daddy got for him, the business he started, even his marriage. My parents were always bailing him out of trouble. Since they moved to Florida, it's been me dealing with his never-ending problems."

Pamela ended the condemning speech out of breath and red-faced. She reached for her tea with a shaking hand and took a sip. Charlie glanced at Judy, who was scribbling rapidly.

"I'm sorry. It's just that Peter's been such a disappointment. The family's black sheep."

Judy stopped writing. Charlie took another sip of tea to signal a white flag for Judy. It didn't occur to Pamela that her words might be inappropriate. In fact, Charlie realized that with Pamela's sheep, and her own flag reference, a lot of black-and-white metaphor was at play in this elegant sitting room. Keeping it going, she made a mental note that she didn't really care for Franklin's new, white, wife.

"Would you describe your relationship with your brother as strained?" Charlie asked.

"He was two years older than me, but I was the one who looked after him. He always had a lot of questionable people around him. People he'd meet God knows where," Pamela said, disgusted.

"So, let's go back to Wednesday. The day he died. How did you find out? Did the security guard call you?"

"No." Pamela described the visit she'd received from the police late Wednesday evening. They had informed her of her brother's death and announced they were looking for Franklin. They had searched the house. They asked about Franklin's gun, and she showed them the safe in the den where it was kept. The safe, door open, contained papers and ammunition. They had taken Franklin's laptop and his extra set of car keys.

"Did the police have a search warrant?" Charlie asked.

"I don't think so," Pamela said. "I was so distraught I just answered their questions. I gave them permission to take Franklin's things. It wasn't until the police were about to leave that I realized they thought Franklin had killed Peter."

"That's exactly what they think," Charlie said. "My other partner and I met with them this afternoon." Charlie looked at her notes. "Was Franklin in the habit of carrying his gun?"

"No. At least I don't think so. He said it was to protect the house. I never really looked inside his safe."

"When was the last time you saw the gun?"

"I don't know. Maybe a few months ago. Franklin showed it to a guy from our insurance company. They were assessing our security measures. We have a lot of valuable pieces in the house."

"I'm sure you do," Charlie said. "May I see where the gun is kept?"

Pamela bypassed the grand staircase across from the entrance and took them up a narrow flight of steps off the corridor between the large formal dining room and the kitchen. Charlie decided that in the home's heyday the stairs might have led to the servants' quarters.

The vibe and style of the den was all Franklin. Charlie recognized a few of his favorite paintings, including, on the desk, a framed picture of him on a fishing trip with his father. His fishing rod was mounted on one wall, and the heavy bronze iguana Franklin had insisted on buying during their Mexican honeymoon was atop a pile of folders on the corner table.

"The safe is here," Pamela said, shoving aside a tapestry hanging from a pole. "That's where he always kept the gun. Our bedroom is just through there," she said, pointing to an adjoining door.

"Do you have the combination?" Charlie asked.

"Yes. I do."

Pamela opened a wood box on the desk and lifted a small card. She stared at the card for a few seconds, then turned to the wall to manipulate the dial. She opened the safe and stepped aside. The safe contained a few papers, a brown banker's folder, a small metal box, and an opened box of ammunition for a nine-millimeter pistol.

"Did the police take anything else from the safe?"

"Not that I know of."

"Does anyone else have the combination?" Judy thought to ask.

"This safe has been here since the house was built and has never been changed out. We never really used this room. It was for our . . . uh, the nanny. I guess my parents and brother might know the combination."

They returned to the parlor but didn't sit. The tea service had been removed. Pamela's parents were returning to Detroit on Saturday to complete the arrangements for the funeral, which would be held in a week. Charlie asked for, and received, a recent photo of Peter, then arranged for Judy to return to the house to ask questions of Pamela's parents.

"I'm sure my father would prefer to meet with you, Charlie," Pamela said. "No offense, Ms. Novak. It's just that Daddy's used to dealing with the person at the top."

"I'll be sure to come by on Monday," Charlie said, "to give you and your parents a report on our activity. Until then it's a better use of my time to be in the field looking for Franklin and gathering the evidence that proves his innocence."

"Of course. That makes sense," Pamela said. She was now sniffing and wiping at her eyes with a handkerchief that matched the color of her outfit.

"Has Franklin called *you?*" Pamela asked, staring at Charlie.

"No. But I called his cell phone this morning. It went directly to voicemail. I left a message."

"I see."

"I'm sure he'll be in touch with you soon," Judy said sympathetically.

Pamela acknowledged the good wish with a nod. "I hope Franklin won't be angry that I got you involved."

"We can't worry about that now," Charlie said. "What's important is that we find him."

Pamela dabbed at more tears. Charlie didn't think it was a good time to share her worst fear about Franklin's incommunicado status.

Don walked into the Lenore in Greektown at 4:30 p.m. Two patrons were at the bar, nursing drinks and watching a PGA tournament. Phil Mickelson was on top of the leaderboard. A back room was being used for a training of some sort. Don sat on the stool farthest away from the TV. He removed his trench coat and pulled a notebook from his jacket pocket, laying it on the counter.

The bartender wiped glasses, but had kept an eye on Don from the moment he stepped into the dim sports bar. "Get something for you?" she asked, discarding her polishing rag and moving to Don's end of the bar. Don saw her eyes click to the notebook for a second before settling on his face.

"A beer and some information," Don said with a smile.

"Draft?"

"That'll be fine."

"Light?"

"Hell no."

The bartender, with a nametag reading Marti, returned with

the cold glass, placed a coaster under the beer, then waited. Don took a sip of beer, swiped at the foam on his lip, then retrieved the photo of Peter that Charlie had brought back to the office. He pushed it toward Marti with the tips of his fingers.

"Did you see this guy yesterday?"

"Yep. I already told the police what I know."

"I'm not the police," Don said.

"Are you a reporter?" Marti asked, looking at the notebook.

"No. A private investigator. The man's family hired me to help the police find his murderer."

"The police told me the guy he was with, the brother-in-law, is the murderer. That's what the papers say too," Marti said, crossing her arms.

"The family doesn't think so."

"Good. Neither do I."

"Why do you say that?" Don flipped the notebook open to a clean page.

"That Peter guy is in here all the time, and always causing trouble. Pissing off some jealous boyfriend, or claiming the server brought the wrong order, or spilling his drink on somebody. There's been at least three times I've cut off his drinks because he was smashed."

"What about the other guy, the brother-in-law? Was he drunk Wednesday night?"

"No. He had a mixed drink and then a beer. The Peter guy had four mixed drinks, one right after another." Marti looked at the photograph again. "After *that* guy began shoving somebody who bumped into him, the brother-in-law, what's his name, Rogers? He stepped in to break it up. Paid for the tab and told me he was driving the drunkard home."

Don picked up the photo and laid a five on the bar. "Okay. Thanks." Don gathered his coat from the seat next to him.

"I hate to hear of anyone dying, but this guy was asking for it, one way or the other," Marti said, giving Don a bartender-wisdom head shake. She grabbed a cloth from below the bar and began polishing the hell out of a tumbler.

Don's next stop was Peter's apartment. It was in a downtown

industrial building converted into lofts, only a short drive from Greektown. Don parked on Gratiot across the street from the Crowley Lofts and leaned against his car. He watched a few drivers use a fob to open the sliding gate for entry to the parking lot. There was a small camera on the corner of the building pointed at the driveway, and two more mounted cameras aimed at the parking lot. Next to the vehicle gate was a pedestrian out-station with a button and an intercom. Don scanned the area, noting the trash-strewn street, the makeshift homeless squats, and the nearby boarded-up storefronts. He double-pumped the car alarm and walked across the street. His push on the entry button was followed by a grumpy male voice: "Help you?"

"I'm here to see the Fairchild apartment. Detective Wallace said he would add my name to the list," Don said, leaning into the speaker.

"What's your name?"

"Rutkowski."

"How you spell that?" This time Don noticed an accent.

"R-U-T-K—," Don didn't get any further before the buzzer sounded and he stepped through the gate.

The security guy wore a wrinkled white shirt and a stained black tie. His jacket, with his name tag, was slung on the back of the chair. He was probably in his late thirties. Now that Don was standing across from the guard, the man's accent was even more pronounced. *Maybe Jamaican, or African, or something like that,* Don thought. He was no style guru, and he certainly didn't begrudge a man having a second job, but he always judged a place by its front desk. Don graded this building a D-minus.

"Do you have the video for the security cameras?" Don asked the guard.

"The manager gave it to the police," the grouchy guard replied. "Here's the key. The unit is on the second floor."

"What's the number?"

"There's only one unit on that floor."

Don lifted his notebook from his inside jacket pocket. "Could you spell your name for me?"

The man squinted at Don. Don stared back unblinking. The man spelled his name, and Don wrote it in the notebook.

"Thank you. Second floor. Which way is the elevator?"

The man pointed with his thumb beyond the brick wall behind him.

There were two elevators, but the floor lights were illuminated on only one. Don noted seven floors. A door marked with the stairs icon was on the opposite wall. The elevator opened revealing an oversized space that could also be used for freight. Don pushed the button marked 2, and waited as the doors closed very slowly, and the ascent started with a jerk. It stopped and opened onto a shallow foyer and a formidable door. A fluorescent light flickered in the foyer. Don saw a small security camera mounted high on the wall. He inserted the key into the door's lock and pushed it open, scanning the areas he could see from where he stood and listening for any noise before he stepped in. Dusk had taken hold. Through the floor-to-ceiling windows shone twinkling streetlights, apartments, and offices. In the southeast corner was a view of the RenCen.

He flipped a light switch on the pillar nearest the door, spilling soft circles of illumination from pot lights around the 2,000-square-foot room. The open floor plan was designed to accommodate the big space. On two sides were a couple of doors leading to rooms, but in the middle was the equivalent of a man cave with a pair of handsome leather couches, chairs, a high-pile rug, and a sixty-inch TV nestled in a chrome entertainment center. A kitchen with a huge island and stools was next to the living area. A sliver of plum sunset hung on for dear life through the patio doors that led to a narrow concrete balcony.

The entire seating area and the open door on the left wall were crisscrossed in police tape. Don walked to the open door, passing a small office area off the kitchen. Behind the yellow crime scene tape was the guest bathroom where the body of Peter Rogers had been found. White chalk outlined his shape on the floor. Don stepped just inside the door, using a handkerchief to switch on the light. Fingerprint powder clung to the mirrors, tile, faucets and fixtures. Small pieces of blue tape marked blood spatter. He would ask to see the photos.

Turning to the main room again, Don walked the perimeter. The ceiling was so high the resident above this second-floor apartment probably wouldn't hear an altercation or gunshots. Don looked down to the street and the parking lot. The windows were incredibly airtight, because Don could barely hear street sounds. Only if the patio doors were open, he thought, could residents hear their neighbors. He checked the bedroom. An impressive iron-platformed bed took up the center. Drywall closed off the closet from the main room. Baffle material, maybe cork, covered the ceiling, giving privacy to the bedroom and the adjacent bathroom.

The blond dresser top was cluttered and untidy, maybe from Peter's own carelessness, but maybe from the police search. A framed photograph, the only one Don saw in the entire loft, showed what must be the Fairchild nuclear family. The mother and father were healthily attractive in the way rich people could be. The father wore an ascot, and the mother was elegant in a floral dress with pearls. The two kids appeared to be in their early teens. Peter was in a dark suit with his tie loosened and a smirk on his face. His younger sister was pretty, thin, and already wearing the countenance of her mother.

Back downstairs at the now-unoccupied front desk, Don waited so he could return the loft keys. After five minutes, he stepped around the desk, wrote a note to the absent guard and folded the keys inside. He noted the views of the security monitors—five in all—with rotating views of the upper hallways, the parking lot, the loading area in the back and two views of each floor's vestibule.

Don had seen similar security-camera control panels with a toggle to stop the rotation cycle and the ability to zoom in on any view. *Of course the monitors don't do much good when no one's here to look at them,* Don thought. He turned to sneer into the camera above the front entrance as he crossed the parking lot. In the car he called Charlie.

19

"There's not much to see here. The police already have the security cameras footage, so I'll make an appointment with Wallace to look at that. I also want to see the crime scene photos."

"So it sounds like security is good at the building," Charlie said.

"I didn't say that. If the guard I spoke to is an example of their personnel, the cameras are doing all the work. How'd the meeting with the new Mrs. Franklin Rogers go?"

"She's rich and snooty. She and Franklin live very well. We got some info about Peter. She called him the black sheep."

"Wow. Even I know you don't use that phrase in front of an African-American person."

"I had to signal Judy to stand down. She wanted to go indignant on her."

"I heard the same assessment of the brother from the bartender. I'll tell you all about it when we debrief tomorrow."

Chapter 3

Hamm was happy and fed and walked Charlie from the front door to the kitchen. Mandy was comfortable in sweats and a T-shirt, and had already begun the dinner preparations. She sat at the breakfast counter peeling potatoes and sipping from a glass of white wine.

"That wine looks good. Is there more?" Charlie asked, nuzzling Mandy's neck.

"Yep. I just opened it. Sauvignon blanc. It's in the refrigerator."

Charlie put her jacket over the back of a chair and rolled up her sleeves. She uncorked the wine, poured a generous amount, took a couple of sips, and with her free hand gave Hamm a rub.

"What are the potatoes for?"

"Garlic mashed. I already sliced tomatoes and mozzarella, and I'm baking swordfish."

"Wow. Sounds great. How was your day?"

"Nothing eventful. Patrol until lunchtime, then we were back to the station for a training on community policing. What did you learn about Franklin's trouble?"

"Quite a bit actually. DPD asked me to come in, so Don and I met with Captain Travers and a few of his detectives. They want to make sure we're being cooperative in finding Franklin. Then Judy and I met with Pam Rogers at her fabulous mansion in Indian Village."

"What's she like?"

"Privileged. White. Barbie-doll pretty."

"Jealous?"

"No way. She reminds me of people I went to college with. She can't really help being snobby. It's the way some people become when they've grown up super-wealthy and spoiled by their parents."

"What was Judy's opinion of her?"

"She thought she was snooty, but also feels sorry for her."

Mandy cut a potato into fours, dropped it into a bowl of cold water, and then took a sip of wine. "But did you like her?"

"Let's just say if she wasn't a client, we wouldn't be sitting down having tea together."

Mandy took another sip of wine. "Well you have one thing in common—Franklin. You both married him, and now you both believe he's innocent. Right?"

Mandy's tone had changed. Charlie stopped petting Hamm and leaned both elbows on the counter. "Are we about to have a talk?"

"It's just that we've not talked a lot about Franklin."

"Yes, we have. I've told you all about him."

"Not really. The last time you mentioned him was when he sent you the invitation to his wedding. What was that—almost two years ago?"

"Right."

"Have you spoken to him since then?"

"Nope. He sent me a text on my birthday last year. I texted back a 'thank you.'"

Charlie watched Mandy drain the potatoes in a colander, then carefully scoop them into a large pot with already boiling water. She remained at the stove to sprinkle garlic, pepper, and sea salt on the swordfish.

"Jealous?" Charlie asked

Mandy wasn't amused. "That really wasn't called for. I'm trying to have a serious conversation."

Mandy looked away, and Charlie sipped wine. Hamm noticed the tension in the room and moved to the center of the kitchen and flopped on the floor so as not to take sides.

"I'm sorry. I was being flippant," Charlie finally said.

"You seem really concerned about Franklin, and I get that. But you didn't even hesitate when his new wife asked you to take the case. Why did she call *you*?"

"I'm an investigator. She said she knew I'd care about proving Franklin innocent."

"You *do* still care about him, don't you?"

"I really can't believe he killed anyone. He doesn't have a bit of meanness in him."

"You didn't answer the question. You still care about Franklin."

"I guess I do."

"I get it. Really."

Charlie took a deep breath. She'd hoped Mandy had put those fears behind her. Early in their relationship, after an attack on her life, Charlie had foolishly initiated a tryst with Franklin. Mandy, it seemed, still thought about it, and now she and Hamm waited for a response.

"Honey, you know I'm in a different place now. I've chosen you. I loved Franklin, but I was never *in* love with him. Not like I am with you."

Mandy turned to the stove. She checked the consistency of the potatoes and put the swordfish into the oven. "Dinner will be ready in twenty minutes. You want to change? Then you can set the table."

"Okay. I can do that."

The swordfish was hot and flaky, and the buttered garlic mashed potatoes melted in the mouth. Mandy and Charlie, both good cooks, enjoyed sharing the food prep duties and eating their meals together. Hamm sat next to Mandy's chair staring for handouts. Charlie prompted him to move away from the table with a look, his name said with a high inflection, and a command. It was part of their mano y doggo training protocol. Hamm looked at Charlie, finally dropped his head, and slinked into the living room.

"Is it okay if I finish the tomatoes?" Charlie asked, topping off their wineglasses.

"Sure, and I have one more question to ask about Franklin," Mandy replied.

"Ask as many questions as you like."

"I've been thinking about that time when you were attacked in Alabama," Mandy said, searching for just the right way to ask her question. "We'd been dating for four months . . ."

Charlie knew what was coming and put down her fork. Mandy looked at Charlie full of emotion, then broke eye contact.

"When you got home, you didn't call *me*; you called Franklin. Why?"

"That was three years ago."

"I know. Answer the question."

Charlie took a long sip of wine. She pushed her plate away and gripped the table. Never good at talking about her feelings, Mandy was giving her practice. It was uncomfortable and unfamiliar territory.

"You and I were new together. I wanted to maintain a certain, strong image, and the truth is I felt afraid, weak, and very, very angry. I didn't want you to see me like that. When I called Franklin, it was a cry for help. An impulse. I needed comfort, and I knew he wouldn't judge me. It was a really dumb thing to do," Charlie added.

They sat quietly for a moment, the silence bringing Hamm back into the room. He stared between them, hoping for scraps. Mandy stood and removed her plate and the bowl of potatoes from the table. Charlie, needing an ally, broke her own rule and offered Hamm a leftover piece of mozzarella. Then she gathered the rest of the bowls, glasses, and plates and carried them to the kitchen.

Mandy was at the sink. Charlie leaned into her back and enfolded her waist.

"That will never happen again," Charlie whispered in her ear. "The only person I will ever want comfort from again is you. I promise."

24

Chapter 4

It was Judy's second visit in as many days to the Fairchild house in Indian Village. She had a 10 a.m. appointment to meet Pamela's parents. The butler, Case, greeted her at the door, took her coat, and led her to the room she'd been in yesterday. Judy had dressed for the visit in a well-fitting blue skirt suit and navy-blue pumps. She'd had her hair cut into a neat bob and wore gold loop earrings. She usually dressed this way only for funerals and emergency parent-teacher conferences.

"Mr. and Mrs. Fairchild will be with you momentarily," Case said, moving unsteadily in the direction of the kitchen and leaving her alone in the room.

Judy took the opportunity to explore. She walked to the front windows. Beyond the trimmed bushes and impeccable grass was her 2005 Chevy Impala parked at the curb. It stood out as a solid middle-class American car on a block of luxury imports.

Turning, she examined the paintings. A couple were signed with names she'd heard before. Charlie had said the more modern pieces belonged to Franklin. Judy preferred those to the ones with thick gold-leaf frames, and oil-painted white faces sitting in portrait. The fireplace mantel held a few photographs. One, a picture of a handsome Franklin and a beautiful Pamela in their nuptial attire. They both smiled, staring at each other with held hands. There was also an outdoor photo of the wedding party.

The groomsmen wore morning suits, and the bride's cohort was elegant in off-the-shoulder, soft-pink, ankle-length gowns. The outfits of both sets of parents echoed the colors, but in more conservative styles. The last photo appeared to be an early family picture of the Fairchilds. Judy recognized Pamela as a teenager. The young man beside her, presumably Peter, stood with a cocky defiance of the camera.

Judy heard a door open behind her and turned to see Pamela and the older version of the husband and wife in the photograph.

"Hello. I was enjoying your family photographs."

Pamela glanced over Judy's shoulder at the mantel, her face dimmed in sadness. She clearly wasn't as collected as she'd been yesterday. Mr. and Mrs. Fairchild looked at Judy with curiosity and murmured hellos. With a hand gesture Pamela directed Judy to the couch she'd sat on the day before.

"Thank you for coming, Ms. Novak. May I introduce my parents, Stanford and Sharon Fairchild."

"I'm very sorry for your loss and regret having to meet you under these circumstances," Judy said before sitting.

The Fairchilds flanked Pamela, sitting comfortably in high-back chairs. Despite experienced execution of makeup, discoloration rimmed Sharon's puffy eyes. She was otherwise very put together. Her straight-spine, cross-ankle, hands-in-lap bearing was that of new-world aristocracy. Stanford's stare took a measure of Judy. He was tall, gray-bearded, with sea-blue eyes and the casual confidence of someone used to being in charge.

Judy silently repeated what her grandfather had always said to her: "No matter what company you're in, no matter how rich or educated the others are, you'll still know how to be the wisest person in the room."

"Ms. Novak," Stanford began. "We understand you want to ask us some questions. They must be very important because as I'm sure you're aware this is a horrible time for us."

"Yes sir. The questions are quite necessary. Otherwise I would not bother you and your family. We want to get to the bottom of your son's untimely death. We're working in tandem with the

26

Detroit police, but as a private agency we can often take short-cuts they can't."

Stanford's single blink told Judy he understood and had taken a few shortcuts around the law himself. Sharon pulled a handkerchief from her pocket and dabbed tears away from her eyeliner.

"First, I have a question for you," Stanford said. "Does your investigation assume that Franklin is innocent of killing our son?"

The question caught Judy off-guard. She parted her lips, then pursed them. She looked at Pamela who wriggled, distressed, in her chair. Judy cleared her throat and made a show of closing her notebook as if to say "if we're not on the same page on this, we have a problem."

"Why yes. That is our clear conclusion. Based on our conversation with Pamela, we thought you were all in agreement."

Stanford crossed his leg, his soft wool slacks undulating in the motion. Judy decided his socks were more expensive than her suit. His clothing, mannerisms, and subtle arrogance reminded her of a foil the Mack team had parried with during the auto show case.

"I don't know what to believe," Stanford said. "I know what I've heard from the chief of police, who called this morning. The evidence points to Franklin."

Now both Pamela and Sharon dabbed at wet eyes. Stanford uncrossed one leg and crossed the other. His tone shifted to neutral and what Judy believed was fake empathy.

"Of course, we don't want that to be true. We've come to know and *like* Franklin," Stanford said, patting Pamela's hand. "However, we hope any assumption you and Ms. Mack may hold won't blind you to the hard evidence you find. In other words, Ms. Novak, I want to get to the truth. Just so we are clear."

Judy took in the remark, making mental adjustments to her list of questions. She reopened her notebook. "That's very clear. For now, let's assume—with all the caveats it implies—that Franklin is *not* your son's murderer."

"I accept that assumption for now," Stanford agreed.

"My first question is, who are Peter's current friends and acquaintances?" Judy asked.

Pamela pulled herself together to answer. She described in more detail what she'd mentioned the day before. Peter had an endless stream of people coming in and out of his life. Friends, associates, and a few hangers-on. Pamela was able to come up with the names of a couple of women friends Peter had mentioned, but didn't have their contact information.

"There was this business associate Peter had been meeting with for a couple of months. Remember, Daddy? I told you about him. Some guy who owns a high-end bourbon distillery. One of those so-called vanity lines with a celebrity name attached to it." Pamela concentrated, trying to remember. "He was Canadian, wasn't he?"

"I remember you mentioning it," Stanford replied.

"I thought you said you were going to check out the company?"

"I may have assigned it to someone. I don't recall. I'll call the home office to see if they have a file."

Judy jotted a few notes.

"What about his current employment? I understand Peter worked for you, Mr. Fairchild. What kind of work did he do?"

Fairchild seemed irritated by the question. "He's paid as a vice president in my R&D division."

"And that involves him meeting with a variety of people on behalf of your company?"

"Yes."

"Had he talked about any particular problems he was having? Any unhappy client, or a meeting that had gone bad?"

"I don't recall anything like that," Stanford said, looking to Pamela for concurrence.

"No. I hadn't heard of any problems like that," Pamela agreed.

"Okay. Let's move in another direction. How would you describe your son's demeanor?"

"What do you mean?" Stanford asked.

"My colleague has been looking into Peter's movements the day of his death. He spoke to the bartender at the watering hole Peter and Franklin visited on Wednesday night." Judy flipped a page in her notebook. "The bartender described Peter as a regular at the bar, and often belligerent."

"He had a quick fuse," Pamela agreed.

"That's true," Stanford said. He was perched on the edge of his chair. "Always a hothead. Ever since he was a boy."

Sharon, who hadn't spoken before, stood. "I will not sit here and listen to you criticize Peter," she interjected angrily. "My boy is dead. How are these questions helping us?"

Sharon began to sob, sinking back into the chair. Stanford moved to give comfort to his wife, putting an arm around her and cupping her face in his hand. Pamela watched, pressing a handkerchief to her nose. Judy took note of the family dynamic—sincere grief and concern for each other. She thought she might lose the Fairchilds if she didn't interrupt the emotions.

"Mrs. Fairchild, I have two sons. Teenagers now. Very different from each other. One is always in some kind of trouble at school. He barely accepts a kiss from his old mom these days," Judy said with a quick smile. "But he's a smart, loving kid."

Sharon's sobbing subsided. She lifted her head as Judy spoke and nodded once.

"My other son, the younger one, is a whole different story. He's sensitive but tries not to show it. He's always concerned for me. He and I still spend time together watching TV or playing cards."

Stanford saw his wife's changed composure and returned to his seat. Judy leaned forward on the couch.

"Mrs. Fairchild, I want to ask you a question. It might seem superfluous, but your answer could lead to a line of inquiry we hadn't considered. It might help us find your son's murderer. Will you help me?"

"Yes, Mrs. Novak," Sharon said.

"What was Peter like?"

The simple question opened a floodgate of memories. Sharon spoke about her son with feelings that belied her aristocratic bearing. She recalled his insecurities in school, trying hard to fit in. Peter and Pamela had grown up in this house, and there hadn't been many other young people on the block. They'd sent him to a boys' academy in Washington, DC, for a time, but he couldn't find his way. He was athletic, but also interested in music, playing the trumpet for a while. Sharon spoke of her husband's many absences from home and how a young Peter sometimes cried himself to sleep missing his father.

Stanford Fairchild listened uncomfortably.

Sharon explained that when Peter became a teenager, he found friends who were also interested in music and he formed a band. He hadn't really been a drinker before that, but the bar atmosphere appealed to him and he eventually developed a drinking problem. They'd sent Peter to a six-month residential program in Connecticut for counseling and to wean himself off of alcohol.

Sharon's voice was strong with compassion for her son's flaws. Sometimes she looked at Judy, but more often she closed her eyes, reciting her words to the place where she hoped Peter's spirit resided. Throughout the account of Peter's ups and downs Pamela sat stoically, occasionally running her hand across the front of her dress. She shook her head almost indiscernibly a few times. But Judy saw it.

Stanford was not as emotionally distant from Peter's story as Pamela, but he was certainly less forgiving than his wife. Judy watched his jaw clench tight for five minutes. A few times he glanced at his wife with a look that bordered on antagonism. By the end of Sharon's telling he was slumped in his chair with his hands folded tightly.

"Thank you for sharing all of that, Mrs. Fairchild," Judy said, mother to mother.

Judy was done with her questioning. There was an awkward twenty seconds of silence as she completed her notes. She raised her head from her task when she heard Stanford rise from his seat. He lifted his wife by her elbow. Pamela and Judy made eye contact, and then Pamela stood too.

"Thank you for your time," Judy said quickly, standing and shoving her notebook and pen into her big purse. "This has been very useful, and I hope I haven't caused you too much additional pain."

"Thank you, Mrs. Novak," Sharon said with sincerity. "You *will* keep us apprised of your findings."

"Of course, Mrs. Fairchild. We'll be making a report to Pamela on a daily basis."

"I'll also want a copy of that report, Ms. Novak." Mr. Fairchild's lips were a tight line.

"Of course."

Clearly, Judy had made a connection with Sharon, but not with her husband. Pam rang for Chase, and he appeared at the couch, holding Judy's coat. "I'll be happy to see you out, ma'am," he said.

They said their goodbyes, and Judy looked over her shoulder as the three Fairchilds stepped through the door to the private residence from which they'd arrived.

Back behind the wheel of the Impala, Judy started the engine to warm it up and reached for her bag. She completed the notes she'd been making before her dismissal. Then she glanced at the Fairchilds' home, trying to imagine what it would be like to grow up there. Beautifully furnished, spacious, staff like Chase to take care of your every need. Still, these opulent surroundings couldn't protect Peter from being a lonely child with a distant father.

Judy grabbed her phone and dialed Gary. The chaos of her house came full force through the speakerphone.

"Why is Abby barking?"

"The appliance repairman is here for the washer. I'm going to put her in the crate because the guy won't come in the house. What's up, sweetie?"

"Nothing. Just wanted to hear your voice. The kids got off to school okay?"

"Abby! In the crate," Gary yelled. "What? Oh yeah, everyone got some version of breakfast, and they're off for the day. Is everything okay?"

"Yes. Sure."

"Great. I have to go before the repair guy decides to leave. I'll see you tonight."

"See you. Love you."

"Love you, too."

Judy disconnected the call and took a last glance at the small mansion. She turned on the now-warm heater and left the idyllic for the normal she preferred.

Chapter 5

On rare occasions Don shared food with his office mates. Today he'd brought in pierogi from Polonia Restaurant in Hamtramck. The steaming hot dumplings oozed grease through the paper bag, and Judy put them on a tray to protect the conference table. Charlie, who usually purchased or made a salad for lunch, offered to spoon out some of the greens, tomatoes, and cucumbers onto their plates. Surprisingly, Don accepted.

"You on some kind of diet?" Judy asked.

Don smirked as best he could with a mouth stuffed with beef and onions. He grabbed a plastic fork and with a flourish speared a cucumber and shoved it in with the meat.

"Speaking of diets, don't let me eat more than two of these things," Charlie pleaded. She followed the bite of vegetarian dumpling with a big swig of water. "Judy, finish telling us about your meeting with the Fairchilds."

"I did get a couple of specific leads. Pamela said there were two women Peter has been seen with recently, and there's some guy he's been meeting with about a bourbon deal."

"A bourbon deal?" Don asked.

"Some whiskey company with a celebrity brand. I think the guy who owns the distillery was trying to get Peter to invest in the company. Mr. Fairchild might have checked out the guy, but he didn't seem sure. I'll ask Pamela to follow up with him on that info." Judy paused to bite into a cheese, potato, and kraut pierogi. She picked up a napkin to swab at greasy lips. "These things are delicious. Thank you, Don."

"You're welcome, Novak. So, what was your takeaway on the blue bloods besides they're rich and have a house no kid should have to grow up in?"

"Well, their feelings about Peter are interesting. There's a clear division when it comes to him. The father and Pamela seem to think he was a mess up all his life. The mom, Sharon, has explanations, or maybe just excuses, for his behavior. She admits Peter was a challenge to raise, but thinks his chronic troubles stemmed from his father not being around enough."

"Did they know if Peter had enemies?" Charlie asked.

"He had lots of potential enemies, according to Pamela. She said people called her all the time saying he owed them money."

"That's something we should look into," Charlie said. "But why would he need money? He comes from wealth and had a steady job with his father, didn't he?"

"The dad wasn't very detailed about the work Peter did; in fact, he was hesitant talking about it. Seemed to me it might have been a placeholder job for his son."

"The guy had rich tastes," Don said. "His loft apartment is nice. Fancy artwork. A 180-degree view of the city. Solid, man-sized furniture. He spent a lot of cash on the decor. Maybe that's why he needed more."

"Does he own or rent that place?"

"He has a three-year lease and has been there a year and a half."

Charlie reached for a vegetarian pierogi. "This makes two. You have permission to shoot me, Don, if I go for a third."

"Right, Mack."

"Have you called Franklin again?" Judy asked.

"Yep. I tried his mobile this morning. The phone is still on, and the mailbox isn't full, so I'm assuming he's ignoring the messages. I spoke with Mom about it. She suggested talking to his parents."

"How is Ernestine?"

"Good. She was very helpful today. Her mind was sharp, and of course she's shocked about Franklin. I hadn't thought to call so she read about it in the newspapers like everybody else."

Don reached for another pierogi. His fourth. "Does your mother think he's innocent, Mack?"

"She thinks there would have to be a darn good reason for Franklin to kill someone. Like he snapped, or it was self-defense."

"Do you know Franklin's parents well?" Judy asked.

"I haven't spoken to them in a long time, but yes I know them. They're very nice people. Mom sees his mother from time to time at funerals."

"Funerals?"

"Franklin's father is a minister at Gethsemane Baptist Church. He's been the pastor there for more than twenty-five years."

"So that's your plan for this afternoon, see the other set of parents?" Judy asked.

Charlie nodded.

"Want me to come along?"

"No. I'm taking Mom. I thought she might help. You should focus on how we can find Peter's friends that Pamela mentioned. The two women."

"Right."

"What about you, Don, what's on your list for the afternoon?" Charlie asked.

"I made an appointment with Wallace to look at the crime photos, and I hope I can look at the security footage they pulled from Peter's building."

"Good," Charlie said, eyeing another pierogi.

"Don't even think about it, Mack," Don warned.

"There's one more thing about the Fairchilds that sort of bothered me," Judy said. "Stanford seems to think it's possible Franklin *did* kill Peter. Maybe because he received a call from the police chief and the cops are convinced, but he practically ordered me to make sure we aren't blinded by any allegiance to Franklin. It was an awkward moment. I think they'd been talking about it before I arrived. They're a close-knit group, but I could see and feel the tension between them."

"He's right you know," Don said. "Franklin *could* be guilty."

"I know it's possible," Charlie conceded for the first time, struggling to believe her own words. "Maybe he and Peter had a fight. I don't know. Judy, what about Sharon Fairchild? Does she believe Franklin's guilty?"

"Hard to say. She seemed as distressed as Pamela when Fairchild insisted that we follow the clues."

"Of course we'll follow the clues. Wherever they lead." Charlie pushed her chair away from the table and stood. "We have plenty to do this afternoon. Let's check in again around five."

Chapter 6

Don sprawled at a workbench in a makeshift library at police headquarters and studied the crime scene photos. He'd shucked his jacket and was on a second cup of ebony-black, head-buzzing coffee. Detective Wallace, second-in-command in the criminal investigation unit, had provided the full manila envelope from the police photographer, two hundred pictures in all. The photos deemed the most important were pinned to the case board, which Wallace had rolled into the room an hour ago.

Don still had good standing with the Detroit Police Department, one of the assets he brought to Mack Private Investigations. Charlie was persona non grata with some members of the department because of a recent case implicating a dirty cop, but Don was still one of them.

The photos certainly told a story. Countering Charlie's notion that Franklin and Peter might have fought, the apartment was in the same organized condition he'd seen yesterday. The only difference was the gun lying on the shag rug and Peter's body lying on the bathroom floor. There were dozens of closeups of the blood spatter on the bathroom floor and walls and mirrors. Don noted the bathroom ceiling baffle, the same kind as in the master bath. *If a shot was fired in this room with the door closed, it might not even be heard in the master bedroom.*

The gun found in the apartment's man-cave area was a Ruger GP100 revolver. The closeup showed the blue-steel alloy frame and black rubber grip. It was a solid workhorse weapon for home security. Don checked the police report; the weapon had been discharged twice. The .357 magnum bullets in the barrel matched the ones extracted from Peter's body and the ones found in Franklin's safe. The one curiosity for Don was the gun's location—on the shag carpeting in the living room. Why would Franklin, or anyone, shoot someone in the bathroom, then leave the gun in another part of the apartment? Don got to ask that question when Wallace returned to the room.

"What's your theory about the Ruger?"

"We figure Rogers panicked. Maybe his coat was on the couch and he ran for it, then dropped the gun."

Don looked dubious. "Possible, I guess. He wouldn't necessarily hear it drop on the carpet."

"That's what we thought."

"What about these photos, Wallace?" Don pointed to a set of six pictures he'd laid aside. They showed the apartment's front entrance and the vestibule. "The door to the apartment was closed?"

"Yes."

"Fingerprints on the doorknob?"

"Yes, but smudged, as if someone had tried to wipe them off. Nothing usable."

"Did you find Franklin's fingerprints anywhere else in the apartment?"

"On the Ruger and a couple on a table in the living area."

"Not on the bathroom door handle?"

"Nope."

Don stood to look at the photos pinned to the case board. "What's the interest in the windows?"

"We found prints on the sills that were fresh. Not Franklin's."

"But those could have come from a party guest or a maintenance guy," Don said. "We hear Peter had a lot of people coming and going at his apartment."

"We've heard the same thing."

"Did you find bloodstains anywhere else? Wouldn't the shooter have gotten shmear on his shoes or clothes?"

"Likely, since that guest bathroom is so small, but it looks like the door was open when the shots were fired because there is almost no blood on the inside of the door," Wallace said.

"So, the killer might have fired the shots from the doorway?"

"That's what it looks like."

"So the guy would have transferred some blood, don't you think? Like to that deep-nap rug?"

"Right. I'm sure the techs checked the rug and the couch."

Don returned to the workbench, and Wallace joined him. "What's the glass here in this one?" Don held out one of the photos he'd laid aside.

Wallace looked at the number on the back of the print, then flipped through a thick set of stapled pages. He traced his finger down one page and stopped. "It says here glass from a broken fixture in the elevator entrance."

"You mean the lightbulb in the vestibule was broken?"

"Yes. I think that's what it means."

"You don't think that's odd? There's a camera in that entryway. Was somebody trying to avoid being seen?"

"Maybe. Or maybe the bulb was just broken, and the maintenance folks hadn't gotten around to repairing it."

"Do you have time to show me the security footage?"

"Yep. I've got it all set up for you. It's on my desktop computer. Come on down."

Don followed as Wallace rolled the case board—cork on one side and a chalk surface on the other—out to the bullpen. Then he entered his office where his desk and a round conference table took up most of the space. The footage, edited by the police media techs, was timecoded and cued to the date and time: 2.06.08/20:48. Wallace used his mouse to start the viewing.

The first scene showed two men, one white, one black, entering the front entrance of the building. Don had only seen photos of Franklin. As chief of staff for the Wayne County executive, Franklin was often in the public eye, substituting for the top elected official of Michigan's largest county.

Franklin was slightly taller and appeared to be assisting Peter through the door. The next scene showed them clearly inside the elevator. They were arguing. More accurately, Peter was pointing his finger at Franklin, who was shaking his head. Then Peter got in Franklin's face so close that Franklin put his hand on Peter's chest to keep him at bay.

The next section of footage, again from inside the elevator, was twenty minutes later. It showed Franklin, sweating and disheveled. He lurched from the elevator as the doors opened on the first floor. Then, on the lobby camera, he retreated through the front door and looked back over his shoulder. The camera caught his shocked and guilty look. Wallace closed out the file, returning the desktop screen to the folder view.

"Wasn't there any footage from the vestibule itself?"

"Too dark to see anything."

Don wasn't buying the coincidence. "That light was fine when I was there yesterday."

"See what I mean? They fixed it."

"How far back did you look at the elevator and vestibule footage?"

"A few hours before the medical examiner's official time of death. We checked the front desk sign-in. No one else had visited Peter's apartment that day."

"What about after Franklin left?"

"Why would we do that?" Wallace asked.

"Maybe somebody else saw or heard something and went to the apartment."

Wallace shook his head. "We interviewed the tenants on the floors above. No one saw anything. Or heard loud noises. The security guard on duty said except for Peter and Franklin, nobody came in or out of the building between 8:45 p.m. and 9:30 p.m."

Don looked skeptical. "Not exactly a gold-star security team in that building."

Wallace nodded his agreement.

"Let's see the footage from the parking lot."

At 8:45 p.m. Peter Fairchild's 2006 Porsche entered the gated parking lot. The car was parked in a spot near the back of the almost-full lot. Two men, one steadying the other, walked toward the front entrance. The footage continued running.

"Did Franklin have a car?"

"He left his car in the lot near Club Lenore. According to the bartender, Peter was too drunk to drive, and Franklin took his keys."

"That's also what the bartender told me," Don offered.

"Franklin's car has been impounded."

"Wait. Look," Don said, pointing.

"Where?"

"There's someone going around the side of the building. Where'd he come from? Wait a minute; roll that back, Wallace."

The detective toggled the footage backward at double speed, then slowed the image. A figure slipped out of the front entrance and, staying in the shadows, moved quickly to the corner of the building. The timecode read 9:10 p.m. Don and Wallace looked at each other.

"Who the hell was that?" Wallace said.

"You're asking me?" Don responded.

"We missed that."

Don shrugged. "Let's watch it again. Can you roll it in slow motion?"

The figure barely opened the front door, before sliding through the narrow opening. He was wearing a hooded jacket and was carrying a bag. The man walked fast, not quite crouching, but hunched and staying close to the shrubbery. At the far side of the building, he hesitated just a moment before turning toward the loading area.

"I don't think that's the security guard," Wallace said.

"Me either. If it is the guard, that means the desk lobby was uncovered for a while. If it isn't, that means someone left the building before Franklin. Can I get a coffee, Wallace? I think we need to look at a lot more footage."

Charlie helped Ernestine into the bucket seat of the Corvette and stretched the seatbelt into the socket. "You good, Mom?"

"I'm fine. I'm so used to being in the van I forgot what it feels like to sit so low. You'll need to help me out of the car."

"I will. We can be in Bloomfield Hills in a half-hour."

The Reverend Percy and Sylvia Rogers lived in a Tudor-style home on a lovely block with mature trees, green lawns, and side drives. The home had a terraced landscape ending in a low retaining wall. Charlie remembered the front of the home ablaze with color in spring and summer. But there was nothing tranquil about today's scene. A police car idled in the driveway, and across the street, three TV news trucks sat parked. Two reporters headed their way as soon as Charlie got out of the Corvette.

"Stay in front of me, Mom. We want to avoid them," Charlie said, pushing the car seat back so her mother could swing her legs out of the car. Once Ernestine was up, they moved swiftly to the front porch.

Sylvia opened the door on the first ring and pulled them into the house. Percy stood behind his wife with his hands on her shoulders.

"I apologize for all that," he said. "They've been out there for two days."

Charlie hadn't spent a lot of time with her former in-laws, but they'd always been supportive and cordial and had borne her no ill will after the divorce. Ernestine greeted Sylvia warmly, and they went off to the kitchen for coffee. Charlie and Percy Rogers sat across from each other in the living room.

"Thanks for agreeing to see me, Reverend Rogers," Charlie began.

"You can still call me Percy, young lady." He smiled.

Charlie gave a strained smile and a nod. "I can only imagine how distraught you and Sylvia must be."

"She hasn't slept much the last few days. Me either. I've decided to let the associate pastor handle duties at the church this Sunday."

Charlie nodded. "As I said on the phone, I've met with Pamela. She's sure of Franklin's innocence, just as I am."

"We both appreciate that," Percy said.

"I've been trying to reach Franklin. I can't help him unless I talk to him. Do you know where he is?" Charlie asked directly.

Percy shook his head, but his continued silence and darting eyes may have told Charlie the truth. Sylvia had prepared a tray of coffee and cookies for them, and Charlie lifted a cup to her lips. This was going to be tricky. She'd need to gain the trust of this man of God. She figured truth was the best way.

"Franklin probably told you that I'm in another relationship now."

"He did."

"Percy, I want you to understand that I loved Franklin when I married him, but I also knew at the time that I was gay."

"Isn't lesbian the correct term?" Percy's eyes had reconnected with hers and, unlike the judgment she expected, they were bright with curiosity.

"Yes, I guess it is. I'm not much into the labels."

"Neither was Jesus."

"I guess I thought most black ministers are adamantly against the gay lifestyle. You're not?"

"The Bible is sprinkled with acts, and omissions, that are considered sins. As members of my church come to me for counsel and guidance, I try to point them in the direction of Jesus's actions. From my reading of the Bible, there were more acts of love than judgment."

Charlie was pleasantly surprised and relieved. Franklin had talked a lot about growing up as a preacher's kid, and apparently his father's views had softened over the years. Eight years of Catholic school had left Charlie more spiritual than religious, but she certainly believed in God, faith, and miracles. Franklin would need a few miracles now, and maybe Charlie could work with his father to make them happen.

"Look, Percy, the police have pretty much decided that Franklin is guilty. I know he's not. Or, if he did shoot and kill Peter, at least there must be an extenuating circumstance. But the police are getting a lot of pressure from very high places for a quick conviction. If I'm going to help Franklin, he needs to talk to me."

"Are you familiar with the parable of the lost sheep?"

"It's something about a shepherd leaving the whole herd of sheep to go after one that's strayed."

"Exactly. It is Jesus' way of speaking about redeeming a lost soul. I think about the numerous families I've counseled who struggle over how, or if, to reconnect with an estranged family member. Those losses can be the most devastating and hurtful." Reverend Rogers removed his glasses and rubbed a finger against the wetness in his eyes. "I have a whole congregation that needs me, but all I can focus on right now is my son."

Charlie listened to the pain in this father's voice. Stanford Fairchild likely carried this kind of pain at the loss of his own son. She took another sip of coffee.

"Something occurs to me, Percy, when you use the lost sheep parable. The Fairchilds have referred to their son as a black sheep. I know it's different, but similar. Two families with two lost sons. One of them dead. The other, I pray, still alive."

Charlie shared a long glance with Percy Rogers before he slowly dipped his head.

"What do you counsel people when they tell you their loved one doesn't want to be found?"

"Sometimes you just have to sit in faith."

"The Fairchilds embraced their wayward son and brother for a long time. They tried very hard to bring Peter back into the fold."

Percy watched the dark liquid in his cup for a moment before putting it on the tray and with his elbows on his knees he leaned toward Charlie. She mimicked the posture.

"Charlene, uh, Charlie. Will you tell me why you resigned from the Department of Homeland Security?"

"Yes sir. During the three years I was an agent, racial profiling of Muslim Americans became a standard practice. I understood the rationale. People in the country were very afraid. But as a black person, I couldn't watch the singling out, and sometimes harassment, of American citizens with Muslim surnames. The policy was unfair, and it wasn't going to change. So I had to leave DHS."

"That's what Franklin told me, and I always admired you for that."

Charlie's face colored.

"No need to be modest. It was the right stance. Justice is often denied when it threatens power. It was true in the days of Jesus. It's the same now."

Charlie knew Percy's curiosity was leading to something, so she waited.

"I'm going to confide in you, Charlie. I *am* in touch with Franklin. He knows we're talking today. I believe it's important that he speak with you, but he's very afraid and doesn't want to pull you into his problems."

Charlie let out a long breath. "I'm just glad to know he's alive. Can I meet with him?"

"No. He won't do that, but I'm sure I can convince him to call you."

"I don't understand why he's staying away. It's one of the reasons the police believe he's guilty. Why hasn't he called Pamela?"

"I'll let him tell you that himself."

"I *never* believed Franklin killed that man," Ernestine said. She was strapped again into the Corvette.

"I can't say for sure that Franklin didn't kill Peter. His father wouldn't tell me. I guess I'll know more after I speak with him. I appreciate your coming along, Mom. I think it really helped."

"Sylvia is a wreck," Ernestine said. "I think it took all her energy to make herself ready for our visit."

"Percy's very concerned about Sylvia. He's putting on a calm front, but I think he's a devastated man. He talked about lost souls, and he's afraid Franklin will get a raw deal if he comes forward."

"Sylvia said Percy is being very secretive," Ernestine said.

"He probably knows where Franklin is, but doesn't want her to know. Technically, he's obstructing justice if he's hiding Franklin."

"I'm really worried about Sylvia," Ernestine admitted. "I'll call her tonight to check on her. Will you remind me to do that, please?"

"You're a gem, Mom."

"Seeing Sylvia really helps me put my own situation into perspective. My worst fear about this Alzheimer's thing is losing control over my life. Now I realize it could be so much worse. My child could be in terrible trouble."

Chapter 7

Judy's superb people skills and innate talent for research had quickly garnered her details on the two women who had been Peter's regular companions the last few months. One of them, Lainey Pratt, was a full-time law student at Michigan State University and a part-time pole dancer. Her stage name was Cursory Brief.

"Cursory Brief? Sheesh, you gotta be kidding," Don said.

"Did you speak with her?" Charlie asked.

"Just briefly," Judy said. "Uh, I didn't mean that as a pun. I spoke to her about five minutes. She was quite shaken up by Peter's death. When I told her we were assisting the police in the investigation, she asked a few questions. She'd been with Peter a half-dozen times at the Club Lenore but hadn't seen him in a while. Actually, she seems like a nice girl."

"What about the other one?" Don asked.

Judy turned the page in her notebook. "Karen Scanlon. A real estate agent and interior designer. She helped Peter pick out some of the furnishings in his apartment."

"When was the last time she'd seen Peter?" Charlie asked.

"Earlier in the week. She'd delivered some artwork he'd purchased. But they had more than just a professional relationship. She said they were dating. She also said she left a few of her own things in the bedroom and asked if she could go to the apartment to get them."

"She has a key?" Charlie asked.

"Hmm. I guess she does. She said she didn't want to get in trouble by just showing up at the apartment."

"Better let Wallace know about her," Charlie said to Don. "How was she reacting to Peter's death?"

"She said all the 'too bad, so very sorry, nice guy,' stuff, but she wasn't torn up like the law student. She said Peter did mention the deal with the whiskey distiller and had already met the guy a couple of times. According to her, Peter needed some big money because he was planning to buy his loft apartment when his lease was up."

"You think we should meet either of them in person?" Charlie asked Don.

"Maybe the pole dancer."

Charlie and Judy gave him the "really?" look.

"Yes, really. She's the one who feels bad about the guy. She's the one most likely to open up about him and give us useful information. The other one sounds like she might want to get her hands on his stuff. He has a lot of expensive furnishings in that apartment."

"Don's probably right about the Lainey woman," Charlie conceded. "Judy, why don't you try to set up a meeting with her for tomorrow? You can go with Don."

"I don't need Novak to tag along."

"Judy's spoken to the woman, shown her some empathy. She can help. Besides, this gives her more experience with field interviews."

Don saw the merit of the idea and answered by not answering. Charlie had already given her partners the highlights of her visit with Franklin's parents. Now she recounted the details of her conversation with his father.

"You really think the dad knows where Franklin is, Mack?"

"I do."

Charlie looked up when there was a tap on the conference room door, and Tamela stuck her head in. "Ms. Mack. There's a call for you on line one."

Judy's new investigative duties had required bringing in a temp three days a week to do general office duties. Tamela Gite had worked with them before. She was efficient, discreet, good-humored, and patient. She'd mastered Judy's convoluted file organization system and laughed off Don's occasional political incorrectness. Don had even come to rely on Tamela's note-taking skills when he held subcontractor meetings. Tamela didn't normally work late on Fridays, but it was all hands on deck until they had some answers in this investigation.

"It's a man, but he wouldn't leave his name," Tamela added.

Charlie jumped up from the table. "I'll be right there."

"Mack, you should take the call in here. Put it on speakerphone. If we have to go to court, it won't be just your word."

"When did you start thinking like a lawyer?"

"I'm not. I'm thinking like a cop," Don said.

"Okay. I'll take the call here, Tamela." Charlie moved to the middle of the table and pulled the speakerphone closer.

"Hello?"

"Charlie. It's Franklin."

"God, Franklin. I'm so glad to hear from you. Are you all right? Are you hurt or anything?"

"No. I'm not hurting now. Not anymore."

"What does that mean? Why haven't you returned my calls? Why haven't you called Pamela?"

"Do you have me on speaker?"

Charlie looked at her partners. Don shook his head. Judy's eyes grew wide. She seemed to be holding her breath.

"Yes."

"I don't want to speak in front of your partners. I want you to meet me. Tonight. I'll answer all your questions then. I'll just say this in earshot of Don Rutkowski and everyone else who's listening: I did *not* kill Peter Fairchild." Franklin paused for a few seconds. "But I think I know who did. Okay, pick up the receiver now, Charlie."

Don and Judy could hear only Charlie's side of the conversation as she arranged to meet Franklin that evening. Judy slid Charlie her notebook to jot down the address and time.

"I'll come alone. Yes, I remember that place. You're not calling

49

on your cell phone, are you? Good. The police have a tap on your phones. Yes, yes. I believe you. I know you couldn't kill anyone. Okay. I'll be there."

Charlie disconnected and faced off with Don, who had been scowling and gesturing during the entire call. "I know you think it's a mistake to meet Franklin. But I'm going. Alone."

"Mack. Not only is that obstruction, but maybe harboring a fugitive."

"You heard him. He wouldn't talk on the phone."

"He won't hurt you, will he?" Judy asked.

"Of course not, Judy. He didn't kill Peter."

"He sounded convincing, that's for sure," Judy said.

"Mack, I'm coming too. You won't see me, and neither will he, but you're not going to some remote location late at night without backup."

"It's not late at night. I'm meeting him at eight."

"It's dark at eight, and I'm sure your gun is at home."

"I don't need a gun."

Judy stood and planted her fists on the desk. She was shaking. She hated guns and any talk about them. She stared at Charlie with a stern look.

"Judy don't worry. I'm not taking a gun."

"Then you need to let Don give you backup. He can be wrong about a lot of things, but he's usually not wrong about danger."

"I'm not wrong *this* time, either, Mack," Don said.

Charlie resisted with a shake of her head.

"If he didn't kill Fairchild, but thinks he should hide, he's afraid of something, or someone," Don said. "I don't think he'd risk being a fugitive just to avoid arrest. He's got a good reputation. People will believe him if he professes his innocence. Damn, I believed it hearing him say it just now."

Don's words rang true. Plus, Charlie could see from the look on his face that he wouldn't back down from his decision. It was probably smart to have Don nearby tonight.

"Okay, okay. It's almost six-thirty now. I need to call Mandy to let her know what's going on. Then you should probably get to the rendezvous point so you can find a place to blend in. Franklin might be watching." Charlie pushed the address toward Don.

"McDonald's?"

"Franklin and I used to go there when we were first married. I'd leave my job, and he would slip away from his office, and we'd meet for lunch. There were a couple of picnic benches. At least there used to be."

"You're meeting him by yourself?" Mandy asked. Charlie could hear her concern.

"There's nothing to worry about. Don will be around somewhere. Out of sight. He thinks someone could be after Franklin."

"But why didn't he just tell you what's going on over the phone?"

Charlie thought she heard more than concern for her safety in the question. Still some lingering doubt about her motivation for helping Franklin?

"I don't know, hon. He wanted to talk face to face. He sounded different than I've ever heard him. I don't know, maybe afraid. But he was very clear about not having killed Peter."

"Are you going to get him to turn himself in?"

"I'll try. Whatever he's afraid of, it can't be worse than being hunted by the police. The longer he's out there, the more guilty he looks."

"Call me when you're done, or else I'll worry."

"Okay."

"Will you have time to get something to eat?"

"I don't think so."

"I'll make up a plate for you."

"Thanks, honey. I love you."

"Same here, Charlie. Please be careful."

Chapter 8

Don drove into the parking lot of McDonald's. It was seven o'clock. Maybe some of the restaurant's sentimental history for Charlie and Franklin had to do with its location on Mack Avenue. Don drove first through the drive-thru, giving him the opportunity to check out the lot and its surroundings in case Franklin had arrived early, too. It also gave him the opportunity to get a quarter-pounder with cheese, large fries, and a soft drink.

This Mickie D's was well lit and always busy. It was bordered by food manufacturing and packing businesses on the south and west corners, a housing complex across Mack Avenue on the east, and on the north side a feeder road to the Chrysler Freeway. He re-cornered the lot and parked in the farthest space near the side street. From there he could watch the entrance, anyone approaching from Sacred Heart Church on Rivard Street, and most of Eliot Street. He lowered his sun visor to block his face, but not his view, and slumped in the seat.

At ten to eight, Charlie's Corvette entered the lot and parked adjacent to the side door. Charlie stepped out, looked around, and shoved her hands into gloves. It was cold tonight, hovering around the freezing mark. She walked toward the rear of the building, scanned the lot, and turned back toward the restaurant. Don watched her enter McDonald's. She remained inside for five minutes, then exited with a large soft drink. Walking slowly to the rear of the lot, she leaned against the low brick perimeter wall, almost parallel to Don's car. A streetlight shone just a few yards from Charlie, and Don remained slumped in his seat.

A figure moved along the sidewalk on the Chrysler service drive, and Don adjusted his rearview mirror to watch. The man, carrying McDonald's bags, crossed the side street and turned into the driveway of the church. Another movement caught Don's eye. Someone walking in the empty lot at Rivard Street turned onto Eliot toward the rear of the McDonald's. The hooded figure stopped, looking in Charlie's direction. Maybe Charlie heard her name called, because she turned toward the person and waved. When the man reached the brick wall, he pulled himself onto the ledge, swung over, and dropped onto the other side. He walked toward Charlie and hesitated. Then they both moved forward and embraced.

"You look terrible," Charlie said.

"Thanks. You don't," Franklin said with a strained laugh. "I've had a rough few days."

"You want to go inside for something to eat?"

"No. I better stay outside."

"I can go in and get you something."

"No thanks, Charlie. I'm not hungry. I've been eating, just not sleeping." Franklin looked toward the open lot and cupped Charlie's elbow. "Let's move farther down. I can't afford to be seen."

"Those picnic tables that used to be here are gone."

"It's okay. We can just stay near the wall. There's a lot I have to tell you, and I don't want to stay too long."

Charlie listened intently as Franklin recounted Wednesday night. He'd met Peter to listen to his pitch for an investment in a new business. Within ninety minutes Peter was drunk and belligerent, and Franklin decided to drive him home. He'd made Peter a cup of black coffee and was about to leave. That's the last he remembered before coming to with a head gash and pain pounding his skull. He staggered to his feet and saw Peter shot and bloodied. He was about to call 911 when he found something on the floor that struck fear into his heart.

"What was it?"

"This," Franklin said pulling a thin fold of metal from his pocket and placing it in Charlie's hand.

In the dim light Charlie could just make out a curlicue of cut stones. Charlie felt its heft and then turned it over. It was a money clip.

"Whose is it?"

"Can you see the monogram?"

Charlie flipped it over and squinted. Small diamonds formed the letter *F* in a fancy calligraphy style.

"Is it yours?"

"No. Stanford Fairchild has them made. He gives money clips to his business associates. It's his trademark."

Charlie didn't understand what Franklin was hinting at. "Did it belong to Peter?"

"I found it on the floor by the front door. It wasn't there when we came in."

"So someone else was in the apartment? This person rapped you on the head, shot Peter, and then dropped this as they left?"

"That's what I think."

"And you believe it was Peter's father?"

"Or someone he knows well enough to give them a money clip. He only gives those to the top people in his company. Charlie, I panicked. I didn't want the police to find the clip, and I didn't want to try to explain it to Pamela. So I took it with me when I left. I called 911 later."

"What about your gun? Did you have your gun with you Wednesday night?"

"No. I never carry it. The last time I saw the gun it was in my safe. When I read that it had been found at the crime scene, I knew somebody was setting me up. As hard as it is to fathom ..." Franklin paused, whipped off his knit cap, used it to swab his brow, and returned the cap snugly to his head. "I think Stan Fairchild was involved in his own son's death."

54

Neither of them said anything for a few seconds. Franklin shoved his hands into his pockets. Charlie stared at the money clip. When she looked up, Franklin was staring at her.

"You believe me, don't you?"

"I believe you didn't kill anyone. Why haven't you called Pamela?"

"How do I explain that her father is trying to frame me for Peter's murder? It's a lot to swallow, right?"

"She wouldn't believe you?"

"I don't know. She's extremely loyal to her father."

"But what would be his motive for wanting Peter dead?"

Franklin shook his head. "He's been an embarrassment to Stan for a long time. I've heard Pam and her father talk about cutting Peter off from his trust fund. Peter had to leave Florida after his name was mentioned in a prostitution ring. The high-society circles in Palm Beach don't like their members involved in scandal."

"When I met with Pamela, she described Peter as the black sheep. Of all things."

Franklin flinched, and Charlie thought he looked ten years older than his thirty-eight years. "Pam can be insensitive sometimes," he said. "She was tired of bailing Peter out of jams. But she didn't want to disown him. Not the way Stan did."

"You think he was so disappointed in his son that he'd . . .?"

"I know Stan's philosophy is if you have privilege you don't take it for granted. You use it to maintain power and standing. To say Peter disappointed him is an understatement. Peter knew it, too. He once told me he thought his father hated him."

"I think you should come with me now and turn yourself in," Charlie said.

Franklin took a step back as if hit by a punch and shook his head. "I'm not going to do that."

"I believe your story, and I think the police will too."

"You're not that naïve, Charlie. Fairchild is an important man in this state. The police won't take my story over his. No. I'm in a deep hole and turning myself in won't get me closer to the surface."

"You think hiding will?"

"As long as I'm on the run, I have the upper hand. You know as well as I do the money clip is just circumstantial evidence. Have the police found any proof of someone else in the apartment?"

"Not yet. But Don is pursuing that idea."

"How is old Don?"

"The same."

"That means he probably thinks I'm guilty."

"He's starting to have his doubts."

"Look Charlie, I'm glad you and Don are trying to help. I know you'll pursue things the police won't. Like that money clip. Someone else *was* in that apartment Wednesday night. Either Fairchild, or someone he hired. Keep pursuing that. I'll try to call you every other day."

"You won't be using your cell phone, I hope."

"I'm only turning it on long enough to retrieve messages."

"The police can still get a location from those pings."

"I'm constantly moving."

"You should get a burn phone."

"I'll try."

"Are you going to call Pamela?"

"No."

"Do you want me to tell her you're okay?"

"Yes. But don't tell her anything else. I can't confront her about her father yet. Not until I have proof."

Charlie had a slew of arguments for Franklin surrendering to the police, but she could see he wouldn't change his mind. He'd always been a relaxed person, comfortable in his own skin and easy to know and like. Tonight he was edgy. Looking over the wall and around the lot as they talked. Shifting from one foot to the other. Sweating. He was high on fear and dejection.

"It's not so much the police I'm worried about. It's Fairchild," Franklin said. "I'm his scapegoat. He might have people out looking for me."

"He and Pamela hired *me* to look for you."

"Yeah. But you don't want me dead."

"Why would he want you dead?"

"He knows I have the money clip, Charlie. I sent him a letter warning him about it."

Don sat gripping the handle of the Buick. He watched Franklin's every move because the guy acted like a junkie. During the entire conversation, he fidgeted. He looked over his shoulder, put his hands in and out of his pockets, kept taking off his cap. At one point he stepped back from Charlie and seemed ready to run. Then toe-to-toe, Charlie looked up at him, listening. She said something that made him shake his head. Then they reversed the scene. Finally, Franklin reached for Charlie's hand and held it, and Charlie pulled back. That's when Franklin lifted his hood over his head and walked briskly toward Mack Avenue. He crossed in the middle of the street and disappeared behind a gas station.

Charlie watched Franklin meld into the darkness. She turned toward the Buick, and Don sat upright as she slipped into the passenger seat. He held his peace while Charlie gathered her thoughts. Then she turned to him.

"We have a fucking mess, Don."

Chapter 9

Charlie stood back from the whiteboard, reviewing the sticky notes that represented facts and questions. As usual, the line of red question notes was a lot longer.

Maybe it was the personal element, but this case had already made Charlie weary. Plus, it was Saturday. She looked at a not-quite-fully-awake Don nursing a coffee. Only Judy seemed fresh and chipper.

"So you believe Franklin's story?" Judy asked.

"Don asked me the same thing last night, and Mandy asked when I got home. Franklin said he was knocked out, and he found Peter dead when he regained consciousness. He's the one who called 911. Yes, I believe him. I don't know if it's true about his father-in-law's complicity, but *he* thinks it's true."

Charlie reached into her pocket and dropped the money clip on the table.

"So that's it," Don said, reaching for the clip. "He let you keep it?"

"For *safekeeping*. He's afraid Stanford has people besides us looking for him."

Don twisted and turned the clip. Reaching into his pocket for his wallet, he took out a few bills, folded them, and tucked them into the clip. "Nice. These things are considered jewelry you know. This one probably cost about a hundred bucks."

Judy reached for it and weighed it in her hand. "Sterling silver, monogrammed, and if those are diamonds, it costs even more."

"The money clip in the apartment connects to Stanford, but it doesn't prove he was involved in the murder," Don said. "Peter probably had one of these, along with lots of other people, if his father hands them out as mementos."

"Franklin says this particular one belongs to Stanford because the souvenir clips have a smaller *F*."

"Okay. That's a start. I'll follow up," Judy said. "Maybe I can find the jeweler who made them for Fairchild. I'll pretend to be with his insurance company."

"That's a good idea."

"Should we brainstorm the questions on the board, Mack?"

"Yes, but I've got something else first." Charlie reached for the packet of blue notes.

"Uh-oh." Don said. "The blue ones."

The blue Post-its were used for gut feelings, the "what ifs," the notions that didn't spring from logic. These ideas often came from Charlie's highly attuned sixth sense. In this case, the idea was more fear than conjecture. Charlie wrote: "What if Pamela is involved?" Instead of placing it on the whiteboard, she placed it in the middle of the table. Don and Judy leaned forward to read it.

"No, Charlie!" Judy exclaimed. "I didn't really care for Pamela either, but she seemed genuinely concerned about Franklin. I can't believe she'd be a party to framing him."

"Franklin says Pamela is extremely loyal to her father. You saw the dynamics between them when you met with the Fairchilds."

Judy nodded.

"Don, what do you think?" Charlie asked.

"I have to mull it over. I've seen it before, of course. A wife gets fed up with a meandering husband. A kid conspires to kill an abusive father. I even investigated a case where two sisters had put out hits on each other. Murder takes on a whole new level of ugliness when it's in a family." Don rubbed at his chin. "To tell you the truth, I find it hard to believe that this Fairchild guy would resort to killing his son. He's rich. He has a lot of resources. Why wouldn't he just buy his son an island and send him away somewhere? That makes more sense to me."

"I see your logic," Charlie said.

"So you think the wife could have set this up on her own?" Don asked, considering the idea.

"Absolutely not," Judy said. She rose to get another cup of coffee and remained at the pot to drink. Charlie stood and put the blue note on the board.

"Judy, I trust your instincts. Talk me through your reservations about Pamela's involvement."

"First, she called you for help. *She* hired *you*."

Charlie shook her head. "Pamela admitted it was Stanford who suggested it. Besides, calling in some help might be a ploy to appear innocent."

"Okay, second," Judy continued. "Pamela was truly hurt that Franklin's in trouble. I saw that with my own eyes. She seemed to be suffering. That wasn't fake."

"I agree. It didn't appear to be an act. She was unnerved when she called to tell me about the charges against him and was visibly shocked when we saw her the next day."

"That doesn't mean a thing," Don said. "I've interviewed a lot of crooks who break down and cry when someone's been killed, and then two days later they're crying again after it's proven *they* were the murderer. You can't go by people's tears and shock. The average criminal can be a great actor."

"Maybe that's true, but I could tell Pamela wasn't faking it," Judy said. "The woman doesn't have a poker face. All through the meeting with her parents, she grimaced and shook and squinted at everything they said. She wasn't even subtle about it."

"If you say so, Novak. What else you got?"

"Third, I did some checking on how Franklin and Pamela met and on their courtship." Judy sneaked a look at Charlie, who had a raised eyebrow. "I was just curious. The local papers and social blogs love to write about a power couple, so there was a lot of stuff."

"And?" Charlie raised the other brow.

"They met at a Focus Hope charity event. They both like to travel and collect art. All the articles talk about what a great-looking couple they make. In all the photos they look so in love. They started a foundation together to support a girls' STEM academy on the east side. Did you know that, Charlie?"

"No."

"It's okay, Mack," Don smirked. "You and Franklin probably made a nice-looking couple, too."

Charlie cut her eyes at Don, shooting darts his way.

"Okay, okay. So maybe Pamela isn't a turncoat. But I want to check her out to make sure. Judy, keep digging on her. What does she do when she isn't being in love and doing good?"

"Got it," Judy said.

"So now that my blue note has been taken down a peg, let's talk about the other questions on the board."

The Mack partners bandied about the missing pieces of the case. Who was the person who knocked Franklin unconscious? Was that the person who killed Peter? If Fairchild was guilty of such an unthinkable act, what was his motivation? Did Fairchild act alone? How did the money clip come to be left in Peter's condo? How was Franklin's gun moved from his safe to the scene of the crime? The usual result of this exercise was to boost the number of questions. This time was no exception.

"You know that last one seems important," Judy mused. "What did Franklin have to say about the gun?"

"He said he knew his suspicions about Fairchild were true when he read about the gun. He never carries it. It's kept locked in that safe we saw," Charlie said.

"So, if Franklin's gun was at the scene, it would have to be an inside job," Judy said. "Right?"

"As far as the police know, Franklin brought the gun to the apartment. But that's pure speculation," Don responded. "But so is the inside job business."

"Well, if the crime scene photos show the weapon lying on a carpet near the living room, and Franklin didn't see it when he came to, someone had to put the gun there after he ran," Judy said.

"I *am* bothered by the location of the gun," Don admitted.

Charlie smiled at the back-and-forth between her two partners. Judy was holding her own, and it was reminiscent of the idea sessions they would have before Gil Acosta left them last year. Charlie had worried about losing Gil's analytical skills, but watching Don and Judy go at the questions this morning was encouraging.

"Do the police say there were signs of a struggle in the apartment?" Judy asked.

"Yes. The report tries to suggest that the shooting resulted from a physical fight between Franklin and Peter. But I've seen the crime scene photos and some of the security footage, and the evidence doesn't sustain that theory. Peter resisted leaving the bar, so he and Franklin had a back-and-forth. That's true. The bartender confirms that. But Wallace and I watched tape from the elevator camera. It shows Peter acting belligerent and getting in Franklin's face, but Franklin wasn't violent. He kept his cool."

"That reminds me, Don, would you follow up with DPD to find out how they justify a first-degree charge against Franklin?"

"Sure," Don said, reaching for the case file and pulling out the police report. "The medical examiner says Peter was killed between 8 and 10 p.m. We know it wasn't eight, because he didn't leave the bar with your ex until around 8:30." Don flipped pages in his notebook. "The security cameras caught the two of them arriving at Peter's building around 8:45, and Franklin leaving at 9:30." Don consulted the report again. "The 911 call came in just before 10 p.m. But before that, at 9:10, there's a guy slinking around the building. There's no way to tell who it is as the footage is too dark, but that might be your killer, Mack."

"I think we have to look at more of the footage, Don."

"Agreed. I need breakfast," he said in one of his regular non sequiturs.

"I know you have to eat, but I have one more thing, and I need advice. I owe Pamela a call to give her a report. Franklin said it's okay to tell Pamela he's all right, but nothing else. What, exactly, can I say without her asking too many questions?"

"You can tell her Franklin finally called you, and he's okay, but doesn't want to give himself up yet," Don said.

"How do I explain that?"

"Let's do a role play," Judy said. "I have an idea how you can satisfy Pamela for the time being."

"Okay," Don said. "But let's make it fast. I'm starving."

"I've been waiting for your call. It's been more than twenty-four hours since I heard from you. What's happening? Have you found Franklin?"

"I apologize, Pamela. We've been very busy." Charlie quickly listed the completed tasks in their investigation, not giving Pamela a chance to interrupt. "I met with Franklin's parents yesterday. One of my partners is a former cop, and he looked at crime photos with the lead detective on the case. After Ms. Novak met with you and your parents, she tracked down Peter's two women friends you mentioned. We have a meeting with one of the women today, and we also have a lead from the security footage to follow up on."

"You met with Franklin's parents?"

Charlie could hear either jealousy or hurt in Pamela's voice. She couldn't tell which.

"Yes. Briefly."

"I called Mr. and Mrs. Rogers and left a message, but they haven't called back," Pamela said. "Have they heard from Franklin? Has anybody?"

"They've sequestered themselves. They're very distraught as you might imagine. They're getting a lot of calls, and police and the media are staked out in front of their house."

Pamela was quiet. Charlie could sense her resentment shaping into a thundercloud.

"There's something else I need to tell you, Pamela. I finally spoke with Franklin. Last night."

Pamela gasped. "Oh my God. I was so worried he might be dead."

"He knows you're worried. He wanted me to tell you he's all right, but he's afraid the person responsible for Peter's death may be after him. That's why he's running."

"Oh my God. That's horrible," Pamela began, then hesitated. "But that doesn't make sense. Even if the police think he's guilty, they'll protect him if he turns himself in."

"He doesn't think so. The main thing he wants you to know is that he loves you, Pamela."

"Why . . . why did he call you, and not me?" She fought back sobs.

"He thinks your phones are being monitored by the police. He doesn't want to get you into trouble, and he doesn't want them to be able to trace his call."

Charlie's half-truths, practiced at the office, helped focus Pamela on Franklin's well-being, not her hurt feelings or details of the case.

"Where is he hiding? Is he safe?"

"He wouldn't tell me where he's hiding. He said he didn't kill Peter. I told him you knew that. He seemed relieved. He was worried you might not believe him. He said he'd try to find a way to call you," Charlie lied.

"Thank you, Charlie. Thank you. I have to let mother and dad know you've heard from him. But, if he didn't kill Peter, who did?"

"That's what we're going to find out."

Charlie disconnected the call and rested her chin on folded hands.

"Did it work?" Judy asked.

"Yes. You were right. She was relieved when I said Franklin sent his love and was worried about her. She's genuinely concerned about him. No doubt about it. Maybe she has no idea what her father's been up to after all."

Chapter 10

Don and Judy met Lainey Pratt at a juice bar in Farmington Hills. She was a small woman, maybe five-foot-four, brunette, in her mid-twenties with sparkling gray eyes. She was dressed in workout clothes, and her arm muscles were a miniature version of Schwarzenegger's in his prime. She noticed Judy and Don staring at her biceps and donned a jacket. Lainey told them she'd met Peter at a gym in downtown Detroit. She'd purchased a membership there because it had a workout space with a pole.

"Pole routines are an excellent workout—takes less time and provides better fitness than running. Peter came to the gym on the weekends. It wasn't far from his place. He'd watch me work out. A lot of the men did. They think a woman doing a pole workout is an easy target, you know."

"I know," Don said.

Lainey gave Don a curious stare before continuing.

"Anyway, a few times he was wearing a Spartan tee. So when he asked to buy me a coffee, I said yes."

Don had a puzzled look.

"Spartan," Judy said. "Michigan State."

"Oh. That's right. Is that what you two talked about? College?" Don asked.

"We did that first day. He went to State ten years before I did. But, you know, he was a funny guy. He didn't come on too strong, took me to music concerts and stuff. He was into music. I took

65

him to a couple of campus parties, and he fit right in. He had a boyish quality about him."

Tears came to Lainey's eyes and she dabbed at them with her napkin, then took a long sip of a green health drink. The juice bar didn't have coffee, so Don had opted for a strawberry-banana-orange juice smoothie. Judy was drinking something called a green tea fusion.

"Were you two serious?" Judy asked.

"Not really. We just had fun together. I sort of like older men."

"We've heard Peter had a drinking problem," Don said.

"Yep." Lainey did another wipe of her eyes with her sleeve. "I don't drink. So he was respectful of that. But when he came to watch me dance, he drank quite a lot. I didn't like it."

"So tell me more about this pole dancer thing," Don started. He saw Judy's warning look and ignored it. "Doesn't seem like a good thing to do for someone who wants to be a lawyer."

Lainey snorted. "That's the same thing my father said when he found out. Look. Law school is intense. There's no time for a full-time job, and my tuition is $35,000 a year. My parents put me through undergrad, but they don't have the money to pay for grad school, and I wouldn't want them to pay. I can make five hundred to eight hundred a night when I do a shift at the club. I make another five hundred every time I teach a class."

"Wow," Judy said.

"Wow," Don repeated.

"You *teach* pole dancing?" Judy asked.

"You'd be surprised how many women want to learn it. A lot of my students are wives whose husbands pay for the class. The ones who stick with the class get really strong and start to feel very independent."

"What about this name," Don said, looking at his notes. "'Cursory Brief'?"

"It's good, isn't it? Nobody uses their real name when they dance. I'm studying law, and the name sounds mysterious and sexy. It seemed to fit."

Don gave Lainey a skeptical look.

"Look. I don't do any stripping, and I wear a modified two-piece swimsuit."

"Okay. So Peter came to see you dance?"

"All the time. But he had a couple of run-ins with my manager. Peter would drink too much and get possessive. I mean we had an intimate relationship, but we were just friends." She began crying again. "I can't believe he's gone. I hadn't seen him for almost a month. Since the new semester began."

"We don't mean to upset you, Lainey, but we have just a few more questions," Judy began. "Is that okay?" Lainey nodded and wiped at her eyes with her sleeve. "Tell us about these run-ins between your manager and Peter."

"I had to get a manager. At first, I didn't have one. But you get better gigs and better contracts if you do. Also, your manager makes sure the management knows there won't be any hanky-panky. When Peter was drunk, he sometimes took offense to the men who wanted to tip me. It was bad for business and bad for the club. So George, that's my manager, asked Peter to stay away. The next time it happened they had words, and George physically threw Peter out of the club."

"Did Peter ever talk to you about any of his other friends or business associates?"

"Sometimes. But not too much."

"Did he mention a man who wanted him to invest in a liquor business?" Don asked.

"I don't think so."

"What about Karen Scanlon?"

"Oh, yeah. He talked about her, and I met her once. I think he really liked Karen. He hired her to help him furnish his place. He was happy with her work, and she helped him get some artwork and light fixtures. But he came home unexpectedly one day and found her in his place with another guy. She said the guy was there to measure for some window treatments, but Peter thought the man was casing the place for a robbery. He didn't really trust her after that, and he took back his key."

Don and Judy shared a look. Don jotted a couple of notes.

Judy leaned toward Lainey and lowered her voice as if she was sharing a secret. "Did you and Peter ever talk about his father?"

"All the time. Our fathers had a lot in common. Except his was rich. We both knew we had disappointed our fathers. That's another thing Peter and I had in common."

"Oh really?" Judy said, encouraging her to go on.

"I live at home, you know. But my dad hardly speaks to me since he found out about the dancing."

"How'd he find out?" Don asked.

"Some guy he works with recognized me at one of my club dates. I guess my father is embarrassed."

"Can you blame him?" Don said.

Judy gave Don a "you're not helping" glance. Lainey's stare was more "you old white guys really stick together, don't you?"

"Anyway," Lainey said, sighing, "Peter's father thought he couldn't do anything right. He had people checking on him all the time. Peter wasn't as interested in business as his dad was, you know? He probably would have been a musician if his father had let him. I saw Peter cry once when he told me about overhearing his father in a phone conversation. Mr. Fairchild told whoever was on the other end that he sometimes wondered if his wife had had an affair, and Peter wasn't really his." Lainey shook her head. "Can you believe that? What an asshole."

Lainey finished off her healthy drink by shaking the cup, removing the top, and tilting it almost upside down.

"I don't think I have any more questions. You, Novak?" Don asked.

"No. You've been very, very helpful," Judy said to Lainey.

"I just can't believe Peter is dead. He was a nice guy, you know? I really liked him."

"How did I do with the questions?" Judy asked Don when they got to the car.

"Not bad, Novak. Charlie's right, you really do know how to make people open up."

"Is that a compliment?"

"Nope."

"Thanks for your support."

"This is tough love, Novak. It's great that you're a whiz at the research, and you can handle yourself in an interview. But that's just half the job. An investigator has to hone his or her instincts, and be attuned to the unexpected."

"If that's code for being able to fight, that's never going to be me."

"I know."

"You think the world is a violent place, don't you?"

"It is."

"There are more good people in the world than bad. I know that in my heart."

"Maybe. But only a few bad ones can make the rest of us afraid. That's why *this* baby is never far from my side." Don patted the gun holster under his jacket.

They rode along the freeway in silence. Don turned on the radio to the all-news station. A light snow was expected tomorrow according to the excited meteorologist.

"If it's going to snow, I hope Franklin has a place to sleep," Judy said.

"He told Charlie he wasn't hungry. I bet someone has taken him in. Maybe his parents or a friend of his father."

"Could Franklin really be right about his father-in-law?"

"I'm leaning toward no. Wanna know why?"

"Sure."

"Peter had a lot of enemies. People he just didn't get along with. So far, the pole dancer is the only person who's had anything good to say about the guy."

"Her name is Lainey. She's a law student. Don't be such a caveman."

"Okay. The law student. But you see my point. Even the guy's family was down on him."

"His mother put him in a favorable light."

Don turned to look at Judy. "Okay, if I'm a caveman, you're a Pollyanna."

Charlie and Don sat wedged into a storage room with two desktop computers and a wall of boxes that blocked the fresh air and light from the slightly open window. Charlie was hunched over, viewing lobby footage from Peter's building. Don focused on footage from the parking lot and a loading area at the rear of the building. They'd been at it for a couple of hours.

"I hate to even say this, but do you think we're going back far enough?" Don asked.

"Who knows," Charlie responded. "Starting the weekend before the murder is just a way to be systematic. Maybe we'll see something of interest, maybe not. It's due diligence."

"I'll need to stop for some dinner soon."

"Your stomach is better than any watch I know."

"It's a fine-tuned machine."

"If you say so. I think you're gaining weight."

"This is my winter weight, Mack. It's why I don't have to be burdened down with a heavy coat."

When they got through the Sunday footage, Don went out for gyros and soft drinks. Charlie checked on Mandy and Hamm, then called Ernestine.

"Hi, Mom. Just calling to check in and see how you're doing. How was your day?"

"Pretty good. The van took us out to Eastland Mall for our indoor walk. We moved it up because it's forecast to snow tomorrow."

"I think it's supposed to start tonight. But I doubt there will be much accumulation."

"How are you? You're at home?"

"Unfortunately, no. I'm working tonight on Franklin's case."

"Sylvia called me today. We chatted a long time. We haven't been close friends before, but she needs someone right now and doesn't want to talk about her situation with people at church."

"How's she doing?"

"Still not sleeping. She told me you spoke to Franklin."

"She knew that? Mom, tell her she has to be careful with her phone. The police can intercept her calls."

"Okay. I'll tell her. Charlene, you know it's supposed to snow tomorrow."

"We already talked about that, Mom, remember? There won't be much accumulation."

"Oh. That's right."

Don returned with the food and drink to accompany their scanning of video. Monday morning at eight-thirty the security cameras picked up Peter, dressed in business attire, exiting the front door of the Crowley Lofts. He walked to his car parked in the second row and drove out of the lot.

At nine-thirty an ostentatious Hummer entered the lot, and a woman resembling the photo Judy had distributed of Karen Scanlon got out. She carried a small package and entered the building. Charlie's lobby footage showed her signing in at the front desk. A few minutes later, on Peter's vestibule camera, she entered his door. The video showed her leaving the building two hours later.

"I guess Scanlon *does* have a key. I keep forgetting to tell Wallace," Don said.

That evening, Peter came home alone around nine o'clock. Charlie watched him ride up the elevator. His tie was loose, and he looked like he'd been drinking. There was nothing of further interest on Monday's video.

"Ready to start Tuesday?" Don asked.

"No. But let's get it over with," Charlie said.

Before they could organize the Tuesday files, Detective Wallace burst into the storage room. "We've got Rogers holed up in a building on the west side. Come on!"

"Oh my God. They'll shoot him!" Charlie shouted.

～ ～ ～

Charlie and Don rode in the back of the unmarked sedan. The radio squawked with information about the hunt going on for Franklin in an empty building on Grand River near West Grand Boulevard. *The suspect was seen entering at 6:30 p.m. Approach with caution. The suspect is considered armed and dangerous.*

The scene was chaos. A dozen police cars were skewed across four lanes with lights flashing. This was a busy intersection, anchored on the south by two large churches. The east and westbound traffic was being diverted in the direction of the churches. Grand River traffic was being halted and turned around. Curious residents lined the police barriers, and spotlights were aimed at a boarded-up building with fluorescent graffiti. A few minutes after Charlie and Don arrived, light snow began to fall.

"Who saw Franklin enter that building?" Charlie asked.

"It was a call from one of the neighbors. His picture is all over the news. And after old man Fairchild offered a reward for any information on Rogers's whereabouts, the phones haven't stopped ringing."

"He did what?" Charlie shouted.

"I thought you knew," Wallace said. "There's a fifteen-thousand-dollar reward for Franklin."

"We didn't know," Don said as Charlie gripped his arm.

"Well, this tip seems credible."

"I'm coming with you," Charlie said reaching for the door handle.

"No you will not. You two stay in the car," Wallace ordered. "We'll be right back."

A SWAT team had been called in to enter and clear the building. Wallace and his partner joined the fray. Additional patrol cars arrived, and the crowd was beginning to surge behind the police line. Four uniformed officers worked to make sure no one breached the perimeter. Charlie and Don watched a six-man special weapons team break down the front door. The plainclothes and uniform cops stood behind the safety of patrol cars with weapons drawn.

"You think Franklin's in there, Mack?"

"I hope not. I don't think he'd be in this neighborhood, nor sleeping in an abandoned building. Last night he wore clean clothes. He looked tired and stressed, but he wasn't hungry. He's getting some help. My guess is he's holed up at his father's church or in one of the properties the church owns."

"Well, he better be careful. If DPD considers him armed and dangerous, he could be shot by some overzealous rookie."

"Yeah. I hope he knows that. I also pray he's heard about that reward Stanford is offering. I've got to get him to turn himself in, Don. The only way to do that is find something that corroborates his story. Anything that will help."

Wallace and his partner returned to the car. "False alarm. You okay, Ms. Mack? You look pale."

"I'm okay. Just worried."

"There were signs of activity inside the building," Wallace reported. "But it's empty now, and there's nothing to suggest Rogers was even there. We'll take you back to headquarters."

"Wallace, I've been meaning to tell you there's an interior designer with a key to Peter's place," Charlie offered. "We've been in touch with her and she wants to get some of her personal items from the apartment."

"The Fairchild family told us they don't want anyone in the apartment except police. So we have a guy posted there now. By the way, you were right about the broken light in the vestibule. It's one of those motion-detector lights and connected to the cameras. If the light doesn't come on, the camera doesn't come on. That would be a very good reason to break out the bulb. How's the security screening going? Have you seen our mystery man again?"

"No. Not yet," Don answered. "We've found nothing of significance from Saturday through Monday. We were just about to tackle Tuesday's footage when you grabbed us."

"We really appreciate your willingness to keep us in the loop, detective," Charlie added.

"No problem really, Ms. Mack. The sooner we have things under wraps the sooner we can go back to the rest of the crime in the city. This case is a huge personnel suck. As you can see from tonight. We like to get crimes involving VIPs in the closed file as soon as we can, so we're happy to have your team's scrutiny, and we're happy to collaborate."

"Wallace, what's your sense of this Fairchild guy, the father?" Don asked.

"Self-important. Used to having things done his way. Appreciates loyalty and rewards it. He doesn't mind using his connections to pull strings. In fact, he kind of gets off on it." Wallace paused in his assessment. "Why do you ask?"

Charlie warned Don with a touch on his arm. "I haven't met him yet, so I was just wondering," Don said. "Sounds like he could be a pain in the ass."

"It's tough work being rich, Rutkowski. Not everyone's up to it."

It was almost ten o'clock, and Charlie and Don were dragging. Wallace had gone home, and Charlie suggested watching the footage together rather than divide up the tapes. "When you're this tired, it's easy to miss something. At least it is for me."

They were toggling through midday Tuesday exterior footage when they got lucky. A man entered the picture from the back of the building. The time code read 16:26.

"What's back there, Don?"

"Loading dock. Wallace was going to request the footage. Let me see." Don peered at the desktop for the folder. "Yep. There it is."

"Okay. We'll look at that next."

The medium-height man dressed in black jeans and covered in a fur-trimmed, hooded black jacket sauntered to the entrance, staring at the parking lot. He paused, completed his scan of the lot, and went inside the building.

"Okay. He's in at 4:30 p.m. on Tuesday," Don said, toggling the footage forward at double speed.

Charlie and Don concentrated on the front entrance. Don

slowed the footage when anyone went in or out. There was a lot of coming and going between four and six o'clock. At 6:30, Peter's Porsche entered the lot and they watched him park and go into the building. The man was still inside, or at least hadn't exited the front door. An hour later Peter came out dressed in sweats, sneakers and a parka. He exited the lot through the pedestrian turnstile. Two hours later, at 9:30, Karen Scanlon's Hummer entered the lot. She stepped down from the driver's side and Peter exited the passenger seat. They disappeared into the building. The mystery man never reappeared.

"I don't think I can watch anymore tonight," Charlie said, massaging the ridge of her nose.

"We can probably zip through the loading dock footage in fifteen minutes," Don said.

"Okay. Okay. Let me go to the ladies' room. Would you call Scanlon and ask if we can meet her?"

When Charlie returned to the storage room, Don had the elevator footage cued. He had an annoyed look on his face.

"What's wrong?"

"The dock footage is too dark to see much. So I've loaded the elevator tape. Why don't they have a working light in the rear? What kind of luxury building is this? Their security sucks."

"Did you talk to Scanlon?"

"I left her a message asking for a Monday meeting."

The camera in the elevator showed a wide view. Most people seemed not to realize a camera was trained on them. Some started checking themselves in the mirror as soon as the door closed. Others scratched in places they wouldn't in public, or picked their noses, and more than a few couples used the ascending compartment as an opportunity for foreplay. They watched Peter arrive and leave and arrive again with Karen. Peter and Karen grabbed at each other until the elevator stopped. The vestibule light came on as soon as the doors slid open. Peter used his key to open the apartment door.

"The light was working Tuesday," Don didn't need to say. His phone rang, and he pushed the speakerphone button. "Rutkowski. Who's calling?"

"It's me, Mr. Rutkowski. Karen Scanlon."

"Oh. I was just thinking about you."

"Oh, really?" she said flirtatiously.

"We need to meet."

"So your message said. But I can't meet on Monday. I have something else to do. Your message said it was important."

"It is. Let's make it Tuesday morning." Don looked at Charlie and pointed to his watch. Charlie shrugged. "How about nine-thirty?"

"That's fine," Scanlon said. "Could we meet at Peter's apartment? I understand there is a patrolman on guard now, but I left a couple of, uh, personal items there I'd really like to retrieve."

"I guess that could be arranged."

"Well, good. I'm looking forward to putting a face to your voice. I guess you're curious about me, too."

"Uh. Sure," Don said, looking at the paused image of Peter's hand on Karen's breast. "I'll see you Tuesday morning." Don disconnected and looked over at a smirking Charlie.

"I can't wait to put a face to your voice," Charlie mocked with singsong exaggeration. "I bet she's put her face a lot of places."

"Jealous, Mack?"

"Ha! Just tired."

"Let's zip through the loading dock footage to see if we can figure out where that guy was coming from," Don said, clicking on the tape. "It'll only take a few minutes."

They both leaned forward to peer at the grainy footage.

"There are a few cars back there, but it's too dark to make them out," Don said. "I wonder where they came from?"

"There must be a rear entrance. Some of these buildings have hidden drives for their VIP tenants. Usually the ones in the penthouse. Go ahead. Keep going in fast forward."

"Okay, there's the guy with the fur coat," Don said. "But, I still can't tell where he came from."

Don rewound the file, then he enlarged the view on the

monitor to look closely at the blurred noses of two cars. The man suddenly appeared between the two vehicles.

"Pause it!" Charlie ordered. "Okay, go back ten seconds and roll it very slowly. There. See that quick glow? That's the interior light of a car just before the guy appears. He must have gotten out of one of those cars."

"I'm going in reverse until we see a car drive into the loading dock," Don said.

They saw a dark sedan pull down a rear road at 4:15 p.m. and back into a parking pad. The footage was shadowy, it was impossible to see a tag. There was no movement at the car until the man with the fur collar exited and moved out of view. They watched as the car left the loading dock the way it had arrived.

"Well, at least we know where the guy came from," Don stated the obvious.

"That's an expensive-looking car," Charlie said.

"Yeah. Maybe a Lincoln or a Mercedes. Too bad we can't see the plate."

"Does it look like the same guy you saw leave the building before Franklin?"

"No way to know for sure. He moves like the guy, but he's wearing different clothes."

"Maybe it's a custodian," Charlie said.

"Who knows. Let's call it a night and get out of here."

Charlie and Mandy lounged on the couch. *The New York Times* and *Detroit News* were scattered on the table and the floor. Hamm snoozed on the carpet, and the Sunday news shows added background to their easy morning.

"You want another cuppa?" Charlie asked, sliding socked feet into her slippers and reaching out for Mandy's cup. Hamm lifted his head from his paws.

"Don't mind if I do."

"How about another piece of toast?" Charlie asked over her shoulder.

"No, but Hamm wants some."

"Hamm wants any food being prepared in this house. Don't you, boy?" Charlie scrunched her face at the dog. "I think he's ready for his walk, too."

Mandy followed them into the kitchen and sat on a stool. She rubbed Hamm under the chin. "He's been out once this morning. He's okay. I'll walk him when you leave."

Hamm endorsed the idea with several tail wags.

"I'm sorry I have to work today . . . and had to last night."

"And don't forget the night before," Mandy reminded. "It's okay."

"Is it really?" Charlie poured coffee in their two mugs and walked over to the counter.

"Yes."

Charlie put an arm around Mandy's shoulder and buried her face in Mandy's lush hair.

"I think your hair is my favorite part of you."

"It's not my brain?"

"Oh yes, it's your brain. Your hair is second to your brain. Oh, and your breasts, especially the left one."

Hamm always wanted to be part of the kissing action, and he stood on hind legs to lean on Mandy's leg. The three of them were held in a love knot for a few seconds.

"Have you spoken to Franklin again?"

"No. I guess I can call his father if I need to speak with him."

"Do you have any evidence of Fairchild's involvement in the murder?"

"No. Nothing we can prove."

"Who are you meeting today?"

"The manager of a woman Peter was dating. She's a pole dancer and a law student."

"Well, good for her," Mandy said after a pause to reflect on the idea. "Does the manager have something to do with Peter's murder?"

"I doubt it. But this guy had a couple of run-ins with Peter, which turned physical. Don and I want to ask him about it."

"Well, I really hope the father didn't do it. That would be horrible. What's that called anyway when a parent kills a child? It's not fratricide. That's killing your brother, right?"

"Right. It's called filicide. The deliberate act of a parent killing his or her son or daughter. Judy looked it up the other day."

"Nasty word."

"Yes. And if it's true, even nastier business."

George Burston had been in and around show business for four decades. Framed eight-by-eleven photos on the walls of his untidy office bore the greetings of entertainment and sports celebrities who were household names in Detroit. While Don schmoozed with the guy, Charlie scanned the pictures. Gordie Howe, James Brown, Madonna, Jackie Wilson, and Dennis Rodman had all scribbled their thank-yous to George. Apparently, he had once been a real player in artist management.

"I know you must be busy," Charlie started the meeting. "So we won't take much of your time, Mr. Burston."

"Lainey said I should speak with you. I like her. She's a talented young lady."

"Not quite Gordie Howe, though," Charlie said, attempting humor.

Burston gave Charlie a hard stare. Shifted his eyes to Don. Then back to her.

"We did a little research and found out you spent two years in prison," Charlie stated.

"Oh, I get it. He's the opening act, and you're the headliner. Or is it good cop, bad cop?"

Charlie ignored his comment. "Tell us about your relationship with Peter Fairchild."

"I didn't have a relationship with him."

"But you knew the guy," Don said. "He hung around your client, didn't he?"

"He hung around Lainey all the time. He was an asshole."

"So you're glad he's dead?" Don asked.

79

George looked amused. He pushed back from his desk and crossed an ankle over his knee. "You guys are great. You kind of remind me of Esther and Barry Gordy. They came to my office once to give me some grief about one of their singers. God, that was a long time ago. I think I was only twenty years old." George smiled, reminiscing. "They put a good scare into me that day, but I've been around the block a few times since then." George uprighted himself and aimed his next words at Charlie. "And you're right. I did spend a few years behind bars. On a trumped-up extortion charge. I didn't get out for good behavior, so you two don't scare me at all. Let's get to the point. I didn't have anything to do with Peter Fairchild's death."

"Lainey told us you fought with Peter," Don said.

"The guy didn't know how to hold his liquor. Lainey was in danger of losing her gigs if Peter kept interfering with her act."

"How did he interfere?" Charlie asked.

"Peter was jealous. Lainey knows the score. She dances the pole, and she's an artist at it. The men come to see her. They pay a cover charge and they drink, which is good for the club. The men also tip, which is good for Lainey's college tuition."

"Where were you on Wednesday?" Charlie asked.

"Seeing to one of my acts at a club in Dearborn. I was there all evening. It's called the Roundtable."

"That's a good alibi. But maybe you *paid* some guys to take Peter out," Don said.

"Look, I told Lainey if she continued to hang around Peter the gigs might dry up. That's all there is to it. I might not be dealing with A-list talent anymore, but I have a good business, and I wouldn't jeopardize it for a client who brings in maybe ten percent of my income. The papers say the Rogers guy killed Peter. I guess you think he didn't. But I didn't do it either. You're looking for someone else."

Chapter 11

The memorial for Peter Fairchild was a small service for family and close friends only. The insignificant amount of snow around St. Aloysius Church had been carefully shoveled and the surfaces treated. A half-dozen black limousines sat parked in the circular drive flanking a simple black hearse. Two of the limo drivers stood off to the side of the rectory smoking. Two security agents stood next to a Lincoln Continental with plates marked "MichGuv."

Charlie was parked across the street in the lot of a rotary club. She'd watched the Fairchilds enter the church a half hour ago, joining what looked like about seventy-five guests. She'd been surprised to see the chief of police arrive, and Franklin's boss, the Wayne County Executive, pulled up to the sanctuary a few minutes later. Charlie was even more surprised to see Karen Scanlon. *So that's what she had to do today.* Karen was dressed in a tasteful black coat and accompanied by a man Charlie recognized as the mayor's brother. An article in yesterday's paper had reported that the Fairchilds would receive friends at their residence in Indian Village after the memorial.

The display of power and influence at this service made Charlie think about something Franklin had said during their McDonald's parking lot conversation. Who would be inclined to believe his suspicions about Stanford Fairchild? In these lofty social circles, the cards were stacked against Franklin.

"I have some dirt on Karen Scanlon," Judy said as soon as Charlie walked through the door of the Mack Agency.

"Let's talk in the conference room."

Judy was still adjusting to her new role of investigator. This morning she worked side by side with Tamela, color-coding and labeling file folders. Tamela handed Charlie six phone messages as she passed the front desk.

"These came in this morning, Ms. Mack."

"Thanks, Tamela. Is there coffee in the conference room?"

"Yes, and it's fresh."

Charlie flipped through the phone slips. One was a puzzling message from her mother, and another was from a number she didn't recognize. She poured a cup of coffee, added half-and-half, and erased the whiteboard. A mainstay of the conference table was the small plastic box with a variety of dry markers and Charlie's green, red, and blue sticky notes. She sipped coffee and stared at the white space. Writing notes and manipulating them on a flat surface was her way of working a case. Dissecting the details, framing ideas, filling in holes, pointing the way for the next steps in the investigation.

Judy entered with her laptop and file folders. Charlie gave her only a glance before returning her attention to the empty board. Judy quietly took a seat. She'd seen Charlie in this meditative state before. It was the way she cleared her mind so she could look at a case or a suspect in a fresh way. Charlie credited her martial arts training for the technique. It wasn't until the Mr. Coffee unit let out a last gasp of steam that Charlie emerged from her reverie and took a seat.

"You have some ideas?" Judy asked.

"Maybe. But first let's hear what you have on Scanlon. She was actually invited to Peter's memorial service. Can you believe it? She walked in big as day with the mayor's brother."

Judy had done an extensive workup on Karen Scanlon. Her

real name was Carrie Sketcher, and she had two more aliases, which she'd used in the half-dozen states where she'd been a resident. Although she'd been charged with larceny and related crimes, she'd never been convicted.

"Mostly witnesses recanted their statements, or prosecutors just couldn't get a grand jury to indict her," Judy said.

"What's her financial situation?"

"I got only a limited credit report. There are two properties in her Scanlon name in Florida, and the other is in Pennsylvania. Her home address is in Ferndale. She has a real estate license, and she's listed as an interior designer."

"Does the report show she owns a design business, or is she a consultant?"

Judy pushed a paper toward Charlie. "That's the application for the business license. She's the owner, but there's a co-owner. It's listed on page two, halfway down the page."

"Motor City Design Suite, LLC?"

"I'll dig into it. I've also put out calls to our FBI contacts about her, and I have one of our subs checking on her family in Allentown."

"That's a great idea, Judy," Charlie responded, obviously distracted.

"What's bothering you?"

"I had the feeling someone was following me today. Have you noticed anything unusual?"

"No. Someone followed you from the memorial service?"

"I think so."

"Maybe it's the police."

"Possibly. I also think Franklin called again this morning," Charlie said, waving one of the phone messages.

"He leave a name and number?"

"He left a coded message and a number."

"Are you going to call?"

"Yes. But first I'm returning Ernestine's call."

ဆ ဆ ဆ

Don sat across from Detective Wallace's desk in the cramped office. A monkey wrench had been thrown into the Peter Fairchild case.

A fingerprint on the windowsill at Peter's apartment was a hit for a convicted felon. Thirty-eight-year-old Caesar Oliver Sturdivant had spent six years in Rikers for armed robbery and had been picked up by Toronto police two days ago for an assault.

Don stared at the photo of the man taken from the New York State Prison archive. A second photo, showing Sturdivant older and heavier, was a mug shot from the database of the national police service of Canada. Wallace pulled up a third photo on his computer screen: a freeze-frame from the security footage at Peter's building. It was the man they'd seen slinking away from the building a half hour before Franklin on the night of the murder, and presumably the man Charlie and Don had watched leave the loading dock on Tuesday afternoon.

"This is good police work, Wallace. You and your team deserve credit."

"I thought so, too."

Don looked at the detective who was leaning back in his chair and thumping a pencil on the desk.

"You're getting pushback from the higher-ups?"

"I can't really talk about it."

"So you called me so we could *not* talk about it."

"I'm just doing what Travis promised you. I'm keeping you and Ms. Mack in the information loop."

"Is anybody going to Canada to question the guy?"

"It's not in the budget. I sent a query to the Toronto PD. Sturdivant has been arraigned, but his case won't come to trial for several months. He's got dual citizenship so even if we could charge him, I'm not sure we can extradite. Meanwhile, he's cooling his heels in a medium-security facility outside the city."

Don studied the file. Sturdivant didn't have a homicide rap, but he had a long list of violent crimes.

"Did you even know he was in Detroit?"

"No. We don't know when he got here or when he left. Peter had a cleaning company come into his place every two weeks, but there's no guarantee they cleaned the woodwork. We found only the one print from Sturdivant."

"Thanks for letting me know, Wallace. I'll share the info with Mack," Don said, sliding the file across the desk.

"That's yours to keep. I made a copy. Look, Rutkowski, what do you know that I don't?"

Don shook his head.

"Do you have an alternate theory about who killed Fairchild?"

"Mack does."

"Who does she think did it?"

"I'd rather not say."

"The sister?"

"Why do you say that?"

"We found out she's been moving around a lot of money. She's made two big cash withdrawals in the last couple of weeks."

"That's interesting," Don said.

"Okay. I understand. I guess you can't talk about it because she's your client, and my superiors wouldn't be too happy that I'm sharing that file with you. But unofficially, Rutkowski, let's stay in touch."

Don sat in his car a block away from police headquarters thumbing through the file. In addition to the photos, there was the fingerprint report, a history of Sturdivant's criminal activity, and a list of his known associates. The folder also included the address and telephone number of a detective at the Toronto Police Service, and a commander at the Ontario Provincial Police.

The last page in the folder was a copy of a Comerica bank statement for an account in the name of Pamela Fairchild. On the statement, two five-thousand-dollar withdrawals were circled. One two weeks ago, the other on Wednesday morning.

Chapter 12

Don greeted Karen Scanlon in the lobby of Peter's building, then introduced Charlie.

"Oh, hello. I didn't know I was meeting anyone else."

"Don and I are partners."

Karen's expression reflected her noodling on the various things that could mean. Charlie didn't try to help. They greeted the officer on duty at the elevator banks. Don showed him his PI license, and the officer checked him against the list he had. On the ride up Charlie self-consciously looked up at the camera. Karen checked herself in the mirror. She wore a white parka and fitted ski pants inside Ugg boots. A Burberry scarf was tied for fashion rather than protection from the cold. Charlie and Karen exchanged strained smiles when their eyes momentarily locked. At the second floor, the elevator opened and the vestibule light and camera sprang to life. The apartment's solid metal door was crisscrossed in crime-scene tape.

"Damn, I forgot to get the key. We'll have to go back down," Don said.

"I have mine," Karen said with no hesitation. She unzipped her designer tote, reaching into a sleeve to retrieve the key, then expertly unlocked the door and pushed it open.

"You'll probably need to turn in that key to the officer when you leave," Charlie said, not smiling.

Karen started to respond, but stopped when she got the same serious expression from Don. "I guess you're right."

"Do you mind if I get my personal items before we talk?" Karen said, discarding her jacket and heading to the bedroom.

"I'll go with you," Charlie said, following.

Karen moved immediately to a dresser drawer, and Charlie watched her pull out a few intimate items. She turned to the closet and took a small cardboard box from the shelf.

"What's that?" Charlie asked.

"A few papers Peter and I were discussing. Nothing of value to your investigation."

"I'll need to take a look at them," Charlie said. "If you're done in here, let's go to the other room."

They sat in the living area near the fireplace. Charlie found certifications of authenticity for several expensive pieces of artwork in the box. Karen aka Carrie might have been planning on claiming the art as her own.

"We understand you were with Peter in his apartment on Tuesday night," Charlie said. "How was he?"

"Who told you that?"

"We saw you on the security cameras," Don said. "By the way, the name's Carrie, isn't it?"

Karen's eyes darted nervously. Under pressure from the truth, her demeanor shifted 180 degrees. She sucked her teeth and shrugged. Karen, the refined and successful interior designer, became Carrie Ann Sketcher from Allentown, Pennsylvania. "Yeah. I was with Peter on Tuesday. I spent the night. What of it?"

"You may be aware we've been hired by Peter's family to investigate his death. I'm sure they'll want to have these documents," Charlie said, tucking the box next to her on the couch.

Scanlon sucked her teeth again. "What did you two want to talk to me about? I have other things to do today."

"Do you know if Peter was in some kind of trouble? Was there anyone with a grudge against him?" Charlie asked.

"If so, he didn't tell me. But there was always somebody pissed off at Peter. He flaunted his wealth when he shouldn't have, and he wasn't a very good judge of character. He was a pushover for any Tom, Dick, or Harry with a business scheme."

"His sister said he was investing in a liquor distillery. You know anything about that?"

Scanlon took a moment to answer, and Charlie prepared herself for a lie or half-truth.

"He told me about it," Karen admitted. "I went with Peter to one of the investor meetings. The guy lives in Windsor. Big house. Big crowd. He's dripping in money. The drinks were flowing pretty heavily that night, and Peter really can't hold his liquor. I think I ended up driving him home. Anyway, Peter told me he was considering the deal, but didn't have all the money. He'd already asked his father for the cash, and maybe his sister, but they weren't interested."

"If the guy had money, why did he need Peter's?" Don asked

"I think he needed an American investor, or something like that."

"You got this guy's name?" Don was taking notes.

"Bobby something," she scrunched her face in concentration. "His last name is like one of those revolutionary guys. You know, like Hamilton or Washington." Karen ran her manicured fingers through dirty-blond, salon-styled hair. "I remember. It was Madison. Uh, Robert Madison, I think."

As Scanlon spoke, she surveyed the room. Sometimes she'd stare at a corner and blink as if taking a photograph. It was clear to Charlie that if Karen got the chance, she'd rob the place blind and then sweet-talk her way past the cop downstairs.

"Did Peter ever talk to you about his father?"

"All the time," Karen said, swiveling her head to Charlie. "He had a complex when it came to the old man."

"Tell me," Charlie said.

"What's there to tell? I've seen it a lot with these trust-fund kids. Either they have no ambition at all, or they want to be successful on their own. Peter wanted to prove he didn't have to depend on his father."

"You ever meet Mr. Fairchild?"

"No. Is that it? I don't know what else I can tell you."

Charlie eyed the woman skeptically. There was probably a *lot* more she could tell, but they suspended the questions for now. The three returned to the lobby with no conversation. The cop was talking to the security guard. While Don signed the three out, Charlie held her palm out to Karen who pretended not to understand the gesture.

"Keys?" Charlie said with a squint.

"Oh yeah."

Karen bypassed Charlie's hand, and dangled the fob in front of the officer. "Mr. Fairchild gave me a key to his apartment. Under the circumstances, I guess I should give it to you." Carrie, the small-town grifter, was Karen the big-city sophisticate again.

Sitting in Don's Buick, they watched Karen navigate her huge vehicle through the exit.

"You know she lied about not having met Fairchild, don't you?"

"Yep. She gave it away with the eye dart and the change in subject."

"What do you make of her?" Charlie asked.

"She'd knife her mother," Don wisecracked. "If the old lady was foolish enough to turn her back."

"Speaking of mothers, I have been summoned by Ernestine this afternoon," Charlie said, reaching for the door handle. "She wouldn't tell me what it's about, but I promised to come by."

"She okay?"

"She's a lot more forgetful, but she sounded fine. Just mysterious. So I told her I'd see her this afternoon. But first I'm meeting with Pamela to lie to her again. It's getting harder and harder."

"Did you reach Franklin?"

"Not yet. I left a message on the number he provided."

"I sure hope you can talk him into giving himself up."

Charlie nodded. "You all packed for Canada?"

"Yep. I'm starting off now. I'll call in this evening."

Chapter 13

An anxious Pamela agreed to meet Charlie at a small restaurant/ bar on East Jefferson. Pamela sipped hot tea. Charlie took a gulp of iced tea, cleared her throat, and reported on the Mack team's efforts to prove Franklin's innocence. The account was rife with omissions, half-truths, and outright lies.

"How well do you know Karen Scanlon?" Charlie asked.

"Karen? Why do you ask? Surely she had nothing to do with Peter's death."

"She's just a person of interest. What can you tell me about her?"

"Not much. She's been helping Peter with furnishing his apartment. She's supposed to be some kind of designer," Pamela said, rolling her eyes. "She and Peter became fast friends. More than friends. He seemed to like her, but I don't think they were serious."

"Do you know how they met?" Charlie asked.

"I think one of my father's associates recommended her services. Why all the questions about Karen?"

Charlie answered the question with one of her own. "Did you know that Scanlon is not her real name?"

"What do you mean?"

"Her name is Carrie Sketcher."

"Why no. I didn't know that."

Pamela stopped moving and fixed her eyes on the table—almost in a trance. She didn't blink. Her manicured hands remained poised just inches from her teacup. Charlie watched her snap back to the present with a shake of the head. Pamela's eyes darted to Charlie, assessing whether her zone-out had been noticed.

"She had her own business and good connections in the city. I knew she was a few years older than Peter," Pamela said with a brief smile. "But otherwise, uh, Karen was one of Peter's more acceptable companions."

"Acceptable enough to be at Peter's memorial service yesterday," Charlie stated.

"Yes. She was there. Were you?"

"I was parked across the street. I wanted to see if anyone out of the ordinary showed up."

"I see. That shows a lot of initiative."

Suddenly Pamela's eyes filled with tears. She wiped at them with her napkin. "I'm sorry."

"No need to be," Charlie said.

"Have . . . have you spoken to Franklin again?"

The tears reappeared.

"No," Charlie lied, and changed the subject. "We also met with Peter's other woman friend. You mentioned her in our first meeting."

"What?" Pamela tried to focus on Charlie's face.

"Lainey Pratt. She seemed to really care about Peter."

"I heard him speak of Lainey, but we never met," Pamela said regaining her composure.

"And one final note. My partner, Don, is following a lead from the police about a possible suspect. He's on his way now to Toronto to investigate."

"That's a lot of paper," Charlie said, staring at the table.

Judy had commandeered the conference table, and it was layered in papers, folders, alphabetized dividers, and clips.

"Yeah. I'm starting to organize the individual files on people of interest in this case. We have quite a menagerie of suspects. How's Pamela?"

"Distraught."

"That's a copy of the master list of files," Judy said, pointing.

"Stanford and Pamela Fairchild, Karen Scanlon, Caesar Sturdivant, and Franklin Rogers?" Charlie asked, looking up from the list.

"I thought we should keep Franklin on the list."

"Right. Of course. Have you heard from Don?"

"He called at noon. He was at the outskirts of Hamilton, Ontario, where he stopped to get something to eat. He's probably in Toronto by now."

"How's the research on Pamela?"

"I started checking, but it's not going to be easy. Most of the time, with a bit of nudging, you can find someone happy to give a negative report. That's not been the case with Pamela. No one's called her warm and friendly, but the people I've spoken to say she's generous with her time and money, and does what she says she's going to do. I checked her school records, reviewed her foundation's 501(c)(3) paperwork, and looked into her financials. I even paid someone to visit the salon where she gets her nails done. So far she's clean, Charlie."

"What about those withdrawals she made?"

"I'm still looking into that. The account's in her name because it's part of her trust fund. But it may be that other people can make withdrawals."

"Okay. And Stanford?"

"One of our subcontractors is working on a dossier. We should have it this afternoon."

Charlie nodded. "Pamela did this weird zone-out thing when I met with her today."

"Zone-out thing?"

"I don't know what else to call it. One minute she was talking to me, and the next she was somewhere else."

"She's got a lot on her mind," Judy said. "What were you talking about when she started, uh, daydreaming?"

"Karen Scanlon."

ᔕ ᔕ ᔕ

Ernestine had insisted Charlie come by her apartment. She said it was important. Charlie waved at the front desk ladies and headed to the elevator.

"Your mother's waiting for you," one of the ladies beamed. "She has company and wants to surprise you."

So much for the surprise. Charlie really loved her mother's independent living facility, and the people who ran it, but it was very hard to keep your business to yourself. It was one of the things her mother regularly complained about. Charlie normally let herself in when she visited her mother, but since Ernestine had company she knocked. Her mother opened the door, looking anxious.

"Hi, Mom." Charlie looked over her mother's shoulder to the dining room and saw Franklin's mother. "What's going on?"

"Come on in, Charlene. Don isn't with you?"

"No, he had to go out of town."

"Sylvia wants to speak with you."

Charlie joined the two at the dining table for a cup of tea. Mrs. Rogers looked thinner and more tired than she had just a few days before. Charlie waited until Franklin's mother was ready to speak.

"I think someone is spying on us. I've seen a car at our curb twice in the last few days, and my phone seems to be acting up. Your mother said you wanted us to be careful on the phone, so I thought you'd want to know, and I didn't want to call."

"It's very likely the police, Mrs. Rogers."

"That's what your mother said. They think we know where Franklin is."

"Don't you?"

"Yes and no. Percy knows, but he won't tell me. I'm worried, Charlie. What if the people outside my house aren't the police? Yesterday, a man came to our door saying he worked for a newspaper, but I didn't like the looks of him. I told Franklin about it, and he wants me and Percy to go out of town for a while. He said now that there's a reward for information leading to his capture, all kinds of crazy people might start bothering us."

Charlie stood to stretch her back. She'd been sitting a lot, and standing helped her think.

"Franklin left a message for me at my office yesterday," Charlie said to Sylvia. "I called back, but I haven't heard from him. Do you know why he called?"

"Like I said, he's worried about me and his father. He's thinking of giving himself up so people will stop harassing us."

"It's a very good idea for him to surrender to the police. You think he's ready?"

"Yes. But . . . Charlie, would you go with Franklin if he turns himself in?"

"Of course. I've already told him that."

Now Sylvia rose and rounded the table to stand next to Charlie. Ernestine shifted in her chair and locked eyes with her daughter.

"Did you hear that, son?" Sylvia shouted. "Charlie will go with you."

"I heard."

Charlie spun as Franklin stepped out of the half-bath where he'd been hidden. He wore a long brown coat, hat, and a beard, and he'd shaved his head. He looked haggard, but not as edgy as the other night.

"Franklin! Why all the cloak and dagger? And why would you come to my mother's apartment if you think someone's after you?" Charlie was angry.

Ernestine interrupted. "It's my fault, Charlene. I told Sylvia to bring Franklin here today. No one would think of looking for him here."

"I'm sure all the ladies downstairs saw him, mom. You know how much they gossip. This place is a fishbowl."

Charlie turned to Franklin. "It was a foolhardy thing to do. I think I'm also being followed. Probably by the same people you're afraid of—the ones who want to keep you from revealing your suspicions about Fairchild. Let's get out of here, Franklin. Now."

They left without a goodbye. Charlie led Franklin to the stairs and down to the first floor, then hurried through the lobby to the front entrance.

"You wait here. I'll bring the car around."

Charlie turned the corner of the building, trotting through the parking lot, almost reaching the Corvette when two shots rang out in quick succession. She darted back toward the entrance but stopped when she saw Franklin heading her way, running in a crouch, holding his left arm. Charlie heard the squeal of tires and shouts from people nearby. She clicked the fob to unlock the car as she ran, jumped in, fired up the engine and burned rubber in Franklin's direction. She screeched to a halt, leaning over to open the door. Franklin tumbled in and slumped.

"I'm shot, Charlie."

"Hold on."

Charlie sped to the lot entrance, braked the 'Vette to check for traffic, and blasted out onto West Grand Boulevard. She was at 50 mph before she checked her rearview mirror. She raced another block on the Boulevard, then doubled back.

"Why are we going back?"

"We're not. I'm taking you to the nearest hospital. That's Henry Ford."

Blood oozed through the grip Franklin had on his arm. Charlie unwrapped the scarf from her neck. "Here, use this. Keep pressure on the wound."

At two o'clock on Tuesday, a dozen people filled the chairs in the emergency room. Charlie guided Franklin past the guard and up to the intake counter.

"I have a gunshot wound here," Charlie said.

The front-desk nurse jumped quickly into action. She shouted a code into the loudspeaker and rounded the counter with a wheelchair. The nurse and Charlie helped Franklin into the chair as all eyes in the emergency room took in the drama. Even the people who appeared lethargic and ill sat on the edge of their seats. Moments later, an attendant burst through the reception door.

"Gunshot wound, upper arm," the reception nurse said with urgency.

The attendant pushed the wheelchair to a set of double doors where he scanned a badge and they slid open. He dashed through with Franklin, followed by the nurse and Charlie at a run. In the examination room the nurse cut Charlie's blood-soaked scarf from Franklin's arm and threw it to the floor, then carefully removed Franklin's coat. They were joined by an emergency-room nurse who, with the desk nurse and attendant, lifted Franklin onto a gurney. The ER nurse cleaned the blood from Franklin's arm to see the wound. The staff, in emergency mode, was grabbing gauze, inserting needles for an IV, and checking Franklin's vital signs.

"Follow me," the reception nurse said, shoving a clipboard into Charlie's hands. The nurse pointed to a chair in the hall and sat next to Charlie. "I need you to fill out that form. Are you a relative?"

Charlie paused.

"If you're not a relative, we need to get in touch with one, pronto!"

"I . . . I'm his wife."

The nurse's eyes indicated she didn't believe Charlie, but she pointed to the form. "I need just the vital info. His name, address, age, is he taking any meds, does he have any allergies. Also, I have to call the police. That's standard with a gunshot injury."

Charlie nodded and reached for the business card in her jeans. "Could you call him?"

The nurse looked at Detective Wallace's business card. "I'll call him now. You stay here. Your friend is going to be okay. He's lost quite a bit of blood. That's the main thing to be concerned with."

The nurse rose and took two steps toward a phone at the wall. "What's your name?"

"Charlene Mack."

"And his?" The nurse nodded toward the interior room.

Charlie hesitated.

"It's Rogers, isn't it?"

Charlie confirmed the nurse's suspicions with a nod.

༄ ༄ ༄

Wallace stared at Charlie and crossed his legs. His coat, hat, and demeanor gave him away as a cop, so people in the emergency room gave the couple a wide berth. Two uniformed officers stood inside the reception door, and Charlie saw the blinking lights of patrol cars through the front entrance.

"You know I could arrest you for obstruction, aiding and abetting, and harboring a criminal," he commented.

Charlie let a blink say I'm sorry. "Under the circumstances, I didn't know what else to do."

"You were at the meeting, Ms. Mack. We're *supposed* to be helping each other."

"I told Franklin he should give himself up."

"When he was with you *this* time, or the time before?"

"So you *are* monitoring the Rogers's phones?"

"We're following the protocols."

They stared at each other for a few moments. Wallace removed his coat and folded it on the chair next to him.

"Don says you've noticed anomalies in the case, and you're trying to help us," Charlie said.

Wallace nodded. "Is he on his way to Toronto?"

"He is. When can I see Franklin?"

"He's in recovery. They'll be moving him to a private room."

"Someone took a shot at him, detective. He needs twenty-four-hour protection."

"We're aware of that, Ms. Mack. Who do *you* think is after him?"

Charlie looked away. The emergency room was now on full tilt. The last time she'd been in this environment, she was recovering from a blow to the head that left her unconscious. The involuntary shudder usually accompanying that memory didn't come this time.

"Rutkowski said you're looking into another angle in the case, but you don't want to talk about it," Wallace said. "Why?"

"Frankly, you wouldn't believe us. Plus, it would put you in an awkward situation. Don and I intended to tell you as soon as we can prove what we suspect."

"Did Rutkowski tell you about the large sums of money the sister withdrew?"

"Yes. We're trying to understand how that might connect to Peter's murder. But, now that you have Franklin, he's going to tell you what he's told us, and things are about to get a lot more complicated."

"What does that mean?"

"It means you won't be getting a pat on the back for having Franklin in custody. Instead, you're about to drive your bosses crazy."

As Detective Wallace leaned in to learn more, the ER doctor interrupted them with the news that they could see Franklin for a few minutes. The surgery to remove the bullet had taken only a half hour, and there were no complications. Franklin's small private room was on the third floor just a few feet away from the nurse's station. Across from the door, a cop balanced on a tilted metal chair. The officer leveled the chair and jumped to his feet when he saw Wallace approaching.

"Everything okay here, Wright?"

"Yes sir, everything's fine. I saw the prisoner a few minutes ago when the nurse changed his IV."

Charlie inched open the door and poked her head in the room. Then she pushed the door all the way and gestured for Wallace to follow. Franklin was awake, propped up on two pillows. His left arm was immobilized with a soft cast and a white sling.

"Charlie." Franklin flashed a silly drug-induced grin. "They took a bullet out of my arm. You wanna see it?"

"No. I think Detective Wallace here already has it."

"Oh. Detective. Like the police? You called the police?"

"The hospital called the police. They do that when anyone gets shot. How do you feel?"

"Good." Franklin smiled, feeling no pain.

"Rogers, are you able to answer a few questions?" Wallace asked.

"Sure." Then glancing at Charlie: "Am I able to answer a few questions?"

"I don't know. You seem kind of out of it."

"Rogers, why did you kill Peter Fairchild?" Wallace blurted.

Franklin shook his head. "No, I didn't kill Peter. Stan did!"

Wallace tried to make sense of what he'd just heard. "Stan?" Suddenly, his face registered the meaning of Franklin's statement. He looked at Charlie. A nurse stepped into the room and confronted the visitors.

"You have to go now. He needs to rest. He just came through a major surgery."

The nurse began checking Franklin's vitals on the monitor, and when Charlie and Wallace didn't move fast enough, she gave them the evil eye. In the hallway, Wallace cupped Charlie's elbow and moved her to the visitor area. He pointed to seats near the windows out of earshot of the others waiting there.

"Did Rogers mean what I think he did?"

Charlie nodded. "It's what he told me when I saw him. It's the reason he's been on the run."

"I'll be goddamned," he said too loudly. A few visitors looked in their direction.

Wallace stood. Charlie watched him walk toward the nurse's station, stop, and shove his hands into his pockets. He turned and looked at Charlie, then slowly walked back to her.

"Could he be right?"

"Maybe," Charlie answered.

"Come on, let's go."

They returned to Franklin's room, and looked in. He was sleeping peacefully. Then Wallace turned his attention to the cop on duty.

"I don't want anyone but medical personnel in this room, officer. I mean it. No priests, no flower deliveries, no cleaning people, no peppermint patties, or whatever you call them."

"Candy stripers," Charlie corrected.

"Right. None of them. Is that clear?"

"Yes sir."

"If there is anything out of the ordinary, call me directly," Wallace said, handing the officer his card.

100

"Yes sir."

Wallace insisted Charlie accompany him to the police station, but allowed her to follow in her car. Arriving, he escorted her to an empty office, left her there, and closed the door. She turned on her phone, retrieved Don's message, and called back.

"What's shaking, Mack? Sorry I missed your call earlier."

"Don, I'm at police headquarters."

"Okay. Did something happen?"

"Franklin was shot. I took him to Henry Ford Hospital. They called the police. Wallace knows about old man Fairchild."

"Well, the bird's out of the coop now. Who shot at him?"

"Franklin said it was someone in a white SUV. We were leaving my mother's apartment, but I didn't see them."

"Your mother's place?"

"Long story. But Ernestine and Franklin's mother were in cahoots."

"What did Wallace say?"

"He hasn't said much of anything. But he gets the gravity of the situation. I'm locked in a back office."

"He could have put you in a cell, Mack."

"I know. I think he's reeling from the allegation about Stanford."

"Without a doubt. Nothing to do now except tell the truth, which will bite someone in the ass. Let's just hope it's not yours."

Chapter 14

Don had an appointment at the Toronto Police Service at 4 p.m. The conversation with the Ontario Provincial Police was a courtesy. To kill time, he walked around the downtown neighborhood. Toronto had a feeling of purpose. Don wouldn't be able to explain it to Charlie or his wife Rita if they asked, but he felt an energy in this city that Detroit was missing.

Don found a McDonald's and took a seat facing Grenville Street. A few teenagers came in, ordered fries and sodas, and left, eating and laughing. The other customers were clusters of older Asian women in animated conversation who commandeered the corners of the restaurant.

"Novak, I need you to check out something for me," Don said into his phone.

"Don, it's customary to say hello when you begin a call."

"Don't start with me. I already spoke with you once today. I'm done with hellos. I might have to stay overnight. Check out some reasonably priced places for me, will ya? A motel is better, so I don't have to pay for parking."

"Okay. You're in Toronto now."

"Yep."

"Did you speak to Charlie?"

"Yep. She called from DPD."

"What should we do?"

"About what?"

"About Charlie! What if they put her in jail?"

"I think she'd already be behind bars if they intended to press charges. Anyway, let's not worry about that until we have to. Did you find anything about the other suspects?"

"Not yet."

"Alright. I have a meeting in a half hour with the Toronto detective. If I don't answer, leave me a message."

Toronto's police and municipal building looked like a museum— glass-block windows, pink granite, and weird angles. Too artsy-fartsy for Don's tastes. The police headquarters in Detroit's Greektown was built like a place where justice and punishment were meted out—for better or for worse.

Detective Harper Li greeted Don in the massive first-floor atrium. It was bright and airy with a floating staircase to the upper levels and a domed ceiling. Li was talkative, and he chattered as they took the stairs to the fourth floor. Don saw an elevator, but apparently this young detective's cardio workout included stair climbing. Li was a seven-year veteran of the police service. He'd been born in Hong Kong, but his parents immigrated to Toronto when he was fifteen years old.

"They were both fans of American culture," Li said. "I know more about the U.S. than most Canadians. My mother read every classic American book she could find. That's why I've got this name, Harper. Get it?" Li joked. "My younger brother's name is Robert E."

Don smiled at the acknowledgment of the confederate general, but hadn't caught the literary reference.

"My mom has a few relatives in Michigan. We might have moved to Detroit, but it was easier for us to migrate to Canada where most of my parents' family and friends were going."

"Toronto's a nice city. I walked around a little before our appointment," Don said. "I think right now it's got a lot more going for it than Detroit. We've had financial problems in the last few years. Our downtown looks nothing like this."

"So I've read. But you still have car bragging rights. I bought a Camaro last year."

"Nice. I saw the new Camaro at the auto show a couple of years ago. It's a whole lotta car. I drive a Buick Lucerne. Eight-cylinder. I need the power and the space. I have a son and a daughter on the way."

Li settled in his chair, ready to shift to business. Don did the same.

"Detective Wallace asked me to pave the way for you to interview Caesar Sturdivant," Li said. "I pulled his sheet. His father is deceased, an émigré from Antigua, but Sturdivant was born here. His mother is American. Still alive and moved back to Ohio a decade ago. His criminal record dates back twenty years. What's your interest?"

"He may be connected to a homicide in Detroit. We, or rather the police, picked up his print at the crime scene. My partner and I are investigating his possible involvement in the murder of our client's brother."

Li looked skeptical. "He's been convicted of assault, breaking and entering, and larceny. He's a chronic criminal, but not a murderer."

Don nodded. "I understand. But the person who may have hired him is very rich. Sturdivant may have gotten an offer he couldn't resist."

"Well, he's in a correctional facility about forty miles from the city. He's agreed to see you tomorrow morning. I'll drive you."

"That's not necessary. I have a car."

"I've been ordered to accompany you on the visit," Li said bluntly.

"Okay. Got it. But I'll pick you up."

Li shook his head. "Nope. We need to show up in a patrol car. I bypassed procedure, and finagled with a lot of gatekeepers to get you in with him on such short notice. Believe me, the Bureau of Prisons does not like changes to the routine. Visiting hours are on weekends. Inmate meetings require a minimum of three guards. I had to tell them you're a bigwig from Detroit just to get you the appointment."

"What time do you need me here?" Don asked.

"Get here at eight-thirty. We can't get into the facility until ten."

Don called Judy from his car. "Hello, Don!" she answered.

"Hello. Satisfied?"

"I am. So, are you staying?"

"Yes. I have an early appointment. So I need a place downtown."

"I already found you a place. You want me to book it?"

"Yes, please."

"I'll text you the info. Meanwhile, Charlie's here now and wants to speak with you."

"So you're not in jail," Don said when Charlie got on the line.

"No. DPD is just glad to have Franklin in custody. Wallace is a good guy. He told his bosses some story about Franklin calling me after he was shot, and he hasn't kicked Franklin's suspicions about Fairchild upstairs."

"Smart man. What's next for your ex?"

"He'll be in the hospital a day or two under protection, then moved to an infirmary. I had to call his parents and Pamela. She was hysterical. She thinks she'll use her father's influence to have Franklin moved to a suburban hospital."

"You know he's still in danger, don't you, Mack? If we're right about things, Fairchild will be trying to keep Franklin from talking."

"I know. I convinced Wallace to double up on the police detail at the hospital. He's on our side, Don, but that means he's way out on a limb. You should give him a call to let him know about your progress with Sturdivant. Are you seeing him tomorrow?"

"Yeah. One of the detectives here pulled some strings to get that done. Nice guy. Young. Talks a lot. Chinese. His name's Harper Li."

"Oh, like the author," Charlie said. "That's a funny name to give a Chinese kid. I guess somebody really liked *To Kill a Mockingbird*."

"I guess so," Don said, clueless.

"Okay, here's Judy with your motel info. I'll call you later tonight. Pamela is insisting on an in-person meeting. She's on her way. I need to figure out what I can tell her."

Pamela arrived at the Mack offices at 6 p.m. dressed down in designer jeans, Jimmy Choo shoes, and a three-quarter black zip-up leather coat. Her blond hair was pulled back with a red leather headband, and her Burberry satchel was the size of overnight luggage.

She assessed the office suite as Charlie and Judy escorted her to the conference room. Judy had made a fresh pot of coffee, but Pamela said she preferred the small bottle of apple-grape juice offered. She didn't show any signs of the anxiety she'd displayed earlier in the day, but her eyes were tinged red, and a few dark circles betrayed the expertly applied concealer.

"I wanted to meet here, rather than the house, because I didn't want Father to be involved," Pam said. "He's not even pretending anymore. He's convinced Franklin killed Peter, and has been on the phone all afternoon with the police chief and the hospital administrator. They all believe he's concerned about his son-in-law, but really Daddy wants Franklin to stand trial for Peter's murder."

Pamela paused to take a deep breath. She unzipped her jacket and removed a Burberry wool scarf.

"How's your mother?" Judy asked.

"Sad and exhausted."

"I'm sure this is very hard on her."

Pam nodded her agreement. "I told Daddy you're following up on other suspects who may have killed Peter."

Charlie and Judy glanced between them momentarily, aware that last bit of info might mean trouble for them.

"How did he respond to that?" Charlie asked.

"He was skeptical. I thought he'd be impressed that your colleague was traveling all the way to Toronto, but he seemed annoyed."

There was an awkward silence while Charlie and Judy waited to see if Pamela had more to say. After all, she'd called this meeting. Charlie moved to the coffeemaker and poured herself another cup from the carafe. She poured more coffee for Judy, too, and returned to the table. Pamela kept her eyes fixed on Charlie.

"I understand you were with Franklin when he was shot."

"Who told you that?"

"It's not difficult for Daddy to get information."

Charlie let that sink in.

"I guess not. Your father has a lot of influence. Franklin's mother arranged for us to meet. He was ready to turn himself in."

"Sylvia called *you?*" Pamela's voice couldn't disguise her anger. Her face twitched. She was not a person used to looking through the lens of green-eyed envy.

Charlie squared her shoulders, clenching her jaw, suddenly feeling her own anger at being challenged.

"My *mother* called me," Charlie said icily. "She and Sylvia are church friends. They thought having me accompany Franklin to the police would be the safest thing to do."

"That turned out not to be right," Pamela said sarcastically.

"We've heard from our partner in Canada," Judy said, trying to lessen the friction. "The police found a fingerprint of a convicted felon at Peter's apartment, and Don has determined this man's whereabouts."

"You think this is who killed Peter?"

"It's a reasonable guess," Charlie said.

"Well, that *is* good. What's this person's name?" Pamela asked, pulling out her phone to make a note.

"He's been identified as Caesar Sturdivant," Charlie said. "Does that name mean anything to you?"

"No. Why should it?"

Charlie shifted in her chair. "Just trying to make a connection between this man and Peter, that's all."

"No. I never heard of him. But I'll ask Daddy."

"I wish you wouldn't do that yet."

107

"Why not?"

"I don't want to get his hopes up," Charlie lied. "I'd like to be able to rule this guy in or out before we share his name too widely. Deal?"

Pamela gave some thought to Charlie's reasoning. "But Daddy's so sure Franklin is guilty. Maybe knowing about this new guy will give him second thoughts."

Charlie shook her head. "It's better to wait. Please, let us do our job."

"I guess I could wait," Pamela said, putting her phone away.

"It occurs to me that I'm making a huge assumption," Charlie said. "Do you want us to stay on the case? Now that Franklin is in custody, you might want to go in a different direction."

"Yes, of course you're still on the case. As soon as the police realize Daddy believes Franklin is guilty, they'll stop looking for any other suspects."

"That's not necessarily true. Franklin still protests his innocence."

Pamela shook her head. "You noted it yourself, Charlie. My husband isn't as influential as my father."

Pamela excused herself to go to the restroom, leaving Judy and Charlie alone in the conference room.

"She's jealous of you," Judy said, unplugging the coffee pot.

"It got a little tense there for a moment, didn't it?"

"I can't blame her, Charlie. As far as she knows it's the second time Franklin has been in touch with you, and she's not heard from him once."

"Yeah, I can understand why she'd be pissed."

"You think the police will let her see him in the hospital?"

"Probably."

"You think he'll tell her his suspicions about her father?"

"I don't think so. But who knows? You still think she's innocent?"

"I think she's a faithful wife grieving for her dead brother, afraid for her husband, and reeling with how much her life has changed. Like I said, everyone I spoke with says Pamela's a good player. I don't care for her nose-in-the-air countenance, but I'm sure it's because that's how she was raised. After all, if she loves Franklin, and he loves her, she can't be too bad, right?" Judy reminded Charlie.

Charlie responded with an "I'm not so sure" smirk, then stepped down from her high horse and smiled. She was proud of how well Judy was doing in her new investigative role.

"You know something, Judy Novak, you're being a show-off. You don't have to be right *all* the time."

"I need to make some points during my probationary status," Judy quipped. "Charlie . . ." Judy lowered her voice. "I think you should go with Pamela to the hospital. She's probably never been to an inner-city hospital. She'll need someone to hold her hand."

Pamela returned from the restroom and began gathering her belongings. She noticed the stares and sudden silence.

"Why do I feel you two have been talking about me?"

Charlie pulled her car into a visitor space in the hospital lot. Pamela had followed in her Mercedes and opted for valet parking. Charlie waited while Pamela gave the attendant instructions and handed him a bill. It was a big tip because he tilted his hat in tribute, and he wasn't wearing one.

Pamela must have called her father on the way over because they'd only been at the hospital five minutes before the automated doors parted and Stanford Fairchild, followed by another man, stepped into the lobby. He entered as if he were at the premiere of a movie starring him.

Pamela immediately jumped to her feet and ran to her father, who enfolded her in a bear hug. He peered over his daughter's shoulder at Charlie as she approached.

"You must be Ms. Mack," he said, sliding Pamela to his left and extending a hand.

"Yes sir. I'm sorry for your loss, Mr. Fairchild."

Fairchild had been hearing those words nonstop for almost a week. He'd become practiced at displaying the remorseful eyes and tightened lips. He flashed it all at Charlie. But beneath the kind words and contrite body language, the two sized up each other.

"I didn't know you were coming, Daddy," Pamela cooed.

Stanford slowly dragged his eyes from Charlie's and looked down onto Pamela's teary cheeks.

"I wanted to make sure you had no trouble seeing Franklin. Have you checked with the front desk yet?"

"Yes. They sent a message to the officer in charge because he has to approve any visitors."

As if on cue, Wallace approached them from the hospital's east corridor. Charlie hoped the detective was as smart as Don seemed to think he was.

"Mrs. Rogers," Wallace said. "I understand you want to see your husband. I came down to escort you personally."

Wallace nodded to Fairchild and Charlie. The man hovering behind Fairchild hadn't said a word, but he had the anxious mannerisms of an attorney ready to attack at the signal of his boss.

"I'm afraid the rest of you will have to wait here," Wallace said.

"I understand, detective," Charlie said, trying to help out. "You're following protocols."

"That's correct, Ms. Mack."

The attorney stepped into the body circle. Wallace listened, stone-faced, while Fairchild and the lawyer, talking simultaneously, made the case for accompanying Pamela to Franklin's guarded room. Finally, Fairchild recognized the set of Wallace's jaw as "hell no" and stopped talking. The lawyer did too. Fairchild glowered at the detective and then at Charlie. He wasn't used to anyone, let alone two African American working stiffs, standing in his way. He turned from the group and began talking into his phone. He was taking his demand up the food chain.

Wallace took advantage of Fairchild's shift in focus to guide Pamela toward the elevators. She looked back toward her father, but Wallace was quick.

"We'll be right back," Wallace said over his shoulder.

Only a few people sat in the lobby. It was a far different scene from yesterday's emergency waiting room, but the lady at the front desk and the smattering of visitors looked upon the group with interest. Perhaps they recognized Fairchild. Perhaps they recognized the tones and animation of the conversation as potential drama. Charlie took a seat. The lawyer lingered near the middle of the room, watching Fairchild's back as he spoke to someone on the phone. Eventually, the attorney came to sit across from Charlie.

"I'm Robert Carlberg with Ziegler and Arnow."

"I'm Charlene Mack with Mack Private Investigations."

"I've heard of you."

"Pamela Rogers hired me to help prove her husband's innocence."

The lawyer gave a two hundred-dollars-an-hour shrug. "The case seems fairly cut-and-dried. The police have some definitive evidence against Rogers."

"We don't think so. We'll know for sure when we complete our investigation," Charlie countered.

Fairchild joined them, standing at the row of seats and looking around the lobby. He seemed impatient and uncomfortable in the setting.

"How is your investigation going, Ms. Mack?" he said, finally sitting. "Oh, and by the way, thank you for the flowers you sent to the service."

Good old Judy.

"You're welcome, sir. As I was telling Pamela this afternoon, we have a few new leads."

"Pam mentioned a name. Caesar Sturdivant I believe."

So she didn't wait to tell her father. Charlie watched the lawyer copy the name in his portfolio.

"Yes. He's incarcerated in Toronto. My associate, Mr. Rutkowski, has arranged a meeting with him. Mr. Fairchild, I know this may be awkward, but Pamela tells me you're convinced Franklin is *guilty* of murdering your son."

"All the evidence points to him."

"It's mostly circumstantial evidence, sir, and we're interviewing Peter's known associates who might have additional information."

"And?"

111

"Nothing so far," Charlie admitted. "But we've found inconsistencies we want to further investigate."

Fairchild gave a look Charlie couldn't quite read. It might be either boredom or concern.

"You know Franklin says he's innocent," Charlie offered.

"Does *he* know who killed Peter?"

Charlie hesitated a second, which she hoped Fairchild didn't notice. "No. He says he was knocked unconscious. When he came to, Peter was dead."

The lawyer's smirk showed skepticism. Fairchild's stare seemed empathetic.

"Given your relationship with Franklin, Ms. Mack, this may be awkward for *you*."

Fairchild used Charlie's words to turn the table on the conversation. It pissed her off.

"I'm trained to separate my personal feelings from facts and circumstances, Mr. Fairchild."

"And we both know how hard that is to do, don't we?" he said.

Charlie didn't respond. She decided she disliked the man. He was too smug, too sure his power and prestige made him smarter than everyone else. Charlie mentally added Pamela to a different category. She had turned out relatively normal given the arrogance of her father.

"I appreciate that you're doing your best to pacify my daughter. I'm sure you both find it hard to believe that Franklin could be capable of this kind of violence."

"You're right, Mr. Fairchild. I don't believe Franklin could commit such a crime. However, I've learned through experience that any man, under the right circumstances, is capable of anything."

Fairchild's nod suggested he didn't get Charlie's dig to his own culpability. He turned to his lawyer, reviewing a document on an opened laptop, already focused on the particulars of business. Sharon Fairchild was more likely involved in the details of mourning. Charlie wanted to be away from them so she moved to a seat closer to the front desk. The receptionist, a middle-aged black woman, made eye contact and they both smiled.

Charlie was a business owner herself, but she knew her priorities were different. Like other industrial cities, Detroit was born of twentieth-century manufacturing, and fueled by the wealth-dreams of white men like Stanford Fairchild who had imagination, ambition, and privilege. The loom of capitalism wove a tapestry of metropolises where laborers had flocked, hoping to live the American dream. A hundred years later, in most of these urban centers a bevy of black women were the gatekeepers of that dream. They were corporate presidents, members of city councils and school boards, and principals of schools—like Charlie's mother. They were social workers, librarians, teachers, homemakers, even private investigators. These women worked to maintain the equilibrium of working-class microstructures sprung from larger systems that were often rigged against the little guy.

Charlie studied the backs of Fairchild and his lawyer. More and more she believed Franklin's suspicions. Like Franklin, Pamela might be just a pawn in her father's life-and-death game of chess.

The swoosh of the sliding doors shifted Charlie's attention to the entrance. She stood when Captain Travers, in uniform and followed by two of his lieutenants, stepped into the lobby and stopped. The three handsome men were a recruitment poster for the Detroit Police Department. Travers stared at Charlie for a few seconds, and then scanned the room until he saw Fairchild. He looked at Charlie again and gestured with the tilt of his head. They moved to the side of the room.

Travers leaned in so he wouldn't be overhead. "What's going on? I got a call from the chief's office."

Charlie pointed toward Fairchild. "His daughter is upstairs with Franklin. We weren't granted access. He's not used to hearing 'no.'"

Travis rolled his eyes. The pressure he'd received from higher-ups in the past week showed in the circular lines at his mouth and under his eyes. Charlie didn't really like Travers, and vice versa, but each understood Detroit's hierarchies.

"Okay. Let's go. I'm taking you all up with me."

113

When they arrived on the hospital's fourth floor, they walked through service units demarcated by signage and carpeting of different colors. Decals on glass doors announced the cardiology unit, pediatrics, internal medicine and infectious diseases until they arrived at the wing for high-security patients. A long hallway led to Franklin's room. Outside the door, a patrol officer sat upright in a metal chair, his back straight and his eyes scanning the group approaching him. Detective Wallace leaned against the wall. Both detective and officer stood at alert when they spotted Travers, and the other two DPD muckety-mucks. Wallace and Charlie shared a wary glance.

"Status report, Wallace," Travers ordered.

"His wife is in there with him," Wallace said.

"You frisked her before she went in?"

Both the patrolman and detective showed guilty looks.

"Uh, no," Wallace said. "She refused to be frisked, but we did take her bag."

The patrol officer removed the giant bag from the arm of his chair and let it dangle on his hand as proof.

"How long has she been in there?"

"Maybe a half hour."

Travers knocked on the door, then held it open as Fairchild, Charlie, Wallace, and the two lieutenants entered. Wallace signaled to the patrolman to remain alert. Fairchild gave a similar signal to his lawyer.

Franklin sat upright on the hospital bed with Pamela next to him. They had sad faces, red-rimmed eyes, and were holding hands. Franklin caught Charlie's eye for a second, and Fairchild went into immediate "I'm in charge" mode.

"Franklin, how are you doing?" His voice boomed through the room.

"I'm okay," Franklin said, adjusting the covers around the waist of his hospital gown. He didn't make eye contact with Fairchild. Travis stood near the empty side chair staring down at Franklin.

The two lieutenants stood near the door with arms crossed over thick belts heavy with the tools of their trade.

Pamela left her perch to stand next to her father near the foot of the bed. Charlie purposely moved up to block Fairchild's view of Franklin.

"I understand you have, so far, declined to provide us a written statement, Mr. Rogers," Travers said.

Charlie felt Fairchild shift behind her to see Franklin's face. She held firm in her spot and hoped Franklin understood the nearly imperceptible shake of her head, which meant now was not the time to come clean. Charlie didn't think he'd confided in Pamela. She looked sad, but not stunned. The issue was cleared up when she spoke.

"We've secured an attorney for Franklin," Pamela said. "Upon her advice, he won't be answering any questions or signing any statements."

Charlie looked over her shoulder. Pamela had squared hers and taken a step away from her father.

"What's this about an attorney?" Fairchild asked, voice raised. His tension surged through the room, and Charlie felt it against her back. There would be another big argument in the Fairchild home tonight.

The head nurse cut off any additional conversation when she opened the door and asked everyone to clear out. Travers and his men left immediately. Pamela moved to Franklin's side, and the husband and wife entwined hands. Fairchild stared at the two for a moment and turned to leave. Charlie fell into line behind him.

After a few minutes, Pamela joined the group in the hallway where Fairchild was barking orders to his attorney and Travers. Charlie pulled Pamela aside.

"Is it true you've retained a lawyer for Franklin?"

"He had the name of someone, and we called her."

"May I ask the name?"

Pamela pulled out her phone, scrolled, and showed Charlie the screen.

"Serena Carruthers."

"You know her?" Pamela asked.

"I've met her. She's a good lawyer." *And a force to be reckoned with,* Charlie decided not to add.

"Franklin said they used to date," Pamela added. "He also said she has a reputation for winning cases and taking down those in power. He thought we might need that if he's going to get the police to look for the real killer."

"Did Franklin say anything more to you about that night, or any ideas he might have about who set him up?"

"No. He said he knows you and I, and this new lawyer, will do all we can to save him. He called us his three musketeers."

If Serena Carruthers is going to be involved, it will be more like Diana Ross and the Supremes, Charlie thought.

Chapter 15

Don and Detective Li arrived at the Ontario Correctional Institute at 10:15. Li's patrol car gained them access to a lot closer to the building than other visitors. Don watched as Li locked his sidearm and Don's Ruger in the trunk. Although he had to fill out visitor information, provide fingerprints, and go through a full-body scan, Don was otherwise expedited through the process. He and Li were taken to a ten-foot-square room for their visit with Caesar Sturdivant who, after a twenty-minute wait, arrived escorted by a corrections officer and his attorney.

Sturdivant was a dark-skinned man built like a sturdy rectangle. There was no clear delineation of torso and legs from his thick head to his cuffed ankles. He wore short-sleeved orange prison-issue, and had an array of tats on both arms and his neck. Sturdivant, realizing he didn't know either of his visitors, looked between the two with curiosity. He gave most of his attention to Don, who stared without breaking the gaze. Don mentally checkmarked Sturdivant's fit to the man seen in the grainy security footage at Peter Fairchild's loft.

The guard shackled Sturdivant to a table-bench combo secured to the floor.

"I'll be right outside," the guard said in a no-nonsense tone. "Hit the light switch when you're ready to leave. Or, uh, if there's any kind of trouble."

Don had been leaning against the far wall and took a seat at the bench. Li opted to remain standing.

"Who are you guys?" Sturdivant asked with darting eyes. "Did somebody send you?"

"Who would send us?" Don asked, shifting quickly to police mode.

"Wait a minute . . ." the attorney raised his hands to block the question.

Li decided to take charge. "I'm Detective Li with the Toronto Metropolitan Police. This is Don Rutkowski. He's a private investigator from Detroit."

At the mention of Detroit, Sturdivant flinched and caught Don's eyes, but this time only for a second.

"Rutkowski wants to question your client about an open police investigation in Detroit."

"I don't have to answer any questions," Sturdivant growled. His lips tightened and he crossed his beefy arms on the table. Don looked at a bejeweled crown tattoo circling the prisoner's bicep, guessing it might have taken six hours of ink work. The prisoner saw Don's interest in his artwork and released his arms into his lap.

"Okay, but you and your attorney did say we could come and have a conversation," Li said. "That's why we're here. So will you listen to what Mr. Rutkowski has to say?"

The attorney leaned over and whispered something in Sturdivant's ear. The prisoner scowled at Don. "Go ahead," the attorney said.

"Caesar, your fingerprints were found at a crime scene," Don began. "Where the member of a prominent Detroit family was murdered."

"I don't know nothing about that."

"You haven't even heard the details."

"I don't need to hear no details. I don't know nothing about a murder."

Don sat quietly for a few seconds, then reached into his jacket pocket and pulled out a folded piece of paper. Sturdivant sat forward in his seat, staring at the paper as Don pretended to read it.

"I've been working with the Detroit police. The man who was murdered is Peter Fairchild. It says here there's security footage of you leaving the scene of the homicide."

"Naw. That ain't right," Sturdivant protested. "I never set foot in that building."

"Who said anything about a building?" Don asked.

Sturdivant's eyes widened and his jaw moved but he didn't speak. His attorney shifted positions in his seat.

"They saw you in the vestibule, Caesar," Don chided. "That's that little hallway outside the elevator. There was a camera!"

"That Frank guy did it. That's what the police say!"

"That's before Franklin told them his side of the story. That's before your fingerprints were found on the windowsill. And that's before Peter's family hired me and my partners to find the real murderer." Don's voice got louder with each declaration.

Sturdivant began to rise from the bench, and Don rose, too. The attorney put a hand on his client's shoulder, pushing him back into his seat. Li moved to the table.

"I need a few words alone with my client," the lawyer asserted.

Forty-five minutes later Sturdivant's attorney signaled the guard. Don and Detective Li, who had been cooling their heels in the hallway, returned to the interrogation room.

Sturdivant's demeanor was changed. His shoulders, previously tense with anger, had given way to sloped resignation. He kept his head down, and his hands rested at his sides.

"My client wants to make a statement," the attorney said somberly. "But he wants assurance the information he provides will allow him to receive consideration."

"What kind of consideration?" Detective Li asked.

"He will want to have his cooperation reflected in the charges brought against him. He may also need future protection."

"Protection?" Don asked.

"His information will, uh, cause the ire of some powerful people."

"Look," Li said. "I can't make any deals without understanding the nature of the information Mr. Sturdivant can provide. Is this related to the crime in Detroit that Mr. Rutkowski mentioned?"

The attorney nodded his affirmation.

"Well, that further complicates any negotiations with Mr. Sturdivant. We'll have to involve the Detroit police and the prosecutors in that jurisdiction." Li looked toward Don.

"That's Wayne County in Michigan," Don said. "The prosecutor will need to feel Sturdivant's information will lead to an indictment."

"We understand," the attorney said. "So I've advised my client to give a partial statement, which will provide the nature of the information and help you get the permissions you need."

All three men turned to Sturdivant. He hadn't raised his head from his chest since they'd returned to the room. He looked up now. First at his attorney, then to Don.

"I was at the apartment where that Fairchild guy was killed. I was hired to help, but I didn't shoot the guy. Somebody else did."

"And you know who?"

Sturdivant nodded.

"And that person paid you to help with the crime?" Don said with a sneer.

"Nope. Somebody else paid me."

"And who was that?"

"You'll have to cut me a deal to find out," Sturdivant said defiantly.

Don was awakened by the motel phone's blare, which seemed to reverberate even after it went silent. Sitting up with a start he looked at the red lights of the clock. 1 a.m. His mobile sat quietly on the side table. The green light showed it was on and fully charged.

"What the hell." Don grabbed the receiver just as a second ring sounded. "What?"

"Rutkowski, it's Detective Li. Get dressed. I'm downstairs and we need to drive to the prison."

"Why?"

"Sturdivant was attacked. He's alive, but he's scared and wants to talk now."

Don's time in the Marines had taught him a few life lessons, which remained with him. One was how to take a five-minute shower. Another was laying out socks in your shoes for a quick dress and, most importantly, keeping your gun close to your line of exit. He had dressed, showered, and swished mouthwash in less than five minutes. He didn't have time to think about packing anything, so he hung the "do not disturb" sign on the door handle.

Li turned on the car's top lights as soon as Don was buckled in, then zipped into the sparse traffic. "That coffee in the holder is for you," he said.

"God bless you," Don responded, taking a sip. "So what happened?"

"I got a call from the lawyer. Just after midnight a guard found Sturdivant lying on the floor of his cell in a pool of blood. He was knifed. They do bed checks every two hours, so somebody attacked him between ten and midnight."

"Did they question his cell mates?"

"He's in a single cell. The two men on either side of him say they didn't see or hear anything."

"Sturdivant is in the infirmary?"

"Yes. But he'll be transferred to a nearby hospital as soon as possible. He may be gone before we get there."

"Damn."

"Who did you tell about our conversation with Sturdivant?" Li asked.

"Nobody but my two partners. I called them last night. Who'd you tell on your end?"

"Well, you heard my call with the Detroit police. What's the detective's name?"

"Wallace."

"Right. Then the chief prosecutor in Wayne County and of course my superiors. Oh, and my wife."

"She's probably not our leak," Don said sourly.

"Nope. But there's a leak somewhere. This can't be coincidence."

"Don't believe in them either."

"I guess your guy, Fairchild, must have a very long reach."

"He's got power and money to buy all sorts of muscle. You'll need to find a safe house for Sturdivant, and he'll need protection at the hospital."

"I'll make those calls as we drive," Li agreed. "You still think he'll be extradited to Michigan?"

"Probably. But the first order of business is to get him locked down. The second is to hear what he has to say. I really hope he's ready to talk. Maybe we can get a deposition out of him before somebody else tries to bump him off."

Chapter 16

Pamela asked Charlie to accompany her to the first meeting with attorney-at-law Serena Carruthers. The firm had swanky offices on the twenty-first floor of Tower 600 in the RenCen complex.

They stepped through the glass doors and were directed to a private seating area and offered coffee, tea, bottled water, gourmet cookies, and chocolates. The posh suite was evidence that even during an economic downturn for Detroit, good lawyers were still a sought-after commodity. They waited less than ten minutes before being escorted to a conference room with floor-to-ceiling windows, and decorated with more live flowers than usually found at a funeral.

Carruthers, two of her associates, and an assistant rose when Charlie and Pamela entered the room. Charlie had first met Serena ten years ago at a fundraising event for the Charles H. Wright Museum of African American History. Charlie owned a public relations firm at the time, and Serena had been recruited to a prestigious law firm where she was on a partner track. Later, they served together in Leadership Detroit, a networking initiative for the city's rising influence leaders. Their social networks included a few shared acquaintances, but they'd never hung out or pursued a friendship.

Serena greeted Pamela. Her employees followed suit. Then she turned to Charlie.

"It's been a long time. We don't seem to move in the same

circles anymore," she said, giving Charlie a hug. "But I hear you're doing well."

"Yes, things are okay for me. But I see you're doing *very* well."

"It's *not* true what they say," Serena said with an eye twinkle. "Crime *does* pay."

"Speaking of paying, I'd like to get our business underway," Pamela said, interrupting the reunion.

"Of course. You're right," Serena said without a missed beat, pointing to two seats at the table. "We do have serious matters to discuss."

The Peter Fairchild murder and the manhunt for Franklin Rogers had been well covered by the newspapers and local broadcast stations in the region, but Serena's thoroughness required a fresh retelling from both Pamela and Charlie. Of course, Charlie left out the most volatile information—Franklin's allegations against his father-in-law. Serena asked about the additional suspects being investigated by the Mack Agency and the attack on Franklin.

"The attack is odd, don't you think?" Serena asked Charlie.

"It's hard to say."

Serena gave Charlie a puzzled look. "What's your line of inquiry around the shooting?"

"I didn't get the license plate, but the police are securing the camera footage."

"That's not what I'm asking. Why would someone shoot at Franklin? That's what I want to understand."

"It's like I said. He felt he was being followed." Charlie weighed her words to tell most of the truth. "Franklin told his mother it could be someone trying to collect the reward for finding him."

"Well, that's a possibility," Serena said, making a note. "Is that what you think?" It was her third attempt to get a straight answer from Charlie.

Charlie shook her head. "I think Peter's real killer is trying to keep Franklin quiet."

"Well. Now that's a theory I can work with. Do the police accept that argument?"

"Not exactly."

"Why not?"

Pamela intercepted. "Because my father has them convinced Franklin is guilty."

"Is that so?" Serena said, squinting her eyes.

She placed her $500 Montblanc ballpoint on top of her monogrammed legal pad. She shifted her gaze between Pamela and Charlie, then at her assistant and junior lawyers, with a "watch this" look. They dutifully kept their pens poised over their notebooks.

"Pamela? May I call you Pamela?"

"Yes, of course."

Charlie noticed a strand of blond hair had escaped Pamela's perfect coif and dangled at her forehead. In the car she'd described the huge row she'd had with her father about hiring Serena. He thought it a waste of money. Pamela had countered that she'd spend all the money at her disposal to prove Franklin's innocence.

"I believe every single person deserves the best defense possible. I've defended clients I knew were guilty, and ones I believed innocent. But I like to know the difference. Do the two of you believe Franklin's story?"

"Yes." Pamela spoke up right away.

Charlie finally answered, affirming Franklin's innocence, and Serena noted the hesitation.

"Do you have doubts, Charlie?"

"No. But there are complications."

"What complications?" Carruthers asked.

Pamela twisted in her chair leaning toward Charlie. Her anxiety filled the distance between them, and Charlie didn't dare look her way. Pamela wouldn't like the decision she'd made last night after talking to Don. It was the only way Charlie could feel comfortable going forward in a case where she had to lie to her client. While everyone waited for Charlie's response, she stared at the luxurious grain in the oak conference table, mentally arranging and rearranging the facts, questions, and speculations. Then she switched from her investigator hat to the lawyer hat.

125

Charlie turned to Pamela. "I hope this doesn't disappoint you, but I think it's best I resign from the case."

"What? . . . you can't do that . . ."

"Wait. Hear me out. I have a proposal. I still absolutely believe in Franklin's innocence, but I think it makes sense, now that you're hiring Serena, to have the investigation run by Serena, with me reporting to the Carruthers firm. Think about it. It was your father's suggestion to hire us. Now that he's on the fence about Franklin, it makes things cleaner. We can report all our findings directly to Serena."

Pamela shook her head, loosening more hair onto her forehead. Her face was getting splotchy, and her chin quivered. "No, I don't like that. We have to work together. I know you believe in Franklin. I need your support to keep the police interested in the case."

Charlie knew things looked promising with Sturdivant's deposition. Don had reported he might be an eyewitness to Peter's murder. That would keep the police interested.

"I'm positive we can keep the police engaged in the case," Charlie said. "But since Serena will be representing Franklin, she'll have more leeway with privileged communications. Technically, anything the Mack Agency discovers now should be shared with the police, whether it works for, or against, Franklin. If we're working for Serena, we won't be obligated to share our information."

Charlie scanned those around the table. Pamela looked confused. Serena skeptical. The associates were waiting for Serena to tell them what to think. Charlie figured there was just enough truth in her reasoning for Pamela to agree to the plan. But she could see from her stare that Serena wasn't buying the ploy.

"We have a team of investigators we usually work with," Serena finally said. "Of course, we'd make an exception if Pamela insists the Mack Agency continue to work on the case."

Pamela was still dubious, but reluctantly agreed to the arrangement and left the conference room with Serena to work out their agreement for legal representation. Charlie stayed to work with the assistant on the mechanics of a work-for-hire contract with Mack Investigations. There were clauses on permissions before expenditures, the release of information gathered to date, and a clear understanding that the expenses related to Don's round trip to Canada would be directly billed to Pamela Fairchild Rogers. It was Wednesday, and the new working arrangement would be effective Friday.

Charlie left Pamela at Serena's office and hailed a cab. She called Don, and when he didn't answer, dialed Judy.

"I'm done with my meeting."

"You okay?"

"Yeah, but I was thinking of heading home unless there's work for me there."

"Nothing that can't wait. Go home."

"Have you heard from Don?"

"Not yet."

"Yeah. Maybe I will go home. Listen, I need to tell you that we're closing out the Fairchild case tomorrow."

"Oh? Pamela decided she didn't need us after all?"

"No. I quit."

Judy's response was silence.

"Don't worry. We'll have a new client on Friday."

"Who?"

"Serena Carruthers. We'll be working for her."

"Well, you have had quite the morning. I'll call if anything comes up. Otherwise see you tomorrow."

Charlie and Mandy had purchased a fixer-upper in Detroit's Barry subdivision last summer, and after a setback a few months ago following a scary home invasion related to a case, they'd finally settled into a comfortable domestic coexistence.

The sound of any car in the driveway brought Hamm to the front door as sentry. As Charlie entered, he stood on long hind legs

127

to lean on her chest. They performed a pas de deux in the foyer for a few seconds before Mandy appeared.

"He is a fickle dog. I thought he loved only me," Mandy said.

She wrapped her arms around Charlie's neck, executing a kiss. They looked down at Hamm whose expression suggested the fickleness of love was not reserved only for his species.

"I was hoping you'd be home," Charlie said, nuzzling Mandy's neck. "I couldn't remember if today was one of your long shifts."

"I've only been home a half hour. I'm working on a roast for dinner. You want a cocktail? Or some wine?"

"I'll have a glass of wine, but first I want to put on my comfort clothes."

"Has it been that kind of day?"

"It's been that kind of day ever since I took this case."

"Is Franklin okay?"

"As far as I know. I'll fill you in on all of it after I change."

With the combination of an oversized flannel shirt, sweatpants, and a few sips of pinot grigio, Charlie released some of the worries of the day. Perched on a counter stool, she watched Mandy finish the application of a cumin-mustard-sea salt rub onto a small chuck roast. She arranged a handful of red potatoes and chunks of onion around the meat, poured in a cup of vegetable stock, and placed the shallow pan into the oven.

After shooing Hamm out of the kitchen a few times, Mandy now called to him and rewarded his good behavior with a chew bone. She poured another glass of wine and sat, their knees touching, next to Charlie at the kitchen island.

"Is this case getting to you because it affects Franklin?"

"No. It's filled with land mines for everybody involved."

"You still believe Fairchild is responsible for Peter's death?"

"Yes. I really do. I just have to be able to prove it."

Mandy shook her head. "It gives me the shivers. Why would a father do such a thing?"

"We can't know for sure. Peter had always been the . . ."

"Black sheep?"

"Yeah, but I'm done using that analogy. Maybe the disappointing offspring. But really, if family members that disappointed was a reason to kill, I imagine the murder rate would skyrocket."

"You think Pamela's involved?"

"No. I don't exactly like her, but I dislike her less than I did. I know it will be difficult for her to learn her father is responsible for her brother's death."

"And is framing her husband to take the fall," Mandy added.

Charlie shook her head. "It's family treachery on the scale of Shakespeare."

She held out her glass for another pour and admired how good Mandy looked in a red-haired ponytail and an apron over chinos. Mandy caught the look and smiled.

"You really look tired."

"I'm drained. It takes a lot of energy to juggle so many half-truths and outright lies. Especially when you're lying to your client."

"But you're working for Serena Carruthers now."

"Starting the day after tomorrow. That's when I'll give Serena the full story, and she'll decide when to tell Pamela. She has to be told sooner or later, and when it happens, she'll be devastated."

"Will Don bring back proof of Fairchild's involvement?"

"I sure as hell hope so, and it will need to be indisputable. The police don't want to go up against Fairchild either." Charlie shook her head again. "Even when we prove Franklin innocent, I don't see how his marriage will survive."

"Is that what makes the case so complicated for you?"

Charlie shrugged.

"After you prove Franklin innocent, and I hope you do, his marriage isn't your business, Charlie."

"I know."

"Do you?"

They shared only a brief moment of unasked questions and unspoken assurances before Charlie reached for Mandy's hand.

"I think after dinner I'll take a bath," Charlie said, taking a sip of wine.

Mandy rose from her seat, picking up the half bottle of white wine. "Come on. The roast has a couple of hours to cook. Let's get you that bath now."

Mandy had drawn a wonderful bath of lavender salts. The bath was followed by lovemaking. Then they'd bundled up in bathrobes in front of the fireplace to eat their roast beef, drink a couple of glasses of red wine, and share a big bowl of dulce de leche ice cream. They'd just cleaned up the kitchen when Charlie's phone rang.

She stared at the phone. *Thank God for good timing.*

"I wasn't sure you'd be home. That's why I called on your mobile," Don said.

"I've been home for hours."

"Must be nice. I've got to stay in Canada another night."

"Sorry, Don. I know you don't like being away from Rita and Rudy too long."

"Yeah. But there's been a complication."

"Another one?"

"Yeah. This one is serious. Somebody knifed Sturdivant last night in his cell."

"Is he alive?" Charlie held her breath.

"Barely. They operated on him this morning. His attorney says that Scanlon broad, or whatever her name is, killed Peter. Sturdivant was hired to take care of Franklin. But, get this, Fairchild himself paid Sturdivant in a wad of hundred-dollar bills."

"Wow. That's the testimony we need to exonerate Franklin," Charlie said.

"Right. *If* Sturdivant is alive to give a full statement. It's touch and go."

"What's tomorrow's plan, Don?"

"I'm headed to the hospital in the morning to meet the attorney."

Charlie and Hamm entered the master bedroom. Mandy was reading and glanced up.

"If it isn't my two favorite people."

"Officially, only one of us is a people."

Mandy laughed. "Shh. Don't say that in front of Hamm."

When Charlie didn't laugh, Mandy put her book down and gave Charlie her full attention.

"Did Don have good news?"

"Yes and no. He's found our Canadian hit man, who admits Fairchild was involved, but last night someone tried to kill the guy, and he may not live to tell his story."

"Oh Charlie. I know you must be frustrated."

Charlie didn't answer. She fell on the bed and curled up with her head on Mandy's lap.

Chapter 17

At noon Don burst into the office. No matter how many times he made this drug-bust entrance it was startling. Tamela leaped to her feet at the front desk. Charlie and Judy appeared around the corner.

"Do you always have to enter a room that way?" Judy yelled.

"I'm not in the mood, Novak." Don hung his trench coat on the clothes tree. "I need some coffee," he said in Tamela's direction.

"In the conference room," Tamela said, heart still pounding. She slumped into her seat.

Don pushed past Charlie and Judy, heading to the coffee. They followed. He threw his overnight bag onto a chair and practically lunged at the coffeemaker. While he was pouring, Judy pulled out the basket of snacks she kept as an emergency supply for Don. He downed a cup of coffee, pulled the basket in front of him, and ripped open a can of Pringles. Judy made another pot of coffee.

"It's been a hell of a morning, Mack," Don finally said. "Some asshole took a fucking shot at me."

"*What?*" Charlie and Judy responded in unison.

"I'd just left the hospital and was heading to the highway when a car pulled up next to me and stayed there. I saw the window go down, so I gunned the accelerator, but a bullet shattered my back window. The car tried to follow me, but I lost him, of course."

"Damn. I'm glad you're okay. That really pisses me off," Charlie exclaimed.

"Tell me about it. The window will cost me at least two hundred dollars. And *this* sucks," Don added. "Sturdivant didn't make it."

"Oh no!" Charlie said.

Don finished the Pringles and ate a package of nuts while recounting the details of his last twenty-four hours in Toronto. Caesar Sturdivant had been pronounced dead at six in the morning—cause of death, an infection related to his injured organs. Don had checked out of the motel and returned to the hospital in his own car to meet Sturdivant's lawyer. They had met for almost two hours, and Don was eager to get on the road for the trip home. Don speculated the white, four-door Honda might have trailed him from the hospital parking lot because within five minutes the shot was fired. He hadn't gotten more than a glimpse at the driver or the shooter in the passenger seat. Nor did he get a look at the license plate. He'd called Detective Li from the road to inform him of the attack, but refused Li's request to stay and file a report.

"We've got to figure this out," Charlie said. "First, someone tries to kill Franklin. Now Sturdivant is dead, and people are taking potshots at you. Things are getting more dangerous by the day."

"And if we're right," Don said, "Stanford Fairchild is behind all the attacks. I arranged for us to meet with Wallace today to fill him in. I'm pretty sure he doesn't want us coming around police headquarters, so I invited him here."

"When?" Judy asked.

"At three."

"Okay. In the meantime, I'll get Tamela to order in some lunch."

"Good idea, Novak."

"I'll have her get comfort food. Something that goes with dodging a bullet."

"How about corned beef sandwiches?" Don proposed.

Judy had seen it many times before. No matter the danger, Don was always ready to eat. She teased him about it, but it was one of his more endearing qualities.

"Done," she said.

While they waited for lunch, Charlie worked her board exercise. Fairchild's name was on one side, Karen Scanlon's on the opposite. Under Fairchild's name was a row of red sticky notes—the questions. *What's the motive for having his son killed? For framing Franklin? What is Fairchild's relationship to Scanlon? Did he pay her to kill Peter? What, if any, connection did Fairchild have to Sturdivant? How do we prove Stanford Fairchild's guilt?*

There was a similar row of questions under Karen's name, along with the facts. Scanlon had a key to the condo. She had a police record, used an alias, and now there was a claim from Sturdivant that Karen shot Peter.

"Is there anything in your research to suggest she's capable of murder?" Charlie asked Judy.

"No. But there's one thing my grandfather used to say. 'If you can lie, you can steal. And if you can steal, you can kill.'"

Charlie gave Judy a pensive look. "You and I are pretty good liars, you know."

Judy shook her head. "It's different. We're lying in the name of justice. Aren't we?"

Charlie smiled. In the center of the board, she replaced the current blue note with another. A conjecture. *Pamela Rogers is unaware of her father's murder conspiracy.*

"You're convinced she's not involved?" Don asked.

"That's my opinion," Charlie said.

"And mine," Judy added.

"What about the two bank withdrawals?" Don asked. "The last one the day Peter was killed."

"I'm still trying to track that down," Judy said. "But she always gives a lot of money to charity."

"The withdrawals were five grand each," Don said, looking at the document he'd received from Detective Wallace.

"I guess we can ask her about that," Charlie said. "We don't officially work for her anymore."

"We still need to get Don's travel expenses paid and get our final check," Judy noted. "So let's not piss off Pamela until we have that money in hand."

"She could tell Carruthers to pull the plug on us anytime she wants," Don observed.

"The fact is, no matter what we do, by the time this case is over Pamela will probably hate the Mack Agency," Judy added.

"I'm afraid you're right," Charlie said.

Wallace arrived alone and in plain clothes. Don still had a lot of police contacts, but the department had graduated a half-dozen classes of officers since he'd left the force. They were well-educated, many with military backgrounds, and some with previous policing experience. Wallace had been a patrolman in Atlanta before joining the Detroit force ten years ago and had quickly worked his way up the ranks to detective status. Wallace stood just inside the conference room door staring at the whiteboard.

"I hope nobody outside of this office has seen that board," Wallace said before reaching out to shake hands with the three Mack partners.

"Nope. Only us," Charlie said. "I guess your case board looks a lot different."

"You'd guess right. I've been trying to figure out a way to get one of the higher-ups interested in investigating the Fairchild connection without kicking it up to the chief. I think if I bring these allegations to Captain Travers, he'll respond based on the politics. He's too interested in being chief himself one day."

"We've worked with Travers before," Charlie said. "I think you're reading him right."

"We have only a matter of hours, not days, to make a legitimate case against Fairchild," Wallace said. "I got a call this morning from the prosecutor's office following up on the Sturdivant information they received from Toronto police. Fairchild's not above going straight to the mayor, or even the governor, to keep our investigation focused on Rogers."

"Right," Charlie agreed.

"I think Fairchild may already know about our extradition inquiries."

"We're pretty sure he *does* know," Don said. "I didn't tell you when I called earlier, but Sturdivant was attacked in his cell yesterday, and he died this morning."

"Aw shit, man!"

"And somebody took a shot at Don before he left Toronto this morning," Charlie added.

Wallace, who always presented as a cool customer, grimaced. His hands turned into fists, and his eyes took on a mean glint. "We've got to get this dude. I don't give a fuck who he is."

"Have a seat, Wallace, and let's compare notes," Don said.

"I want to get a closer look at that board first," Wallace said, moving around the table and reading each note. He stepped back and crossed his arms. "This is pretty good. Whose work is it?"

"It's Mack's way of figuring out a case," Don replied.

"I'm impressed," Wallace said with an admiring look for Charlie. "What's the category for the blue note?"

"Conjecture. Sometimes just a gut feeling," Charlie said.

"I'm not sure you're on the right track with that one. Pam Rogers withdrew $10,000 over two weeks. That feels like a payoff to me."

"We're going to find out more about that. She gives a lot of money to charity. It could simply be that," Charlie said.

"Don't donors usually write checks?" Wallace asked.

Charlie conceded the point. "The more I get to know her, I can't believe she knows about her father's treachery, and I'm positive she wouldn't be involved in framing Franklin for murder."

"Woman's intuition?"

"Call it whatever you like. I'm a pretty good judge of people. We think Fairchild is behind this conspiracy. Probably with Karen Scanlon. Maybe with others."

"Okay, okay," Wallace raised his hands in surrender. "Let's talk about what evidence we have to prove your theory."

Wallace refused a sandwich, but accepted a cup of coffee and settled into a seat next to Charlie. Using the board diagram, the Mack partners brainstormed with Wallace for almost three hours. In the end, they had very little proof of Fairchild's guilt that would stand up in court.

"Can't we get a deposition from Sturdivant's attorney as to what his client confessed?" Judy asked.

"We could. I think he'd cooperate. He's a decent guy," Don said.

"I'm not even sure Sturdivant's direct testimony would have been enough to convince a jury over the word of Stan Fairchild," Charlie said. "But it's worth a conversation with the attorney. Don, would you take that on?"

"Sure. As long as the conversation is over the phone. I've had my fill of Toronto."

"Judy, I want you to continue checking on Scanlon," Charlie said. "Find a connection between her and Fairchild. We really need that."

"Okay," Judy said, making a note.

"How do you think you'll start?" Wallace directed his question at Judy.

Judy had the attention of the other three in the room. She shifted in her chair. "Well, I've already found a few records on her. They're in that folder," Judy said pointing, and Charlie pushed the folder toward Wallace. "I've been using our regular subscription service for financial and criminal checks. But I can pay for a more extensive backgrounder, and I have a subcontractor checking on her connections in Allentown and Sarasota, Florida where she owns property."

"I can check in with the departments there," Wallace offered. "And run her prints through the national database."

"That would be very helpful," Charlie said.

"What else, Novak?" Don challenged.

Judy squared her shoulders. "I want to follow up with Sharon Fairchild. We haven't heard much from her. She's much more in touch with Peter's life than Mr. Fairchild or Pamela. I think she'll know what was going on between Peter and Karen."

"That seems really smart," Charlie encouraged.

Empowered by Charlie's support, Judy offered another idea. "When I met with the family, it was really clear the Fairchilds didn't see eye to eye on Peter *or* Franklin. Stanford was constantly trying to throw Franklin under the bus, and he practically rolled his eyes any time I asked about his son. Maybe Sharon will provide more insight about her husband. That would help us to understand the guy, and how he could possibly be involved in Peter's death. Maybe I can also get her to open up about Stanford's feelings regarding Franklin."

"If anyone can get her to talk it's you, Judy," Charlie said.

"Yeah. That's a good use of your time," Don said begrudgingly.

"Is there anything else I need to know?" Wallace asked.

Don and Charlie shared a look, and Charlie gave an almost imperceptible nod.

"We know of another piece of evidence you haven't heard about. Something that was found at the crime scene," Don began.

Wallace sat upright, his face grimacing in astonishment. "What do you mean?"

"When Rogers came to, he found a money clip on the floor. He took it with him. The clip belongs to Stanford Fairchild," Don said.

"And you're just telling me about it now, Rutkowski? I thought we were sharing intel on this case."

"We are, but . . ."

Charlie interrupted. "It's my fault, Detective. I didn't want anyone else to know because Franklin doesn't want Pamela to hear about it. The clip implicates her father, and he can't figure out how to explain it to her."

"Where is it now?" Wallace asked.

"I have it," Charlie explained.

"Let's see it."

Charlie left the conference room to retrieve the clip from her desk in the bullpen. The desk had belonged to her late father, and she kept the key to the bottom drawer on her key chain. Charlie returned to a tense and silent conference room. She placed the plastic bag containing the money clip in front of Wallace.

He stared at the bag for almost thirty-seconds before unzipping it and removing the evidence with a handkerchief. He held it up to the light for a closer examination.

"I guess nobody bothered to preserve the fingerprints," Wallace growled.

The group looked sheepish. Wallace put the clip back into the bag and pushed it to Charlie.

"Put this back wherever you had it."

"Don't you want the lab to run it for fingerprints?" Charlie asked.

"Yes, but not now. There will need to be paperwork, and the chain of evidence is already screwed up, so it doesn't matter if we test it now or later. How do you know the clip belongs to Fairchild?"

Judy spoke up. "They're specially made for him by a jeweler in New York. Fairchild orders other clips—a dozen or so a year—for business associates, but this one is a special run. The clip is sterling, the diamonds are high quality, and the stem at the top of the *F* is an emerald. Only three of these clips exist, and they're for Fairchild's personal use."

"Hmm. Well, depending on how many prints we can pull, and exclude, from those who touched it," Wallace said, looking around the table and scowling again, "this might turn out to be useful evidence."

"There's one more thing," Charlie said. "Fairchild knows Franklin found the clip in Peter's apartment."

"How does he know that?"

"Franklin sent a note to him."

"Why in hell did he do that?"

"He was under stress. Still on the run. I think he thought Fairchild might back off on trying to frame him if he knew about the clip."

"It probably had just the opposite effect," Wallace said. "That's probably why Franklin came under attack in your mother's parking lot."

"That's what we thought too," Don said.

"Do you think Fairchild knows you have the clip?"

"I don't think so."

"We better double up on guards at Franklin's hospital room. I'm going to take care of that now," Wallace said, standing. "Say, do you guys want police protection?"

"Hell no," Don said. "In fact, maybe we should be part of the security rotation at the hospital."

"I doubt that I can get clearance for that, but let me see what I can do."

After Wallace left, Tamela appeared in the doorway. "Can I leave now, Ms. Mack?"

"I'm sorry Tamela. Yes, you can leave. Thanks for staying late. Oh, and one more thing. Starting tomorrow, one of our contractors will be doing some work around the office. I'll introduce you to him in the morning."

"Okay, Ms. Mack. See you all in the morning."

"What's that all about?" Judy asked.

"I agree with Don. We can take care of ourselves, but Fairchild has shown his hand, and we should take a few precautions. Let's start locking the office door. I want to bring in Hoyt Timbermann to be in the office. Don, will you see if he's available?"

"Okay. And if not, I'll find someone else."

"Starting tomorrow, I'll carry my revolver," Charlie said.

"Judy, except for the interview with Sharon Fairchild, I want you to stay in the office."

"I already sent her a message. She can see me at Pamela's house tomorrow at nine."

"Great. She liked you, and I know it helped that you sent flowers to the memorial service. That was good thinking."

"Mack, we should have our people at the hospital. Even if Wallace can't make it official," Don said.

"You're probably right. I'll discuss it with Serena tomorrow. Pamela can always insist on a private detail."

"Do you really think we're in danger?" Judy asked, looking worried.

"I think the failed attack on Don proves we are. Now that Sturdivant is out of the way, Fairchild may feel he can relax a bit. But when he finds out we're about to start fishing in all of his ponds, he'll get nervous again."

"It'll be okay, Novak," Don said. "We probably have twenty-four hours before the shit hits the fan. Take your meeting with the mother tomorrow. Then you'll be laying low."

"Let's all go home and get some rest," Charlie said. "Things are about to get interesting."

"Yeah," Don said. "Interesting, like a house fire."

Chapter 18

Serena's office had a one-eighty view of downtown Detroit. Her desk was an enormous plexiglass structure decorated with lovely paperweights and mementoes. There was a framed picture of Serena posed with the mayor; another of her in tennis togs with her name counterpart, Serena Williams; and a photograph of a young Serena with former President Jimmy Carter. Neatly stacked folders covered the wings of her desk, and Serena sat in an expensive white Eaton swivel chair. Across from the desk, Charlie sat in an upholstered chair cupping a mug of hot coffee.

Serena had carefully established the hierarchy in their new working relationship. They were both lawyers, but Charlie kept her license only so she could handle occasional paperwork. Serena, on the other hand, was a legal power broker in the city and the region.

They'd begun the meeting with the execution of the contract drafted during Charlie's last visit. It was a simple work-for-hire agreement with a beefed-up confidentiality and nondisclosure addendum protecting the work, clients, and proprietary information of both signatories. Serena's associate, who sat in for the first part of the meeting, was off to make the appropriate copies of the agreement. That's when Serena shifted the conversation.

"What do you think of Pamela?"

Charlie took a sip of coffee before speaking. She and Serena had never considered themselves sister-friends, who would gossip over lunch or cocktails about relationships, the people they knew in common, or the latest rumor about the mayor's shenanigans. Charlie's therapist asked her once if she had girlfriends who were her confidantes, her sounding boards, and could provide her a shoulder to cry on. She had none. What she had were her partners, her mother, and now Mandy. For the time being she would keep it that way.

"Pamela is okay. I hadn't met or even talked to her before she called me about Franklin. I got an invitation to the wedding, but I decided I shouldn't go."

"I went. It was lovely. Expensive. Actually, I was surprised Frank was marrying a white girl, and I wanted to get a good look at her and her family."

"In the first meeting with her, I left thinking she was snooty," Charlie admitted. "My partner, Judy Novak, went with me and she agreed. We chalked it up to her family upbringing. But now I believe she truly loves Franklin and will do anything to help him."

"That's good." Serena hesitated, but didn't take her eyes from Charlie's. "I was kind of surprised to hear you were also with a white woman. I'm not judging, believe me," Serena hurried to say. "Just curious. I didn't know you were gay."

"I guess I've known since college that I was attracted to both men and women," Charlie began. "I didn't mean to fall in love with Mandy; it just happened. But all the time I was with Franklin, I wasn't completely fulfilled. Now I am."

Charlie watched Serena formulate more questions, then decide not to ask them. Part street fighter, part diva, and all political operative, Serena could easily move from Detroit to Washington, DC, and be a force in the halls of Congress. Charlie wondered, after all this was over, if they *could* be friends.

"Well, good for you, Charlie," Serena said. "Now tell me, before Gary comes back in, why you wanted to sever your working relationship with Pamela. All that bullshit you were shoveling the other day was laughable."

Charlie smiled. "I'm trying to remember why we never became running buddies."

It was Serena's turn to smile. "I was doing my thing. You were doing your thing. But yeah. It's good to have a chance to work together now. So, what's up with this case?"

"Serena, I have every reason to believe Stanford Fairchild paid to have his son killed and to have Franklin set up for the crime."

"What?" Serena sat upright so suddenly her chair moved backward. "Please tell me you're kidding."

Charlie shook her head. "Believe me, I wish I were. It's a hot mess."

"How do you know this?"

"Franklin suspected it as soon as he regained consciousness at Peter's apartment. He found a money clip belonging to his father-in-law. He was so surprised and confused he took the clip with him. He didn't know what to tell Pamela. That's why he didn't call her. When he read in the papers the police had found his gun at the scene, he knew he was being set up by someone with access to his safe."

"He didn't suspect Pamela?"

"I don't think he ever suspected her. He just wanted to protect her from the truth about her father. And old man Fairchild knows Franklin suspects him."

"How?"

"Franklin sent a letter telling him he had the money clip."

"That was bright," Serena said sarcastically.

"He wasn't thinking straight. He was on the run by then. Maybe he thought Fairchild would just confess to the crime."

"Fat chance," Serena said. She absentmindedly tapped her desk with her pen, then turned to stare through the window toward Detroit's near-east suburbs. Finally, she swiveled to face Charlie. "There's more, isn't there?"

"Remember the person of interest my partner followed to Canada?"

"I do. He's a prisoner, right?"

"He was. He died in a Toronto hospital early yesterday of wounds he suffered in an attack while he was in his cell. We think Fairchild put a hit on him. Someone also took a shot at Don while he was in Canada."

"All this happened since I saw you?" Serena was honestly shocked.

Charlie answered with a grim face. "Some of it was already in play, but I didn't know at the time we met."

"And Pamela doesn't know any of the suspicions about her father?"

Charlie shook her head.

Just then the junior associate entered the room with more folders, stopping short at the sight of his boss's face.

"Gary, Ms. Mack and I are going to need a couple of hours before we do a hand-off on the case. Please go ahead and set up the electronic and hard copy files. I'll buzz you when we're ready. Oh, and would you ask Jenny to bring us a pot of coffee."

They moved to the sitting area—Charlie on the sofa, and Serena in one of the overstuffed leather chairs. Charlie gave Serena another account of the case, this time starting with Pamela's late-night phone call to her ten days ago and ending with yesterday's meeting with Detective Wallace. Serena made a few notes and asked a couple of questions. By the time Charlie was done, they'd finished the coffee.

"So, what do you think?" Charlie asked.

"I think this case will either elevate our careers, or we'll never work in Detroit—or Michigan—again."

"At this point, I'd settle for just coming out alive."

"Don't forget about getting paid."

Charlie laughed. "Well yes. That would be good, too."

"Something else occurs to me, Charlie. Did the hit man in Canada confess to killing Peter?"

"No. I forgot to tell you that part. Sturdivant made only a partial statement to police, but his attorney alleges Karen Scanlon killed Peter."

"The interior designer? Hmm. Interesting. Is she connected to Fairchild?"

"We're trying now to prove that."

"I'm not sure we can rely on the lawyer's statement. That gets us into privileged communications territory," Serena said. "And as you know, it survives a client's death."

Charlie nodded. "Don and the Toronto detective were witnesses to some of Sturdivant's confession. That might help."

"Yes. It might, and maybe we can win the point that revealing the one attorney-client conversation furthers Sturdivant's interests by sparing his mother the burden of having her son labeled a murderer."

"Now I see why you make the money you do," Charlie said.

Serena laughed. "Thanks." She quickly returned to the situation at hand. "Look, Charlie, I can appreciate you and your partners wanting to protect Franklin and prove Fairchild's guilt, but I have a slightly different focus for you. I need to prove Franklin's innocence."

"How does that put us at cross-purposes? It's the same thing."

"Not exactly. It's a slightly different emphasis on where to focus the investigation. For instance, I think we need to follow up on Franklin's gun. I want to know who had access to it, what prints were found on it, and what the chain of possession was at the crime scene. It's good you're doing a deep dive on Karen Scanlon, that's helpful. But I want to know more about Peter's other associates."

"We already checked on a few of them," Charlie responded.

"I specifically want to know more about this Windsor distiller you mentioned."

"Why him?"

"I've heard of this Madison. His name has come up before with some of my other clients."

"Okay. I'll put Judy on the gun, and on this Madison guy. But I still think we need to involve ourselves in protecting Franklin at the hospital."

"Won't the police do that?"

"Yes. But we care about the guy, so we'll be more conscientious."

"You mean *you* care about the guy. Okay. I agree. The best-paying clients tend to be the ones who are alive."

"What's your thinking on how and when to tell Pamela everything?" Charlie asked.

"To be honest, I don't know. But I think you and I should do it together."

"And that will start the ball rolling at breakneck speed. Pamela will confront her father. He'll call his friend, the police chief, and we'll lose all cooperation from DPD."

"And if Fairchild really did conspire to kill his son," Serena said, picking up the list, "he'll feel like a caged rat. He'll escalate his efforts to get rid of anybody he sees as a threat. That means Franklin, but also anyone else who supports the narrative that he's a murderer."

"Like me and Don. That's why I've started carrying my gun."

"I know. Our detector signaled you were armed."

"You have a metal detector?"

"A very discreet one at the front door, and believe me, discreet costs money." Serena rose from her chair. "I'll call Pamela. Let's get her in here this afternoon and lay the cards on the table. You want to warn Franklin first?"

Charlie considered the question. "I really think Franklin ought to be the one to tell Pamela his suspicions. The two of us can be there to provide moral support, but it feels like that's his job."

Serena paused to give it thought. "That's sound reasoning," she agreed.

"Why don't we meet at the hospital? You can tell Pamela we want to go over the defense strategy with Franklin."

"Good idea. What time?"

"Let's say two o'clock," Charlie said. "That gives me time to contact Franklin, get my people on the same page, and give Wallace a heads-up."

Judy had been escorted by the butler to the front sitting room, but when Sharon Fairchild arrived downstairs, she suggested they meet in the conservatory attached to the rear of the home. It was a magnificent place. Flowers were in brilliant bloom, and even on a cold winter morning the space was delightfully warm. Sharon requested a coffee service, and they sat at a round garden table in comfy draped chairs.

Sharon's face and eyes were puffy. Her only makeup was a light pink lip gloss. Her hair had gold clips holding back each side, and she wore a plum-colored sweater tunic over dark slacks and black flats.

"I'm happy you called and wanted to meet, Mrs. Novak," Sharon said as she poured coffee. "The rush of phone calls and sympathy cards are waning. I really welcome the opportunity to speak with someone about Peter."

"I understand that. I was very close to my grandfather, and I remember my entire family coming together for his funeral. We all grieved and supported each other during the time of his death, and the days leading to his funeral, but then everyone went back to their own lives. They forgot about Grandpa. But I never did, and I never will."

"You *do* understand," Sharon said with welling eyes. "My friends try to hide their annoyance when I bring up Peter. Pam mentions her brother now only when she's arguing with Stan about Franklin."

"We're still trying to prove Franklin had nothing to do with Peter's murder," Judy said.

"Yes, I know. I don't really believe he's guilty either."

"Your husband doesn't seem to share that opinion."

Sharon shook her head. "I know."

"How was their relationship?"

"Stan and Peter?"

"Well, yes, I'd like to hear about that as well. But first, I'd like to understand why your husband is so ready to throw Franklin to the wolves."

"I wouldn't quite put it that way," Sharon said slowly. "I think he believes the evidence. Stan is a very logical man. He's more moved by numbers and facts than feelings."

"Did he *like* Franklin?"

Sharon hesitated. "He didn't approve of Franklin at first. He didn't think he was, uh, right for Pamela."

"Because Franklin is black?"

"Oh, no. Nothing like that. Stan isn't a racist. He works with a lot of black people and, uh, Mexican and Chinese people. He has a lot of employees. He knows how to get along with everybody."

"I guess he would have to," Judy said, lifting her cup for a sip. "What kind of man *is* your husband? I mean, what's his personality? I've always wondered what makes successful men like him tick."

"Stan is very ambitious. Driven."

"And used to getting what he wants?" Judy offered. Then she aimed her first lie at Sharon. "My husband can be like that. He doesn't suffer fools lightly."

"Yes. Exactly. Stan admires men who have good business acumen and work hard to make something of themselves. Initially, he didn't believe Franklin had the right prospects. He doesn't think much of politicians, but Pamela knows how to wrap her father around her little finger, so he accepted Franklin."

"What about more recently? Did Franklin and Mr. Fairchild have any disagreements?"

"I don't think so. Why do you ask?"

Avoiding the question, Judy turned a page in her notebook and looked around the nursery. "This is really a lovely room. Are you the one with the green thumb?"

Sharon's mood lightened. "Do you know about flowers?"

"I know a bit. Grandpa was a gardener. I'd stay with him every summer in Queens. He had a vegetable garden and a large area for flowers in his backyard. We'd spend hours together fertilizing and planting and pruning. He had wonderful roses. But they certainly weren't as beautiful as these."

"It's my passion really. Gardening. At our place in Florida, I have a couple of people who work the garden, but I help the staff several times a week." Sharon paused, and her face slackened. "I miss my garden." She paused again, and when she finally spoke, her voice was pensive. "Peter used to help me with the care of the plants. He was very good with roses and orchids, all of it really. When Stan and I are in town, Peter and I would usually work together here."

Sadness overtook Sharon. Judy sat quietly for a while before asking her next question.

"You say your husband admires ambition. Did he think Peter was ambitious enough?"

Sharon fixed a gaze on her hands as she answered. "Peter never lived up to his father's expectations. He tried to take initiative and worked hard to please Stan . . ." Sharon glanced up momentarily before her eyes dipped again. "But Stan is . . . a perfectionist."

"What was Peter like as a little boy?"

Sharon's face lit up a bit at this question. "Oh, he was a delightful boy. So full of mischief. He loved sports and music. He played on the basketball and soccer teams at school, and he had a lot of friends."

"Did Peter and your husband spend time together around sports?"

Sharon didn't answer immediately, so Judy shared some of her own experience. "I have two sons. When they were boys, they were always throwing some ball with their dad." Judy chuckled. "I also remember attending a lot of Little League and basketball games."

Sharon smiled and nodded. "I recall a never-ending stream of scrimmages, practices, and games. Stan traveled a lot for business back then, more than he does now, so I was usually the one who attended Peter's sporting events." Sharon couldn't stop a blush of embarrassment.

"What was their more recent relationship? I understand from our earlier interview that Peter had a position in one of the Fairchild businesses."

"Yes. Peter worked for the home office for a while. I'm not sure what he did there before he was assigned to one of the subsidiaries. I think he was a junior executive or something. He never really liked the work. Stan invested in a music company Peter owned once, and then there was a sports management venture. Nothing came of them, I'm afraid."

"What about a more recent investment opportunity? Franklin mentioned Peter asked him to invest in a Canadian distillery."

Sharon nodded. "Pam said something about Peter asking for a loan, but I don't know any more about it than that. I don't get involved in those issues. Pam has a head for it, but Stan is always saying I shouldn't trouble myself with business matters."

"I see," Judy said, turning a page in her notebook. She wasn't sure how much more to dig on the father-son relationship, so she introduced another line of questioning. "How was Pamela's relationship with her brother? I imagine the normal sibling rivalry, but I sense a sweet big-sister feeling for him."

"Yes. Yes, you're right. They're only two years apart." Sharon turned inward, not moving or speaking. Judy didn't press. She poured another coffee and sipped at it. After a few minutes of quiet that might have been awkward for two other people, Sharon returned to the room.

"I'm sorry. I slipped away for a moment. I apologize."

"No need. This is such a pleasant room, and quiet is good for the soul."

"You're very easy to talk to, Mrs. Novak. I'm sure you've heard that before."

"Grandpa would say you have two ears and one mouth, and that means God wanted us to listen more than talk."

"Your grandfather must have been a good man."

Judy nodded.

"You have just the two sons?"

"I also have a daughter."

"Tell me something, Mrs. Novak. As a mother. Do you *like* your children?"

151

Judy laughed. "It depends on the day and the circumstances. Sometimes one of them will do something that just exasperates me. My daughter is my joy, and my middle child, Tommy, makes me laugh. He's the kind of person who just gets along with everyone. But my oldest son—he's seventeen now—announced a few weeks ago that he wants to drop out of high school, buy a used motorcycle, and ride cross-country to California. He told me and his father he'll work on a GED when he gets back. I thought my husband would kill him." Judy winced, remembering the situation with Fairchild, but Sharon responded with a smile and a nod. Judy recovered and wrapped her hands around the warm cup before continuing. "The answer to your question is, I love all of my children. When they do or say things I don't like, I try to remember they are individuals. They're a part of me and their father, but also their own unique beings."

"It was always difficult for Stan to accept that Peter was never going to follow in his footsteps. At first, Stan thought he could groom Peter for the work. Then he tried shaming him, by comparing him to his sister or to the other young men in the company. When that didn't work, well . . . he just turned hard toward Peter. After that, every kindness or consideration he showed Peter was because I asked for it."

"That had to be stressful for you," Judy said.

Sharon reached for a handkerchief in the sleeve of her tunic and brought it to her eyes. "I'm sorry. I don't even know you. Please, forgive me."

"Really. There's nothing to forgive. Mothers love their children in a way that's different from their fathers. The vow we take at marriage—sickness and health, richer or poorer, for better or worse—might be more apt for the love we give our children than for our spouses."

Judy ended the interview, realizing she'd got everything she could from this grieving mother.

152

Chapter 19

When Judy arrived just before noon at the Mack office, the door was locked. She searched for her key in her tote and found it, but decided to knock. She looked up at the camera over the door and winked. The door was flung open and her entry blocked by Hoyt Timbermann.

"Judy Novak," he proclaimed.

"Hoyt," Judy said, pushing past him. "You know you can see who's at the door by flipping on the monitor at Tamela's desk."

Tamela smiled and turned the monitor toward them so they could see the empty hallway and Hoyt's shadow on the floor.

"Yeah. I forgot that. But I figured your knock was too polite to be trouble."

Judy rolled her eyes in Tamela's direction, checked the message box and strolled into the bullpen, followed by Hoyt. She dumped her tote on the desk that had been used by the agency's former partner, but was now designated for her. She moved around the desk to sit.

"Don and Charlie aren't in?"

"They went out to pick up lunch," Hoyt said. "Say, I heard you made partner. That's nice. How are you fitting that seat?"

"Today I think it fits okay. I'm grateful for the opportunity to try my hand at the investigation work, but to be honest, Hoyt, I still miss Gil every day."

"Yeah. He was a tough guy. What *about* the rough stuff? You know, like we had in the auto show case. You okay with that part of the work?"

"Charlie promised me I wouldn't be involved in that, and I don't have to get a gun."

"Yeah. I guess that's why I'm here, huh?"

The Mack partners, freelancer Hoyt, and Tamela sat around the conference table sharing pizza and salad. Charlie thought the food might make what she had to say about their situation easier to hear. She was ready to explain that their work was about to take a new and very dangerous turn. Everyone needed to understand the stakes.

"As of today the Franklin Rogers case is moving into high gear. Our client of record is now Serena Carruthers. She's signed on as Franklin's attorney, and we're working as her investigative team. We have three main priorities. First, we're going to add another layer of protection for Franklin at the hospital. Second, we're researching two elements of the case Serena wants to focus on: Franklin's gun and Peter's known associates. Third, we're going to make sure we stay safe."

On the last point, Tamela's eyes grew wider. She'd been quiet since coming into the conference room, stopping short at the sight of Charlie, Don and Hoyt wearing gun holsters. Now she dropped her slice of pizza onto her plate and picked up her soda. Charlie could tell she wanted to ask questions.

"We've already looked into Peter's friends and associates," Judy said.

"Right, and we're going to dig some more. This new work will be all yours, and maybe Tamela will assist. Serena wants us to continue sifting through Karen Scanlon's life, and she wants us to find out as much as we can about the Canadian bourbon deal and the man who approached Peter about it. Madison. I don't think we ever got a first name, did we?"

Don held up a finger. "I got it." He flipped through his notebook. "Robert Madison."

"Right. Those are your tasks, Judy. Scanlon and Madison. Pick over them like a vulture over a carcass."

"Got it."

"Don, how many freelancers did you line up for the hospital security detail?"

"Two others, besides you and me. Wallace says Franklin will be leaving the hospital for one of the prison facilities this weekend. So we'll only need to work the next couple of days."

"Hoyt, I want you to keep an eye on this office during business hours," Charlie said. "Use your own discretion, work with the security guys downstairs if you want. Make sure nobody comes into this office unannounced."

"Okay, Ms. Mack."

"Judy, let's hear about your meeting with Sharon Fairchild."

"She's still mourning. That's understandable. She talked a lot about Peter. She finally admitted her husband was—in her words—'hard' toward Peter. He runs his business and family the same way. He sees each person as having a role to play. In Fairchild's estimation, Peter never lived up to his role."

"Does that mean he could kill Peter?" Don asked.

Judy shrugged. "I think it means he found Peter expendable."

"What about Fairchild's relationship with Franklin?" Charlie asked.

"Rocky at the start. I think he tolerates Franklin and doesn't think he's good enough for his daughter."

Charlie nodded. "Okay. This is what will happen today. Serena, Don, and I are meeting Pamela at the hospital. I've left word for Franklin that we're coming. The idea is Franklin will tell his wife of his suspicions about her father. That conversation is going to set off a chain of events."

"You mean you really believe Fairchild killed his own son?" Hoyt asked.

"We do," Charlie responded.

155

"That's a goddamn shame," Hoyt blurted. "Oh, sorry."

"No doubt Pamela will be worked up," Charlie continued. "There will be crying and yelling. And anger. She'll confront her father. He'll be pissed. Scared. Dangerous. I believe he'll make another attempt on Franklin's life."

"*Another* attempt?" Hoyt asked.

"We think he's behind the shooting that put Rogers in the hospital in the first place," Don said.

"I didn't know that," Hoyt said. "So you were fired upon in Toronto, the prisoner witness was killed, and Franklin was hit by a bullet. That's nasty. No wonder you're bringing in help."

Charlie watched Tamela. Her eyes bulged, and she had a white-knuckled grip on her can of soda. Charlie signaled Judy with a flick of the eye, and Judy turned to face Tamela.

"Yeah, but things are under control. Right, Don?" Judy asked. "We'll be okay here in the office. Especially with Hoyt around."

"I suppose so, Novak. I don't know how brazen Fairchild's henchmen might be, but we'll be ready for them."

"Tamela," Charlie said calmly. "I know what you're hearing is scary. Is there anything you want to ask? Do you want to stay away from the office for a few days? It's all right if you want to do that."

"No, Ms. Mack. I'm not scared. This is exciting. When I told my brother I was working for a private investigator, he thought I was fooling him. Every time I get home he asks about my day, and I tell him about filing and taking notes, and answering phones. Just wait until I tell my brother that you have a gun, we have a guard at the office, and somebody tried to shoot Mr. Rutkowski," Tamela exclaimed. "He'll be so jealous."

Chapter 20

"Charlene Mack is a pain in my ass!" Captain Travers said, slamming his hand on the desk. He had been listening to an update from Detective Wallace on the Rogers case, but was now on his feet staring down onto Beaubien Street.

"This is going to be a fucking debacle, Wallace. You realize, of course, everything you have on Fairchild will be dismantled by his million-dollar lawyers?"

"I know, sir. But we can't ignore the information we've received. Too many other people know about it, plus the Mack team has a couple of other irons in the fire." Wallace paused to assess Travers's demeanor. "Also, Serena Carruthers is defending Rogers."

Travers looked over his shoulder. "Carruthers, huh?"

"Yes, sir."

"I'm pissed you didn't bring this to me earlier. How long have you known?"

"For a while. This case is nothing but trouble for the whole damn city. I wanted to bring you hard proof."

"And yet you haven't, Detective. All you've brought me is misery." Travers gave Wallace a hard look and turned back to the window. "You know I had plans to become the next chief. With this mess I'll be lucky to work long enough to get my pension."

"I'm sure it won't be that bad, Captain. All we're doing is fol-lowing the leads. Everyone will understand that."

Travers took two long strides to his desk, and fell into his chair. He took a long drink of water from the glass on his desk.

"My wife is making me drink more water. It helps with my blood pressure. You want some?"

"No thanks," Wallace said anxiously.

"You're originally from Atlanta, aren't you?"

"That's right. My folks are still there. My dad was in uniform in the eighties."

"Detroit is not Atlanta, Wallace. You've been here long enough to know class and race politics is front and center with every-thing."

"That's not so different in Atlanta," Wallace said.

"Right. But for every Peachtree Street or Ponce De Leon Avenue you have in Atlanta, we have four streets named after white industrialists. We're different from the South. Our rich white men have a deeper foothold on what goes and what doesn't go. Believe me, Stanford Fairchild is going to bring the full power of his influence down on us. You and me."

Wallace nodded. "Then I think you should call the chief now. Rogers is telling his wife what he knows this afternoon. It won't be long before your phone starts ringing."

"Ms. Novak, I think I've found something about that company you asked me to look up."

Judy walked to Tamela's desk and peered over her shoulder at the computer screen.

"Right there," Tamela said, pointing.

"How'd you find this?"

"First, I just googled the company. A bunch of stuff came up that didn't seem to have anything to do with anything. I searched through a dozen pages. Then I got the idea to focus on keywords.

I put in 'Scanlon,' 'design,' and 'Detroit.' That's when I found this blog. It's written by a party planner who specializes in celebrity events. I had to dig through his archive, but I found this post and picture."

The photo showed a glamorous group at a house party. The blogger wrote about the fun time he'd had at the magnificent home of a Windsor businessman. The exquisite furnishings, he noted, were courtesy of Karen Scanlon of Motor City Interior Designs, shown second from the left in the photo. Third from the left, with an arm around Scanlon, was a smiling, handsome, gray-haired man in a beige suit. The caption identified him as Robert Madison.

"Isn't that the name of the man Ms. Mack mentioned?"

"It is indeed. This may be the break we were looking for. Can you print out this page and make several copies? Make the quality of the photo as good as you can get it, and bookmark the web page. Bring everything to the conference room when you're done. That's really good work, Tamela."

"You got something, Judy?" Hoyt asked, sticking his head in the conference room.

He'd been sitting in the bullpen looking bored all afternoon. The only excitement he'd had was when a delivery guy knocked on the door with office supplies. While Tamela signed for the order, Hoyt kept a gun on the young man who backed out of the office with raised hands and then ran to the stairs, not bothering to wait for the elevator. Judy made a notation about the incident on the invoice before filing it away. This was likely the last delivery they'd have from that store.

"I think we do, Hoyt. It looks like our secret lady, Karen Scanlon, knows more about Peter's bourbon company investor than she let on."

"What's the guy's name?" Hoyt asked.

"Robert Madison."

"Oh yeah. Right. His name rang a bell when it came up earlier. I think he may have organized-crime connections. You want me to check that out with some people I know?"

"That would be great. The guy lives in Windsor. Meanwhile, I need to call the secretary of state's office before it closes. Let me know what you find out."

"You got it."

Chapter 21

Charlie and Don met their new freelancer in the parking lot. Chuck Denton had the first shift in their hospital security detail. He was young, too young, Don thought, but had been recommended by one of their regular guys who wasn't available. The deal with Wallace called for their sentries to be outside the building and in the lobby. They would have walkie-talkies for communications with the cops guarding Franklin on the fourth-floor wing. Only uniformed police and hospital staff would be allowed on the floor where Franklin was laid up.

"You good, Denton?" Don asked.

"Yes, sir."

"Don't call me sir. You'll work until eleven. Then Mack, uh, Ms. Mack and I will take the overnight shift."

"Yes, sir," Denton said.

Don turned his back on the boy and started toward the hospital entrance. Charlie leaned into the car window and winked. "Thanks, Denton. Keep your eyes open. Call Don or me if you see anything unusual."

"Yes, ma'am. I sure will."

Charlie signed in at the desk and took a seat next to Don. At 1:55 Serena Carruthers arrived wearing a fur coat and dark brown Jimmy Choo boots.

"This is my partner, Don Rutkowski," Charlie said in introduction.

"Rutkowski. I've heard a lot about you."

"I've heard a lot about you, too," Don replied, deadpan.

Introductions over, Serena walked to the front desk.

"Thanks for being so warm," Charlie said in Don's direction.

"What did you want me to do, kiss her ring?"

"No. But she's paying our bills so let's at least keep it friendly."

"I *was* friendly."

At ten after two, Pamela Fairchild entered the lobby, breathless and beautiful. She was recently coiffed and manicured. Her hair was pinned back in a bun and, like Serena, she wore a fur coat.

"I hope I'm not too late," Pamela said with an envious glimpse at Serena's shoes. "I called the doctor from the car, and he's on the way down to meet us. Are you joining us?" Pamela said to Don after introductions.

"No. I'm leaving. Detective Wallace and I are meeting to discuss the security plans for Franklin."

"Well, that's very good."

Escorted by Franklin's doctor, Charlie, Pamela, and Serena walked through the maze of hallways to Franklin's room. An officer stood outside the door.

"So he'll be released soon?" Pamela asked the doctor.

"He'll need to do a bit of physical therapy for that arm, but the wound is healing excellently. So yes. He could be discharged in the next couple of days."

Franklin sat in a chair near the bed, looking anxious. His beard was filling in, and so was his hair. He wore a dark blue robe over hospital pajamas, white socks, and paper slippers. His left arm was still in a sling.

"Hi," he said to the group with a half-smile. When Pamela moved up to hug him, he peeked over her shoulder at Charlie with a nervous look. "Since I knew there would be four of us, I asked the guard for a few more chairs."

"He didn't leave his station, did he?" Charlie asked with concern.

"No. No. The officer asked one of the nurses, and she had someone bring the chairs."

Pam commandeered the seat next to Franklin and clasped his good hand. Serena and Charlie sat across from them in the now very tight room.

"Serena wanted us all to meet and go over your defense strategy, honey," Pamela said. "By the way, the doctor says you'll be out of here soon. That means we need a court date so we can get you back home. Right, Serena?"

"We do need a court date, but I doubt any judge will grant Franklin bail. He's considered a flight risk," Serena said.

"A flight risk? Why?"

"Because I ran before, Pam. Remember?"

"I didn't think of it like that," Pamela said, caressing his hand.

Franklin's eyes darted between Charlie and Serena. Charlie returned a look of encouragement and empathy. Franklin cleared his throat and shifted in his seat before speaking.

"Honey. I need to tell you something. I didn't tell you the whole truth about why I ran away from Peter's apartment."

"What do you mean? You said you ran because you were scared."

"I *was* scared. But not just because I discovered Peter dead. That was horrible, but it was because of something I found when I regained consciousness."

"What did you find?"

"One of your father's money clips."

Pamela stared at Franklin with a confused expression. "I don't understand. What money clip?"

"The one with the emerald chip. I found it on the floor next to me. I got scared, took the clip, and fled. The next day, when I heard on the news that my gun was found at Peter's apartment, I was even more afraid. Honey, you know I don't carry my gun. I didn't have it that night. Someone's trying to frame me."

"So what are you saying?"

"Look, I know this is hard to hear. It's why I got lost for a few days. It's why I haven't told you the truth. It's almost impossible to believe that Stan would do something like this, but I think he did."

Pamela let go of Franklin's hand and brought her own to her temple. "Franklin!" Pamela's voice had become cold and unwavering. "Are you saying you think Daddy killed Peter?"

"Yes, Pam, I do. And he's trying to set me up for the murder."

Pamela leaped from the chair, slamming it into the wall, and leaned over the bed on her elbows as if she'd been punched in the stomach. The sound she made began as a whoop and ended in a hysterical cackle. The high-pitched yowl reminded Charlie of a jackal she'd seen last week on a PBS nature program. Charlie and Serena stared as Franklin rose to put his good arm around Pamela's waist.

"No. You don't get to touch me," she screamed. "I know who put these wild ideas in your head. That bitch right there," she said, pointing to Charlie.

Charlie began to protest, but Serena laid a hand on her arm. The door to the room opened, and the police officer stuck in his head. "Is everything all right in here?"

"Get out!" Pamela shouted.

The officer's ego kicked in. He stepped into the room and pointed at her. "Ma'am, you need to calm down, right now."

"It's okay, officer," Franklin said. "I'm okay. My wife is just upset. I'm really sorry, and we'll hold it down."

The officer didn't move at first. He'd received the lecture from Detective Wallace about the sensitivity of this assignment. He cut Pamela an ugly look, then turned and left.

Charlie had known it would be an emotional scene, but hadn't anticipated this reaction. Nor had she considered how easily her empathy for Pamela could switch to anger. She and Pamela shot eye darts at each other. Charlie was tempted to grab Pamela by the throat, but Serena continued the grip on her arm.

"Pamela," Serena pleaded. "I know this information is upsetting, but please hear us out."

"Us? So you're all in on it. You expect me to believe my father would kill Peter. You all must be crazy!"

Pamela's voice grew louder, and Franklin tried to pull her back into her seat. She slapped his hand away, and gave him a ferocious glare.

"I said don't touch me! How dare you accuse my father of this . . . this madness. My father is a good man. I guess he was right about you. I guess you *did* kill my brother. And to think I defended you and took your side against his," she said, sobbing.

"Pamela. Please listen," Serena shouted to get Pamela's attention. "There was a witness to your brother's murder. He implicates your father and another person."

"What witness?" Pamela hissed.

"The man we tracked to Canada," Charlie said. "Don spoke to him. We were preparing to bring him back to Detroit . . ."

"You!" Pamela pointed to Charlie. "You've known about this craziness from the beginning, haven't you? You've been lying to me all along. You knew where Franklin was hiding, and didn't tell me. It's true, isn't it?"

"Franklin didn't want me to tell you . . ."

"You claimed to be helping me. Following up on leads," Pamela shouted. "But all the while you were working against me."

"That's not the case," Charlie tried to explain.

"Shut up!" Pamela spit the words. "This morning you sent your mousy little office worker to my house to win over my mother. To fish for information. And all the while you and your partners were conspiring to blame my father for Peter's death. No," Pamela said, shaking her head. "I don't want to hear another word from you, and I may sue you for defamation."

"Pamela," Franklin shouted. "Stop it! Charlie was only trying to help me. I never wanted her to be involved. *You* called *her*."

His words seemed to get through. She stopped shrieking and turned away from Charlie to face her husband. She was shaking so hard the fur on her coat trembled. Franklin squinted at first, but Charlie watched his eyes widen and water with tenderness.

"Listen to me," Franklin's voice was quiet and hoarse. "No one else has access to, or knowledge of, my gun safe except you and your family. I wrote a letter to Stan telling him I had the money clip. I didn't know what else to do. Honey, two days later someone put a bullet in me. Charlie's colleague escaped an attack in Canada, and then a witness—whose fingerprints were found in Peter's apartment—was attacked in a jail cell in Toronto. He's dead. Only a few people have the resources and reach to orchestrate that kind of retaliation. Don't you see?" Franklin was pleading for his wife's understanding. "It has to be Stan."

Charlie couldn't see Pamela's face, but she saw her shoulders stiffen and heard her release a sigh. Was it resignation? Despair? Pamela reached for her handbag.

"I've got to get out of here," she said.

She didn't make eye contact with Charlie as she maneuvered around the chairs and headed for the door. Franklin, Charlie and Serena, still stunned by her emotional outburst, didn't try to stop her.

"I should go after her," Franklin finally said.

"You can't leave this room. I'll go," Charlie said.

"Both of you stay here," Serena ordered, racing after Pamela.

Franklin looked stricken. He cradled his injured arm and bowed his head. Charlie didn't speak. His manner recalled the day, five years ago, when she'd asked him for a divorce. They'd been separated for a year, but it was a sad moment as they both acknowledged the pain of their failed marriage. Charlie stood and took the seat Pamela had abandoned.

"I'm sorry. I knew this would be a tough confrontation."

"Yeah. Me too," Franklin said. "After I left Peter's place, when I was hiding, I considered just walking away from my marriage, my job, Detroit—everything. I thought leaving would be easier than having to face Pam. She's in agony, Charlie."

"And angry."

"Yes, but mostly caused by her pain. She's lost everything."

"You always did try to see the other person's side of things," Charlie said. "It's one of the things I loved about you."

Franklin tried to smile when Charlie touched his arm, then took his hand.

When Serena returned, they released hands and Franklin swiped at his wet cheek. Serena pretended not to notice. She took off her coat and tossed it across the bed.

"I've been fired," she said.

"No. You haven't," Franklin responded. "You're still on the case. The money will be coming from me. And I still want Charlie and her team working with you."

"Well, all right then," Serena said.

"Did you get to talk to her?" Charlie asked.

Serena shook her head. "No. She just fired me, and slammed the car door in my face. She was already on the phone, probably to her father, when she pulled off."

Charlie nodded. "Let the games begin."

Chapter 22

Don was waiting in Wallace's office. He'd moved to the small conference table, and helped himself to coffee. It had been more than an hour since Wallace went upstairs to talk to Travers, so he tried to keep busy. He spoke with Detective Li in Toronto, and left a message for Caesar Sturdivant's attorney, hoping the hit man's confession could still help somehow. After Charlie called to report on the explosive meeting in Franklin's hospital room, Don checked in with the freelancer in the parking lot for his take on the action.

"Denton? Rutkowski here. Is everything okay down there?"

"Yes, sir. Twenty minutes ago, Mrs. Rogers rushed out of the hospital. Another lady followed her. It looked like maybe they had an argument. Then Mrs. Rogers got in her Mercedes and drove away, and the other lady went back into the hospital. Other than that, it's been quiet."

"Okay, Denton. Keep your eyes open. Call me if anything else goes down. And before you say it, don't call me sir."

"Oh. Right. Got it, Mr. Rutkowski."

Wallace came back to the office with a mournful look and a need for coffee.

"I take it Travers was angry."

"Angry and feeling sorry for himself. He's taking it personally. Rutkowski, this is the God's honest truth. We're gonna need more evidence. Without it, this guy will go free."

"Believe me. We're working on it."

"I had to talk Travers down from arresting your partner."

"Why?"

"The money clip."

"You told him about the clip?"

"What else was I supposed to do? He said he was tired of the Mack agency's meddling."

"We weren't exactly meddling. We had a client paying us to investigate."

"Yeah, I know. But withholding evidence. That's straddling the line. Hell, it's over the damn line."

"This isn't exactly a straight-line case."

"I know. I know." Wallace wedged himself in at the table, winced from the stiff coffee, and ran a hand through his thick hair. "Travers doesn't like to rock the boat. That's how he stays above the fray. Unfortunately, everybody involved in this case is knee-deep in fray. If I know him, he's already trying to buy himself an out with the chief."

"This is going to be really ugly," Don said.

"As ugly as it gets."

"I think Fairchild will get more reckless. It was an amateur move to have his people take a shot at me in Toronto."

"I know. Everything's quiet at the hospital, but I'm adding another man to the detail."

"I spoke with my guy, too. He's got an eye on the parking lot and the front door."

"Good."

Don looked at his phone. "I have a call coming in I've got to take."

"You need privacy?"

"No. You should hear this, too. It's Sturdivant's attorney. I have a bunch of questions, and maybe some of his answers will give us that evidence you need."

"God, I hope so."

༖ ༖ ༖

169

At 6 p.m. on Friday, the Mack partners would usually be closing the office for the weekend. But tonight Charlie, Don, and Judy held an emergency meeting. Tamela was gone, but Hoyt Timbermann was on hand.

"The attorney is willing to give us a deposition of his communication with Sturdivant, and copies of his notes," Don said. "Wallace was relieved to hear that."

"I guess a dead client makes attorney-client confidentiality a moot point," Judy said.

"Actually, no. Privileged communication survives a client's death," Charlie explained. "But Serena thinks we can make the case for a waiver. I hope she's right."

"Travers is pissed at you," Don announced.

Charlie smirked. "What else is new."

"And Wallace has added men to the hospital security detail."

"Is Denton working out okay?" Hoyt asked Don.

"He seems to be. Charlie and I will take over for him at eleven. We'll play it by ear for the morning. Rogers may be moved to Ionia County to keep him in a safe environment."

"That's a long way from the city," Charlie said. "Pamela won't like it."

"From what you said about this morning's meeting, do you think she'll even care?" Judy asked.

"I hope so. She was angry and insulting, but I think it was just shock."

"She called you a bitch," Judy said indignantly.

"I know. But I can take it. We *did* lie to her. In fact, everyone's been lying to her. Her husband, her father . . . I'd be upset, too."

"Well, we received her check in the mail yesterday, and I deposited it this morning. I hope she doesn't put a stop payment on it," Judy mused.

"Anyway," Don said, annoyed at the interruption. "At Ionia, Franklin will be isolated and secure, and he can get the rehab he still needs for that arm. Wallace thinks that's better than having him at the Wayne County Jail."

"Did you ask about Franklin's gun?" Charlie asked. "Serena seemed to think it might lead to something."

"Yes. We talked about the gun. The evidence handling was standard operating procedure, and so was the chain of possession. The only fingerprints they could recover were Franklin's. I did ask Wallace to try to take prints from Franklin's safe, which will require a search warrant. He said he would. We also looked at the crime scene photos again. I still think it's odd that Peter was shot in the bathroom, but the gun ends up on the carpet in the sitting area. That feels like an inconsistency."

"I agree," Charlie said. "But it's not enough to help Franklin in court."

"It might have if your ex hadn't run. Then the police report could show that his hands and clothing didn't have gunpowder residue. But that horse has crossed the tape."

"Your point is taken. *Again.* So that's enough about the gun. I want to talk about this new Scanlon information that Judy's discovered," Charlie said. "It may be the *real* smoking gun."

"So, what do you have, Novak?" Don asked.

Judy began pulling several items from her folder. "I can't take all the credit for this. It was Tamela who found the first bit of information. Scanlon had a lot more involvement with Fairchild, and this bourbon deal, than she let on," Judy said, passing a sheet of paper to Don. "This is a photo of her with Robert Madison. He's the Canadian distiller. The photo is taken at his house in Windsor. Scanlon is Madison's interior designer."

"You gotta be kidding," Don said. "So that business about 'I can't quite remember his name' was just bullshit."

"Total. Madison is on the board of Scanlon's design company. I got the articles of incorporation from the secretary of state. I kept digging and found out that two years ago Scanlon's interior design company became a subsidiary of Fairchild Enterprises."

"So old man Fairchild and Scanlon have a business relationship? Damn."

"And that relationship predates the one she had with Peter. She told you and Charlie she'd never met Papa Fairchild."

"She's a conniving broad. I bet she and this Madison guy were trying to take Peter for his money," Don said. "This guy might not even own a distillery."

"You might be right, Rutkowski," Hoyt agreed. "I checked out Madison with some union guys I know in Canada. He's got a couple of different businesses and owns some delivery trucks and warehouses, but nobody knew anything about a liquor business."

"I also did some checking on Madison," Judy said, looking at a paper in front of her. "He has applied for, and been granted, a couple of liquor licenses, but that's as much of a connection to a bourbon business as I can find. He's owned a lot of businesses in Ontario. You want me to keep checking?"

"Yes," Charlie said. "When we add this information to the mix, *and* if we can use Sturdivant's confession to his attorney, we'll have something solid to hand to Serena."

"And to Wallace," Don added. "We also might get lucky with fingerprints on Franklin's safe. Mack, we should meet with Scanlon tonight. If Fairchild spooks her, she could disappear before we can get her to talk."

"How do we get her to see us?" Charlie asked. "Our last meeting wasn't exactly warm and fuzzy."

"I could invite her for a drink," Don suggested.

"That would work?" Judy asked.

"Novak, I am a lot more charming to women than you think."

"Obviously," Judy said, smirking.

"Charm notwithstanding, you'll need to dangle more than a drink to get a meeting with her," Charlie said. "Karen's pretending to be someone she isn't, and we know it. We are not her favorite people."

"What's important to her?" Judy asked.

"Money," Don replied.

"That's right," Charlie agreed. "So, let's reel her in with something we already know she wants. How about those artwork certifications she was trying to steal from Peter's apartment? They're probably worth a lot."

Don looked skeptical. "Really?"

"Look, I'll write out what to say. Then you give her a call."

Chapter 23

Don arranged to meet Karen Scanlon at the Pioneer Bar in Ferndale. Charlie followed in her Corvette, and was across the street from the bar when Scanlon drove by, made a U-turn, and parked a few cars behind.

Charlie watched through the mirror as Scanlon jumped down from the Hummer. She wore a leather coat and tight jeans tucked into heeled boots. She had a red tam pulled down over her straight blond hair. She whipped off the tam before entering the bar.

Don would buy Karen a drink and inform her Charlie was bringing the portfolio for the artwork. In the phone call he'd informed her the Mack Agency was no longer on the case, but the police had released the certificates and asked that they be returned to her. She seemed to buy the story, and agreed to meet them, which meant Fairchild hadn't yet warned her away from them. It also confirmed her intent to scheme Peter's estate out of the paintings he'd purchased.

Charlie waited ten minutes before approaching them at a back booth. Don had an almost-full glass of scotch in front of him, and Karen was lifting the orange slice from what looked like a screwdriver.

"Oh. Here's Ms. Mack now," Don said, sliding over in the booth. "You want something to drink, Charlie?"

"No, thank you," Charlie said, sitting. She and Karen shared stony looks.

"I hope this is the last time we'll have to meet, Ms. Mack," Karen said with a searing stare.

"Me too, Ms. Scanlon, or Ms. Sketcher, or whoever you are today," Charlie said sarcastically.

Karen never stopped staring as she picked up her drink and swirled the ice cubes. Don sipped his scotch and observed the drama. When Charlie reached into her backpack and laid a folder on the table, Karen glanced at it and warmed up with a smile.

"I hope that's for me."

"It's more *about* you," Charlie said, opening the folder and turning over three sheets of paper. "This is a photo of you standing next to Robert Madison. This is a copy of a business directory showing your company as a subsidiary of Fairchild Enterprises, and this is a copy of your board of directors, including Madison."

Karen Scanlon was a con master. Her eyes glinted her surprise for only a millisecond. Charlie and Don watched as she lifted her glass to her mouth for the last finger of her drink. "So what does that prove?"

"It proves you lied to us," Don said.

"We've all been lying, haven't we? I don't suppose you have any art certificates in that folder."

Charlie shook her head. "Karen, you're in trouble. Are you aware that an inmate in a Toronto prison implicated you in the murder of Peter Fairchild?"

Scanlon dropped the coolness. "What the hell are you talking about?"

"Caesar Sturdivant," Don said. "Any alarm bells ringing? Sturdivant told me and a Toronto detective that you shot Peter with Franklin's gun. He says he was in the room but only there to coldcock Rogers and help you with cleanup."

"I don't know the guy, and I didn't shoot Peter. Franklin did."

"That's what you and Fairchild would have us believe," Charlie said.

Scanlon sat upright and still. "You don't know a damn thing, lady."

"We think we do. Karen, I don't know what Fairchild has on you to turn you into a murderer. But if I were you, I'd be worried."

Scanlon tried to make sense of this. "Look, I just offered my design expertise to Peter Fairchild. His father recommended my services."

"Why would this Sturdivant guy implicate you in Peter's murder?" Charlie asked.

"I have no idea. I have no connection to this Caesar Sturdivant."

Scanlon was still trying to be calm, but Charlie noticed the tic in her left eye and the tint of red on her cheeks. It could be the screwdriver, but she had also reached into her purse and pulled out a cigarette before remembering they were in a nonsmoking bar.

"Did you know Sturdivant was attacked in his cell two days ago? It's a funny coincidence. It was right after Pamela Fairchild told her father Don was in Toronto to talk to the guy."

"After I visited Sturdivant, two guys shot up my car," Don added. "That was probably just a coincidence too, Charlie."

"Maybe. But then there are the guys who tried to kill Franklin, and now he's in protective custody."

"Oh, I forgot about that. That's too many attacks to be coincidence, isn't it?" Don teased.

"Yeah. I'm thinking maybe Fairchild is not the kind of man to leave loose ends," Charlie said. "And as soon as he hears the police are interested in Karen, he'll get nervous."

They both stared directly at Scanlon.

"Look, I need to leave," she said, pulling a ten-dollar bill from her purse and dropping it on the table.

"Karen," Charlie said. "Why should you take the fall for something Fairchild orchestrated? We've checked. You've committed a few minor crimes, but never anything like murder. If the prosecutors prove you killed Peter, you'll go to prison for the rest of your life."

"That would be premeditated murder," Don added.

"No. No. You can't pin this on me."

"Fairchild will be the one pinning it on you. You're no dummy. Look at the facts. This witness is implicating both you and Fairchild, but if it comes down to you versus him, how do you think this will turn out?" Charlie asked.

"With his high-priced attorneys, and his political connections, will a jury believe Stanford Fairchild, or Carrie Anne Sketcher?" Don enjoyed adding this bit of fuel to Charlie's fire.

They remained in the bar while outside, officers took a frightened Scanlon into custody when she exited. She would be questioned as a person of interest in the Peter Fairchild murder. It wouldn't take long for her lawyer to arrange her release, but even less time before inside information—from the prosecutor's office, the police department, Wayne County Sheriff's office, or some other source—leaked to Fairchild.

Charlie ordered a ginger ale, chicken wings, and a coffee for Don.

"I don't need coffee."

"You just had a large scotch, and we're going on overnight patrol."

"In that case, get me another coffee to go. I have my thermos in the car. Oh, and I'm eating some of your chicken wings."

"Get your own."

"Won't this meal be expensed?"

"I guess so."

"Then what's yours is mine." Don's phone beeped a message. "They have Scanlon at police headquarters."

"You think we shook her?"

"I know we did. If DPD hadn't picked her up tonight, she'd be home packing up a few things and hitting I-75 south."

"What's to keep her from doing that after she's released?"

"Wallace is putting a patrol car at her house."

"You think she'll roll on Fairchild?"

"Absolutely," Don said.

"I think so, too," Charlie said. "Scanlon may be a liar, a cheat, and a scam artist, but she's nobody's fool. Maybe she conspired with Fairchild because he gave her a boatload of money, or because he has something on her that's worse than anything she's ever been charged with. She's always had to scrap for a living. It takes nerve, tenacity, and brains to reinvent yourself. She's used every tool she has to get where she is, and she's not going down for some man. Any man."

"Wow. It sounds as if you like her, Mack."

"No. But I understand women who want to make a name for themselves and have their own independence. There is a not-so-thick line between what I do and what Scanlon does."

"I'm not going to agree with that, Mack. I know you. You have a conscience. Scanlon doesn't. The only feelings she has are printed by the U.S. Mint."

"Hi, hon, hope I'm not calling too late. I'm on my way to my security shift at the hospital."

"Hamm and I are still up. Is Don with you?"

"I'm following his car. We met with Karen Scanlon, then had a quick bite."

"Hamm's been walking back and forth to the front door looking for you, but I'm about to lock up for the night. Once we go upstairs and he sees his bed he'll be out like a light."

"I hope he isn't the only one missing me."

"He's not. You're being careful, right?"

"Yes."

"Have you heard anything from Pamela or Fairchild?"

"No."

"Or Franklin?"

"Franklin is a prisoner. He doesn't have access to a phone."

"Will you be home in the morning?"

"We get off at eight. I want to check with Wallace to see what time they plan to transport Franklin to a facility. If they're moving him early, Don and I will probably stay around."

"Okay. Be safe," Mandy said, yawning. "Love you."

"Love you, too. I'll call in the morning. Sleep well."

∾ ∾ ∾

Detective Wallace was waiting in the parking lot when Don and Charlie arrived, and they gathered in front of his unmarked car. He gave Charlie a radio unit and advised them they would move Franklin early tomorrow. He'd ordered a patrol car to the hospital's service entrance and had stationed a second officer on the fourth floor. Wallace also reported that Karen Scanlon had been released from custody.

"We didn't have enough to hold her, but we questioned her long enough to put a tracking device on her vehicle and dispatch a car to watch the front of her house. Now we'll wait and see," Wallace said.

"Any directive from your brass?" Charlie asked.

"There's been a meeting in the chief's office for the last three hours. I wasn't invited, but Travers is there. I'm headed back to headquarters now."

"You're relieved, Denton," Don said, leaning into the car window.

Relieved is how Denton looked as he turned in his walkie-talkie. He'd spent more than nine hours sitting, standing, walking, and hovering around the hospital parking lot. He'd had only a half-hour bathroom and food break. It was the most tedious detail he'd had since becoming a freelance investigator. Still, he wanted to impress the owners of the Mack Agency so he could get work with them again.

"Thanks, uh, Mr. Rutkowski. Say, there's one thing that occurred to me. It might make sense to put a man on the rear service entrance. I doubt there are many deliveries at night, but at least three trucks and a service van took that access road to the rear. When I checked with the parking booth guard, he said vehicles can go back there only if they have a delivery order, and he can watch them on his security monitor."

"That's good thinking, Denton. The police are already dispatching a patrol car for the rear. But we'll be sure to check with the parking guy."

Charlie and Don parked on opposite sides of the lot. Charlie had a close view of the emergency room and the hospital's main entry, and Don was parked in the farthest corner near the access road. His driver-side back window was still splintered, secured inside and out with duct tape. He got out, punched the door lock on his Buick fob, and walked over to where Charlie sat in the Corvette. After rapping lightly on Charlie's window, he stuffed himself into the passenger seat.

"Damn, this is like sitting in a coffin."

"You're here without an invite you know. Did you already talk to Rita?"

"I called her before I got to the bar. She wasn't happy about me spending another night away from home."

Charlie nodded. "You'll make it up to her. What do you think of Denton? Would you work with him again?"

"I think so. This wasn't the most exciting assignment, but he managed to keep his eyes open, and he made a good suggestion."

"What was that?"

"To check in with the parking attendant. Apparently, he has a monitor for the service entry camera. Denton said there were a half-dozen deliveries during the day, and he took the time to check them out. I'm about to walk over there now. You want to come?"

Charlie caught a whiff of alcohol as soon as the attendant slid the window open. "Can I help you?" the man said.

"I'm Charlie Mack, and this is my partner. We're doing guard duty in the lot tonight and thought we'd just introduce ourselves."

"I'm Rivers. The note from my supervisor said we'd have some private security around. Y'all are protecting that killer upstairs on four. Right?"

"Uh. Yeah, we are," Charlie said, deciding not to argue the point. "I assume it's usually pretty quiet at night. Do you get any deliveries?"

"A few. But most of the action at night comes from the drop-offs or pickups at emergency. I been doin' this twenty-two years. Got a year to go before retirement."

"Is that the service entry?" Don asked, pointing to a couple of monitors mounted on the wall.

"Yep. Service dock and waste management area. The trash guys come around four. We sometimes get a laundry pickup and delivery, but that's about the size of it."

Charlie heard the drone of the local news/sports channel, and spotted a small radio perched on the inside ledge. Next to it was an old-fashioned metal lunch box and thermos. As they talked, a patrol car eased up to the booth.

"I'm headed to the back," the female officer said, leaning over from the driver's seat.

"Go on through," Rivers replied, waving.

"Well Mr. Rivers, I'm parked over there," Charlie said, pointing toward the emergency building. "My partner is at the back of the lot. We'll see you later."

There was constant traffic at the emergency room entrance. Not unusual for the start of the weekend. Charlie noted that this was her fourth visit to this hospital in as many days. The past ten days of stress, surprise, and suspense around her ex seemed like a month. Don and Judy were feeling it, too. This case had disrupted their work and home lives.

Charlie didn't have a thermos of coffee, so she headed to the lobby for a vending machine purchase. She exchanged a nod with the guard as she entered. The waiting room had a few people sitting in various corners, and the lady behind the desk was busy on her computer. Charlie slid a few bills into the cash slot for a Snickers bar and a bottled water, then returned to the parking lot. It was a cold night, but clear. It hadn't snowed much all week.

Charlie looked toward Don's car, and he flashed his lights. She responded with a raised hand. She strolled to the parking booth and found Mr. Rivers sleeping, his head resting on his chest, so she didn't bother him. When she returned to the car, she turned over the engine to get some heat pumping through the vehicle. It was going to be a long night.

At two a van marked "Allied Laundry and Linens" pulled into the hospital access lane and drove up to the parking booth. The van driver honked once, and Rivers stepped outside and around to the driver's side. Within a minute Rivers returned to his booth and the van continued along the road. Twenty minutes later the laundry van left the same way it came. The emergency room traffic quieted around 3 a.m., and Charlie was having a hard time staying awake. She called Don.

"What is it, Mack?"

"Single surveillance is boring as hell!"

"Staying awake is just mind over matter."

"Is that what they teach you in the Marines?"

"No. They tell you if you fall asleep, you'll probably die. So you're more prone to insomnia. Plus you're not alone out there. There's always some guy who keeps you awake by chattering all night."

"I'm listening to a news talk station."

"Is that helping?"

"Not really. They keep reminding me how cold it is."

"I'm using a portable heater that plugs into my lighter unit, so I don't have to keep the engine running."

Charlie responded with silent envy.

Don laughed. "I have a nice large trunk for my work tools. It's one of the advantages of having a car that isn't built like a sardine can."

"Maybe I should sit with you. The ER is quiet."

"Okay. Come on over now. I have a good view of the whole place."

It was roomier and warmer in Don's car even with the cracked back window letting in a bit of air. Although he was parked farther from the lobby, his vantage included the parking booth, the access road, and both the front and emergency entrances.

"So Rivers was sound asleep?" Don asked.

"I didn't see any point in waking him."

"He might be more alert if he didn't have a thermos full of booze," Don said.

"Yeah. I smelled it too."

"Look, it's after four, and the trash guys should be here any minute, but Mother Nature is calling now."

"Okay. Bring me back a coffee."

"I'll be back in five minutes," Don said, grabbing the walkie-talkie.

Charlie watched him walk up the row of cars toward the main entrance. He stopped when he heard the trash truck and turned to watch it rumble up the access road. He lifted a thumbs up. The lobby doors swooshed open and then closed behind Don.

The trash vehicle had the logo "Dooley Brothers" on the side. It stopped at the parking booth, and Rivers walked around to the driver's side holding a clipboard. After a few moments, the truck continued up the west side of the building. Charlie looked at Don's thermos, thinking of unscrewing the top for a quick sip. But a brown sedan pulled quickly into the lot, and Charlie sat up with alarm. She watched as the car pulled into a space at the front of the lot, and a man jumped down from the driver's seat. He ran to the open passenger door and reached in to take a small child from a woman. The three hurried to the emergency room.

Charlie sighed and leaned back into the seat. A red SUV and a white four-door sedan drove into the lot and parked, but Charlie was concentrating on the source of the tinny sound she heard coming through Don's cracked window. Finally, she made it out as the radio in the parking booth. The window to the booth must be open. Don had left the keys in his ignition, so she pulled them out as she exited and tucked the two-way radio in her jacket pocket. As she approached the booth, she saw the open door. She looked inside at the service bay monitor and saw the trash truck with its doors open. Two steps more and she spotted Mr. Rivers lying lifeless on the access road.

Shots fired! Shots fired! came the shout through the two-way in her pocket. *We have a fourth-floor breach,* the voice sounded again. Charlie started at a run toward the front entrance, then changed directions. "Don, I'm headed to the rear. Rivers has been shot!" Charlie shouted into the radio.

At a trot Charlie shoved the walkie-talkie into her jacket and drew her revolver. *Officer down, Officer down* the radio sounded again. When she reached the corner of the building, she paused to look. The garbage truck, doors open, was stopped behind the patrol car. There was no movement at the police car, and its driver-side door and trunk stood open. Charlie held her gun in a firing position and walked quickly toward the two vehicles. She circled the garbage truck. It was empty. She came up slowly behind the police car.

"Officer?" Charlie shouted. "I'm private security."

There was no response, and Charlie peeked into the trunk as she moved up to the driver side of the empty patrol car. She looked ahead at the building's rear door, then moved up toward it and yanked on the handle. It opened easily. She carefully stepped inside. The hallway was awash in fluorescent light. And empty. At the end of the hallway was a set of double doors. Charlie approached the doors cautiously, turned the knob slowly, and opened the door a crack. As she stepped through, her radio blared again. *We have gunfire at the front of the building. I need assistance.* It was Don.

"I'm coming, Don," Charlie shouted into the radio.

She was backing out the double doors when she heard moaning. In an alcove, ten yards ahead, the female officer lay on top of a pile of boxes. With gun extended, Charlie moved fast up the hall. The officer's face and head were bleeding, and her eyes were swollen shut. The cop's lips were a reddish-blue.

"I'm here as private security. What happened?" Charlie asked, kneeling next to the woman.

"Attacked."

Charlie could barely hear the whispered response. She leaned over the cop, putting her ear to her mouth.

"He's got my gun," she said through a thick tongue.

"Did he shoot you? I didn't hear any shots."

"No. Not shot. He sprayed my face, then hit me with something. Hard. I followed him."

The officer's face contorted in pain. With some effort, she lifted herself to a seated position.

"Stay still. You might have a concussion."

"I can't see," the officer replied.

"I'll get you some help."

Charlie used the cop's vest radio to speak directly to the police dispatcher. "Officer down in the rear service hallway of Henry Ford Hospital. We need an ambulance immediately."

"Who is this?" the dispatcher asked.

"Private security detail authorized by Detective Wallace. This is Charlie Mack."

"We have an ambulance en route, Ms. Mack," the dispatcher said. "We also have units responding to an officer down at the same address."

Charlie leaned over the officer. "An ambulance is on the way. Will you be all right if I leave you here?"

"I'll be okay," the cop said, speaking more clearly now. "I still got this," she said, yanking her shotgun from behind the boxes.

"Okay, but get yourself behind those boxes too, in case they come back this way."

Chapter 24

Charlie slammed through the exterior service door and onto the landing at a run. She jumped to the ground and kept running. At the front of the building she saw gun flashes and ducked back. She darted toward the parking booth, crouching low. Rivers' body was sprawled face down, blood pooling near his head. Charlie ducked into the booth.

From the window she saw Don and the lobby guard pinned down behind cement planters at the left side of the hospital entrance. The two men firing handguns used the late-arriving red SUV as cover.

Charlie's mind raced. If she shot at the men from her position, she could draw fire from one or both, giving Don and the guard a chance to tag them, or at least move to a safer position. That idea fell apart immediately when one of the men sprinted to the next row of cars for a better line of fire.

Charlie had another idea, and leaped over the shrubs at the perimeter of the booth and ran along the fence line for Don's car. With the volley of gunfire, nobody heard the Buick's engine turn over. With the headlights off, she steered parallel to the back gate, then turned up the row where the SUV was parked. She was a right-handed shooter, but her left hand would have to do for tonight. She rolled down the driver-side window, turned on the high beams, and slammed the accelerator to the floor. The gunmen turned toward the headlights and Charlie fired. Four times. She saw one man go down, and the other run toward the parking booth as she passed the SUV at forty miles per hour. Charlie braced as the Buick plowed into a concrete planter.

She hadn't bothered with the seat belt, but the airbag caught most of the force of the impact. Her chest felt heavy as air escaped her lungs. She flung open the door, then dropped to a squat near the front of the Buick. Don, who was crouching behind one of the planters, stood and fired two shots in the direction of the running man. As he did, the garbage vehicle reappeared, moving in reverse. Don ran toward it, and Charlie followed as two squad cars careened into the access road blocking the truck's exit.

When the truck stopped short, a man jumped down and joined the escaping parking lot shooter heading up the service road to the back of the hospital. Charlie was a few yards behind when Don cornered the building at full speed. She heard two shots and hugged the wall for a peek. Don was on the ground.

"You hit?" Charlie shouted.

"No. They were firing so I hit the deck."

Don rose to his feet and Charlie joined him.

"Where are they?"

"They took off. Somewhere in those trees." Don pointed beyond the trash bins. "There's an eight-foot iron fence on that side, so they aren't going anywhere."

"Yeah, but they're still armed."

"I think they might be out of ammo."

Renee Young had been a Detroit police officer for six years. During her time in uniform, she'd dodged bullets, broken a collarbone while tussling with a suspect, and received two commendations. She had her heart set on a detective slot in a year or two.

Her eyes were still stinging, and her face was swollen, particularly her mouth, which felt the size of a tennis ball. But worse than her discomfort was the embarrassment she felt at being caught off guard and ambushed by the thugs who breached the hospital.

She'd crouched low when she heard the voices of two panicked men running along the service hallway. When they passed her position, she ducked behind the pile of cardboard boxes. Her eyes were still closed and swollen, but she heard the slamming door as they fled the building. She could make out only a sliver of light as she scrambled to her feet, wiped the back of her hand against her protruding lips, and cradled her Remington pump-action shotgun in the crook of her arm. She leaned against the cold wall, her shoulder brushing the surface, and used the toe of her boot to serve as a blind man's cane to inch toward the double doors. In what felt like five minutes she reached the doors and pushed through to the hall that led to the outdoors. Here she couldn't use the walls because wood platforms, boxes, and dollies lined the perimeter. With the shotgun balanced in her right arm and her left outstretched and sweeping from side to side, she moved slowly to the heavy metal door. When she leaned on the push bar, cold air slammed her body, stopping her for only a moment. Once on the loading dock, the fresh air eased her breathing and cleared her head.

She froze in place when she heard running footsteps beyond the trash dumpsters.

"Over there," an out-of-breath man shouted. "Maybe we can get out there."

"Okay," another answered.

The sound of shoes running on pavement turned to the snapping of twigs and pinecones when the men broke through the tree line. Gripping the banister, Officer Young descended the steps as quickly as possible and followed the noises. She counted twenty-six steps, nearly stumbling on a curb, before she reached the mulch-covered ground near the rear fencing.

It was impossible for anyone to squeeze through the eight-foot wrought-iron fence or scale its barbed top, but the pepper-spray thug and his buddy didn't know that. They thrashed and grunted and cursed and whimpered. Young couldn't see much, but at night, in these dark trees, the men she pursued couldn't see very well either. She could make out the two figures groping at the fence—their backs to her. She was only a few feet away when she raised the shotgun in their direction. She was taking a risk, but if she was lucky, she could get off a round or two before one of them killed her with her own service weapon.

"Put your hands in the air," she ordered. "Do it now and move slowly."

The thrashing stopped. Young took a shooting stance, knees bent, prepared to fire at any sound of sudden movement.

"Shit," one of the men said. "She has a shotgun."

"Drop your weapons," Young shouted.

She held her breath so she could hear the guns hit the ground. She heard one thud. She jiggled the gun up and down once. "Where's the other one?"

"I don't have a gun, lady. I dropped mine by the truck."

"Okay. You guys get moving back to the parking lot. No sudden moves. This is pump action and I'm in no mood to play."

Young took two steps back and gestured with the gun. She kept it aimed in the direction of their movements. She saw a bit of light from the streetlamp as they approached the edge of the trees. When they were about to enter the parking lot, one of the men stopped.

"You keep moving," Young said. "Or I swear I'll put a load of buckshot in your back."

"Freeze," a voice ordered behind them. "Drop those guns."

Charlie and Don released their revolvers and turned around, hands raised. Four uniformed officers faced them, guns drawn. Wallace and the security guard quickly joined them.

"Stand down. They're not the ones," Wallace shouted. "They're with me. I said stand down!"

Charlie and Don waited a few beats before lowering their hands.

"You've got two bad guys somewhere in those trees." Don pointed behind him.

"Where's my downed officer?" Wallace asked.

"I left her inside," Charlie said. "She was okay. Not shot. But they sprayed something in her eyes and hit her on the head. Can we pick up our guns?"

Don leaned over to retrieve his Glock. "It's okay, Mack. Get your damn gun," Don growled.

From the trash area came a ruckus and everyone looked. "Don't shoot, don't shoot," a man was pleading.

The group of officers moved forward cautiously, weapons ready. The outdoor lights didn't quite pick up the tree line, but they could make out three people emerging from the shadows.

"Halt right there," one of the officers shouted.

"Don't shoot," Officer Young shouted. "I'm on duty. I have two of the men you're looking for. Come and get them."

"There's your officer right there, Wallace," Charlie said with a smile.

Charlie figured the morning news shows would already be blaring the events of the night, so she gave Mandy a quick call.

"I'm just seeing it on TV," Mandy said. "Thank God you called. Are you all right?"

"I'm okay. No, not really. But I'm not hurt."

"Is Franklin okay? The newscast didn't say."

"Yes. He's safe. Look, I'm going into a debriefing with the police, but I didn't want you to worry. I'll call you back with the details. I love you."

"More than Franklin?" Mandy said, clearly kidding this time.

"Absolutely. I'll call you again as soon as I can."

Wallace sat in the office of one of the hospital administrators, leading the debrief on the hospital attack. A dozen uniformed cops, two hospital security guards, and Charlie and Don tried to make sense of the hospital breach by at least five bad guys.

In addition to the fatal shooting of the parking guard, an officer was dead. Charlie had killed one of the van shooters, and another gunman had been killed inside the hospital. Two officers—including the female cop—were severely injured, and one of the attackers had suffered injuries. The two men captured by the female officer were already in central lockup.

It had been a horrible night. Despite the losses Franklin was still safe, moved to a new location in the hospital and with even more security. Now all they had to figure out was how this mess happened—although they suspected they knew who the mastermind was.

Nathanson, the officer on watch, spoke up. "I was right outside Rogers's door when I heard the service elevator. It was quiet; the only people on the fourth floor were the nurses at their station. I sent the rookie down the hall to investigate." The distraught duty cop shook his head and cleared his throat before continuing. "I heard Conrad shout 'stop right there,' but then they just opened up on him. It happened so fast. I couldn't get to him."

"It wasn't your fault. You got one of them," Wallace said to comfort the man.

There were only grim faces in the room. Charlie felt the collective pain of the blue line, especially the anger and distress from Officer Nathanson, who'd been unable to save his partner.

He'd made the first call of trouble when he heard the shots fired and rushed into the melee. Fifteen shots had been fired before he took down one of the gunmen and the other fled back into the service elevator.

"I think the plan was to try to take Rogers out through the emergency room," another officer said. "When the 'shots fired' call came through my radio, a guy who had been in the waiting room for more than an hour looked at me and bolted toward the door. I tackled and cuffed him, but he was shouting for somebody."

"Probably the two guys at the SUV," Don said. "I grabbed Akens here in the lobby when Charlie, uh, Ms. Mack, radioed about the parking guard. As soon as the front door opened, they started shooting at us. We were just lucky they didn't have assault weapons."

"They had a lot of guys, but not a lot of sophistication," Wallace said. "The two in lockup have Canadian driver's licenses. So did the dead man in the parking lot. By the way, Ms. Mack, that was a good shot. That took some guts."

"She's got plenty of that," Don said proudly.

Charlie had been quiet in the meeting, letting this band of brothers deal with their stress and anger. She smiled now as they gave her nods of respect.

"Is your female officer going to be all right?" Charlie asked.

"Officer Young has first-degree chemical burns on her face. She was sprayed with a military-grade pepper spray. She's also being treated for a concussion and needed four stitches in her scalp. But she's expected to recover from her injuries."

"She was ambushed in her car, but she still went in after them," Charlie said.

"Yes, her bravery is noted."

Wallace talked about the movements of the gunmen, their weapons, and vehicles. He also talked about the report he'd give to Travers and what information should be shared with the media, whose news trucks still lined the front of the hospital. He concluded the debriefing with an announcement about the arrangements being made to notify the fallen officer's family.

The room emptied slowly, officers filing out in singles and pairs, all with slumped shoulders. Wallace stayed back to speak with Charlie and Don.

"I got a call from headquarters. The chief is taking the accusations against Fairchild seriously. He doesn't have a choice now that a cop is dead. Also, one of the captured punks is already talking. Says he was hired by some big shot in Windsor."

"We think we know who that might be," Charlie said.

"Oh yeah?"

"A guy with ties to Scanlon, Peter, and maybe Fairchild."

"There are too many dotted lines to Canada for this guy's involvement to be a coincidence," Don said. "Also, I maybe recognized one of the guys in the parking lot as the dude who shot at me in Toronto."

"Well, they were sure as hell shooting at you tonight, Rutkowski," Wallace said. "I'm glad you two were here, and I'll need written reports from both of you."

"How did these men know you were moving Franklin this morning?" Charlie asked.

"What? You think they knew?"

"They must have known about the six o'clock transport," Charlie said. "They were putting their people into place. Two on the fourth-floor wing. One near the emergency room exit. Two in the getaway vehicle. You've got a leak in the department, Wallace."

"You're right. Has to be someone in my unit," Wallace said, rubbing his hands through his hair.

"What are you doing about Franklin?"

"Well, he's staying put for now. They'd have to be bat-shit crazy to make another attempt on him here."

"You should let Scanlon know what went down tonight, Wallace. I bet that'll make her talk about Fairchild," Don said.

"Yeah. I'll need to find someplace safe for her, too."

"What's next, detective?" Charlie asked.

"You mean besides finding the leak, getting signed confessions from our two gunmen, moving Rogers, and keeping Karen Scanlon safe?"

Wallace looked ready to drop. He was juggling procedures, protocols, politics, and people he didn't usually have to deal with.

"Sorry to pile on," Charlie said. "What can we do to help?"

"Send me the information on the Windsor businessman."

"I'll have Judy send you what she's got."

"And get your written statements about tonight to me. I'll drive to Scanlon's house and tell her what's happened here. Offer her protection. It shouldn't be difficult to convince her she's on Fairchild's hit list."

"Do you have enough yet to arrest the asshole?" Don asked.

"I will with the deposition from Sturdivant's attorney, the confessions from tonight's attackers, and, hopefully, a statement from Scanlon. I'll take what I have to a prosecutor this afternoon. You know, the mayor and the chief and all the others will probably want to give Fairchild the opportunity to turn himself in. So don't expect to see a perp walk on the news. Even with the killing of a cop, Peter's murder, and the conspiracy charges, Fairchild will use all his white-collar power to fight us. Ultimately, we may see more men in pinstripes than in prison stripes."

Don's car had already been towed to his dealership where it now had more than a shattered window to repair. Rita was on her way to pick him up. Charlie wanted to see Franklin before she left the hospital, and Wallace had given his permission.

"Sorry about your car, Don. You shouldn't have left me with the keys," Charlie offered contritely. "Kidding aside. Whatever the insurance company doesn't pay for, we'll make you whole."

"This work can be hard on cars, Mack. Maybe we can file it under expenses. You call Carruthers?"

"Already did."

"Okay. See you tomorrow."

Upstairs, in an out-of-the-way hospital wing, Charlie visited Franklin, who'd been sedated. He opened one eye and slowly smiled when he saw her at the door.

"They tried to take me out again, Charlie."

"Yeah. But we stopped them."

"You're my hero. Always were," he said before drifting back to sleep.

Charlie leaned into the Corvette seat, and hit redial.

"Hey," Mandy answered. "Is the police briefing over?"

"Look, honey, I need to talk to you about something else." Charlie paused a minute, but knew she needed to share. "Several people were killed this morning. A nice old man who was just biding his time until retirement, a rookie cop, and another guy— a murderer, maybe. But *I* killed *him*."

"Oh no, Charlie. I'm so sorry."

"It was just like last time. I had no choice." Charlie's voice wavered. "The guy was firing on Don and a security guard." Charlie fought back tears and tried to collect herself. "I know it couldn't be helped, but it feels awful."

"I know. When can you come home?"

"I'm waiting for Serena. I need to fill her in."

"You've been up all night. You really need to get some rest and take some time to put this into perspective."

"I guess I could suggest to Serena that she speak directly with Detective Wallace."

"That's a good idea."

"Well, she's pulling into the parking lot now. I'll sit with her for a half hour and come home."

"Good. I want you all to myself tonight. No Franklin, no Fairchild, no Pamela, no Serena, nobody but us."

They sat talking in Serena's luxury sedan. "You know, Charlie, they call me a killer in the courtroom but in reality, it can't be easy."

"It's not. I've talked to my partners about it many times. Killing another human being takes a toll. No matter the circumstances."

"The closest I've come to grappling with it is when I do the walk-a-mile-in-my-shoes thing with my regular clientele. It helps. Especially with closing arguments."

"I've heard you're quite good at closing, and also cross-exam."

"That's my reputation," Serena said matter-of-factly. "But what about you? Are you okay?"

"Not so much. I'm going home, take a hot bath, and sleep."

"You should do that. Uh, by the way, I got a call from Pamela."

Charlie raised an eyebrow. "I thought she fired you."

"She wants to meet. At her house. She says she has something to tell us about her father."

"Us?"

"Yes. She wants you there."

Charlie protested with a head shake. "What else could she possibly have to say to me? No way. The way I feel right now, if she gets nasty again, you'll have to pull me off her."

"And I would, too," Serena said laughing. "After you've gotten in a couple of blows."

Charlie couldn't help laughing, too. The first laugh she'd allowed herself in about twelve hours. She considered how tense she was, and tired. Serena's extremely comfortable Lincoln Town Car had plush heated seats and molded backs. Charlie felt her body wanting to succumb to the urge to sleep.

"I can't meet anyone in the shape I'm in."

"I'll set it up for tomorrow or Monday," Serena said.

Charlie grunted.

"I'll take your sullenness as a 'yes.'"

"Did Pamela know about the attack on Franklin?"

"She'd heard it on the news. That's why she called. She apologized for her outburst yesterday."

Charlie's phone rang, and she looked at the display. Somehow she'd already missed several calls.

"What is it, Don?"

"Wallace has been trying to reach you."

"I've been on the phone with Mandy. Now I'm talking to Serena. I know Wallace needs our reports, but it'll have to wait. I have to get some rest."

"Mack, listen!" Don shouted. "Karen Scanlon was found hanging in her home this morning. It's an apparent suicide, and there's a note."

"Oh shit!"

Don approached Charlie's car as she pulled up to the crazy scene in front of Karen Scanlon's house. Crime scene tape was wrapped around trees and extended the length of the block. Six police vehicles—including the medical examiner's van, a fire truck, and an ambulance—joined two tracking dogs, Channels 7 and 4 satellite trucks, and a crowd three people deep, videotaping with their phones. In the middle of the street, blue lights flashing, a car marked Chief of Police notified the neighborhood there was some serious shit going on.

"Wallace said to bring you right in."

"Damn it all to hell, Don," Charlie replied. "This is a circus. Why in the world do they have dogs here?"

"They found boot tracks in the rear of the house. Come on," he said and grabbed her arm.

Charlie counted eighteen people in Scanlon's living room. The counting was a way to keep alert. Several people looked their way as an ashen-faced Wallace shepherded them into the small dining room and closed the door.

"What the hell happened?" Charlie started.

Wallace gave Charlie a sharp look, then rubbed at the stubble on his chin. He slumped into a padded leather chair. Charlie and Don followed suit.

"I was on my way here. I called ahead to my patrolman and told him to notify Scanlon that I wanted a meeting. He rang the bell and knocked on the door. When there was no response, he jimmied the lock. He found her upstairs hanging from a ceiling fan. Broken neck."

"Don said something about a note?"

"Typed. Confessing her involvement in Peter's murder and implicating Franklin. Said Peter had cheated her and Rogers out of money for his investment in the Canadian liquor deal. According to the note, the plan was just to scare him, but Peter was drunk, and things went wrong."

"That's pure poppycock," Don said. "The evidence doesn't back it up. Where is she on the surveillance camera? How did the gun get left behind?"

"Are you buying this as a suicide?" Charlie asked.

"Come see for yourself."

Karen Scanlon's modest two-bedroom townhome was relatively small and uninterestingly decorated. But her bedroom suite was magnificent. The massive four-poster bed was made of cherry-wood with ornate wood carvings. A beautiful damask bed covering in burgundy, rust, and orange was interwoven with gold threads. A seating area near the front windows was framed in lined drapes and a round contemporary rug.

Wallace wouldn't allow them entry into the bathroom, but through the pocket door they saw a large claw-foot tub. A gold-leaf framed mirror ran the length of the two-sink marble vanity. An upholstered bench was pushed under the counter, and hanging from the collar of a ceiling fan was an open noose. A footstool under the light fixture was toppled on its side.

"How did she tie the rope?" Charlie asked

"We think she climbed up on the vanity. We cut down the body, and we're still processing the scene. I wanted you to see it before we dusted for prints or moved anything else."

"What do you make of it, Don?" Charlie asked.

"She used the footstool to get onto the vanity. Tied the rope to the fixture and climbed down. She stepped on the footstool again, looped the rope around her neck, and then kicked it out from under her."

There were a couple moments of silence while they all pictured it. A shiver streaked up Charlie's spine.

"Where are the rope remnants?" Charlie asked.

"I'm not sure. Perez, I need to see you," Wallace spoke into his radio. "I'm in the bathroom of the deceased."

A few minutes later, Officer Jerry Perez stepped into the bedroom. He was tall, lean, and stern. He wore a short uniform jacket and a knit hat.

"You wanted to see me, Detective?"

"This is Ms. Mack and Mr. Rutkowski. They're helping us on this case. Perez was the officer on duty who found Scanlon," Wallace said in his introduction.

"Was the light on when you found the body?" Charlie asked.

Perez didn't hesitate. "Yes, ma'am. The light was on, and the door was open. I could see her hanging before I stepped into the room."

"I'm sure you didn't disturb anything," Charlie said.

"No, ma'am. At least not much. I cut her down and checked for a pulse."

"Where's the rope you cut?"

"I didn't remove any rope."

Charlie looked up at the dangling noose.

"And you climbed onto the vanity to do that?"

"No. I didn't have to. She wasn't hanging that high. Just lifted her on my shoulder and cut the loop. She was only a couple of feet from the floor."

"A couple of feet?"

"Yes, ma'am."

"What was she wearing?"

Perez closed his eyes for a second. "Black pants, sweater."

"Shoes?" Charlie asked.

"Uh, no. She was barefoot."

"Did you move the stool?"

"Nope. I stepped around it."

"Then there's a problem," Charlie said. "The footstool would be too short for Scanlon to use to hang herself. Not enough force for a broken neck."

"I see what you mean, Mack," Don said. "Maybe she stepped off the bench instead."

"The bench is right where it was when I found her," Perez said.

Wallace dismissed Perez, and Charlie, Wallace, and Don conferred around a Louis XIV desk. Charlie was sure it was a replica, but nonetheless expensive.

"The suicide note was here on the desk. I had it dusted and bagged. We also retrieved a laptop and printer. The desk has already been dusted for prints," Wallace said.

"Can we see the note?" Charlie asked.

"Let's go back downstairs."

Charlie looked over her shoulder as they exited, staring at one large oil painting. She was sure she'd seen the certificate for that painting in the box in Peter's bedroom closet.

A forensic tech knocked at the dining-room door and stepped inside to hand Wallace a plastic evidence bag and three sets of gloves. Wallace removed the eight-by-eleven sheet of white paper and passed it to Charlie who held it in gloved hands. Don leaned to join her in reading the note. It was long—in four paragraph blocks.

As Wallace reported, Scanlon's note implicated Franklin in Peter's accidental death and Caesar Sturdivant in the subsequent cover-up. The note claimed she was desperate, on the verge of bankruptcy as a result of her involvement in Peter's bad business deal. Peter had been dismissive and unsympathetic to her attempts to recoup her investment, saying he had to keep a supply of cash on hand. She'd finally called Franklin and recruited him to help talk some sense into Peter. She'd also asked, as an afterthought, to borrow his gun so she could emphasize to Peter the seriousness of her situation.

Peter had refused her demands and they had argued. When Peter became violent, she tried to lock herself in his bathroom, but Peter had followed and lunged for her. That's when Franklin intervened. As the two men struggled, the gun accidentally discharged. Franklin panicked, fleeing the apartment and leaving the gun behind. Scanlon called upon Sturdivant, who had done some real estate work for her, to help remove incriminating evidence. Somehow the gun was missed.

With the knowledge that Sturdivant had already implicated her in Peter's death, the impending ruin of her finances and reputation, and her own guilt about Franklin's arrest, she saw no other option but to take her own life.

Charlie slipped the note into the plastic sleeve and pushed it to Wallace. Don sat back in his chair and sucked his teeth.

"I hope you're not buying any of that," Charlie stated.

"Nope. It defies logic and the evidence."

"Wallace, you have to arrest Fairchild before he kills somebody else."

"We're getting a warrant now."

Chapter 25

Charlie woke up to gentle nudging. She opened her eyes to a light-filled room and Mandy's face hovering over her. Charlie yawned and stretched.

"I feel so refreshed. I must have slept twelve hours."

"More like five. Serena Carruthers is here."

"Here at the house?"

"Yes."

"What time is it?"

"Eight o'clock. Serena said she called you several times and you didn't pick up. You have a meeting in ninety minutes with Pam Fairchild."

"What?"

"She said you knew about it."

"What day is it?"

"Sunday."

"I did tell her she could schedule the meeting for today, but . . ."

"She said she sent you a message," Mandy said. Her look was quizzical. Not angry but annoyed. "Charlie, if you don't get some rest, you'll get sick. I thought you could stay home today."

"So did I." Charlie tossed bedcovers aside to sit on the edge of the bed. "Do you mind, honey? It won't be a long meeting."

Mandy didn't respond.

"Where is Serena now?"

"In the kitchen. I'm going to make her a cup of tea."

"Okay. Tell her I'll be ready in fifteen minutes."

"You're a suburban cop, right?" Serena asked Mandy, sipping tea. When Mandy gave a look of surprise, she added, "Oh, Detroit is a small big town. Word gets around about everyone and everything."

"What's the word on Charlie being in a lesbian relationship?" Mandy asked directly.

"Surprise. Curiosity. A few snide remarks."

"Which camp are you in?"

"Definitely the curiosity camp. How did you two meet?"

Mandy described her first introduction to Charlie at a fundraising gala for the Police Benevolent Association four years ago. Charlie had been escorted by her already-ex, Franklin, and Mandy was with a male colleague. Their eyes met over the shoulders of their dance partners. Later in the evening Charlie gave Mandy a business card. There was instant chemistry, and a year-long whirlwind romance had followed.

"Last year we both sold our places and bought this home together."

"I don't know Charlie very well. Just through professional circles, but I thought she'd always had relationships with men," Serena noted.

"I'll leave it up to Charlie to tell you about her past relationships. But there *are* people who are bisexual, and have romantic attractions to both women and men."

"I see," Serena said.

"I've been out, meaning an open lesbian, since I was in my late teens," Mandy explained. "Charlie, on the other hand, hasn't really been vocal about her sexual orientation."

Serena nodded. "It's complicated in black communities. Black churches and families don't exactly give the Good Housekeeping seal of approval to homosexuality," Serena said. "Like I said, Detroit's a big town. But it's also parochial about some things. That may be starting to change."

"One would hope so," Mandy said.

"What do you think of Franklin?"

"I've never met him, but Charlie has told me a lot about him."

"Hmm," Serena said. "I dated him a couple of times after he and Charlie got divorced."

"I didn't know that."

"He's a smart, ambitious, successful brother. A lot of women had their eyes on him. It was sort of a surprise when he . . ."

"Fell in love with a white woman?" Mandy finished.

When Charlie stepped into the kitchen, Mandy and Serena were quietly sipping their teas. "So, what have you two been talking about?"

"Would you believe me if I said the weather?" Mandy responded.

"Partly you, Charlie, with a smattering of Franklin," Serena quipped.

Mandy gave a little smile and nod at Serena's joke. Charlie raised an eyebrow in Mandy's direction, and Serena took a last gulp of tea. She stepped down from the counter stool. Her brown heeled boots and purse were of the same butter-smooth leather, and her brown herringbone suit was accessorized with a Chanel scarf. Charlie was the sidekick, in flat boots, black slacks, a turtleneck, and a three-quarter black leather coat.

"Ready to go?" Serena asked. "I'm driving."

"I'm feeling underdressed," Charlie responded.

"You look good. Not like you were up most of the night strategizing with cops."

"She's only had a few hours of sleep in the last twenty-four hours," Mandy said with concern.

"Don't worry. We'll only be a few hours. I'll bring her back to you in one piece," Serena said.

When they arrived at the Fairchild house, a patrol car and a four-door unmarked police vehicle were in the circular drive. Serena parked behind them. Charlie led the way to the side gate and rang the bell. They rang a second time, and a buzzer released the gate. When the front door opened, a visibly upset Pamela Rogers greeted them. She directed them to follow her to the back of the house where they entered the conservatory Judy had raved about. The space really was beautiful. They sat at a table covered in cut flowers.

"Thank you for coming. Both of you," Pamela said, looking at Charlie. "I . . . I'm sorry for my appearance. We've had some hard news. The police are here to question Daddy."

"Does your father have his attorney with him?" Serena asked, going into lawyer mode.

"He's on the way. The police say they only want to clear up some of the false accusations against Daddy."

"I see," Serena said.

"I'm so sorry for the things I said to you," Pamela said, extending her hand to touch Charlie's arm. "Please forgive me. I'm under a lot of pressure."

"I know you are, Pamela, and I accept your apology. This has been very hard on all of us. How is your mother?"

"She's so upset that Daddy sent her to her room."

Serena and Charlie flashed an appalled look at the patriarchal gall in that statement.

"Pamela, why did you want to see us?" Serena asked.

"I want to reinstate you to Franklin's case."

"Franklin has already done that. Didn't he tell you?"

"No. I was only allowed to speak to him for a few minutes," Pamela said sadly. "He was appalled at my behavior toward you, Charlie. I know you meant well in everything you've done. I brought you in to look after Franklin, and that's just what you've done. I don't know what else to say. It's been a living hell for me and my family, but it looks like it's almost over."

"What do you mean?" Serena asked.

"Karen Scanlon's confession. She killed Peter and set up Franklin."

"Who told you that?" Charlie asked.

"Daddy. He says she confessed to the whole thing."

Serena and Charlie shared another glance. They'd discussed the staged suicide and the obviously forged note on the ride to the Fairchild home. Now they both decided to remain silent on the subject.

"Well, that's right, isn't it?"

When Charlie gave no indication she might respond, Serena squared her shoulders and answered.

"The police have reasons to believe Scanlon's suicide note isn't authentic."

Pamela looked between them, searching for the veracity of that statement.

"Tell her the rest," Charlie said. "About the men who tried, again, to kill Franklin."

"Two of the men who tried to get to Franklin's room last night were arrested and questioned," Serena said. "One of them implicates your father and one of his business associates. That man has already signed a statement to that effect."

"You can't be serious. You *still* think my father killed Peter and now is trying to kill Franklin?"

"Pamela," Charlie said with all the sympathy she could muster. "All the evidence points to your father's involvement in Peter's death, the attacks on Franklin, and the killing of witnesses. I don't know what would drive a man of his wealth and influence to behave this way, but he's guilty of these crimes."

Pamela began to cry and then to sob. Neither Charlie nor Serena knew the appropriate thing to say or do. Finally, Charlie stood.

"I have to go home and rest. I was on duty yesterday when those men tried to storm Franklin's room. I had to kill one of them.

You're going to have to make a choice. A hard one. Between your husband, and your father. I'm glad I'm not in your shoes."

Chase, the butler, was nowhere to be seen so Charlie and Serena let themselves out. Serena turned over the engine and let it warm.

"That was some tough love in there, Charlie," Serena said. "She needed to hear it from someone, and it really could only have come from you or her mother."

"I'm too exhausted to be gentle anymore," Charlie said. "I just want to go home now."

"Sit back and relax and enjoy your ride," Serena said, putting the car in gear and coaxing a hum out of the Lincoln.

Chapter 26

On Monday morning Charlie and Don met with Detective Wallace in his office. The three sat at his tiny conference table holding files in their laps. They read the transcript of what was the first of a two-part statement from Stanford Fairchild. His smart lawyers had negotiated the parameters of the interviews. They were taking place at his daughter's home. Second, they could last no more than two hours. Third, they were not being videotaped, although there could be an audio recording.

The transcript began with questions about Fairchild's knowledge of, and association with, persons of interest in the murder investigation of his son. Fairchild claimed to know Karen Scanlon only as a person involved in one of his subsidiaries, and as Peter's friend. He stuck to the story that he'd met the woman only once, and that was at his son's memorial service. He denied knowing Caesar Sturdivant at all and said his business dealings with Robert Madison had been infrequent and a long time ago.

"The next interview is at the end of the week. We have an assistant prosecutor sitting in, and one of our detectives from the Criminal Investigations Unit."

"He's really calling the shots," Charlie noted.

"As you and I knew he would, Ms. Mack."

"You might as well start calling me Charlie, or Mack if you prefer, like Don. I've been spending more time with you recently than at home."

"Well, maybe you can hire me after I'm fired from the department. The chief has already told me my job is on the line." Wallace gave more of a grimace than a smile. Then, in an unusual request, he asked Charlie and Don to participate in Fairchild's second interview.

"Let me think about it, Wallace," Charlie said, "I'd like to look at the witness statements first. How long is Franklin's video?"

"Almost an hour. We can take a look at that now," Wallace suggested.

In the video, Franklin was dressed in a prison-issue blue denim shirt. The strap of a sling crossed his shoulders in the medium-closeup shot. Charlie recognized the wall behind him as the one in his hospital room. He looked tired, had a full beard, and needed a haircut, but was otherwise himself.

The off-camera questioner was Serena. Her first prompt to Franklin was to talk about the day Peter died. Franklin's story didn't hold any surprises as he recounted meeting Peter at Club Lenore and talked about the hours that followed. He described the trip to Peter's apartment and his last memory before he was rendered unconscious.

Peter was sick. About to vomit. I helped him to the bathroom. I didn't hear the noise at the front door, but I felt someone behind me, and before I could turn around, I was hit. I felt my legs turn to rubber, and I blacked out. When I came to and lifted myself from the floor I found the money clip. I didn't pick it up at first. I was confused and groggy. Then I saw part of the bathroom wall through the partially open door. I could see the blood. Then I saw Peter.

Franklin's head fell to his chest, and he wiped at his eyes. The camera stopped recording. When the tape picked up again, Franklin's face was drawn. Off camera came a question from Serena: *I want to clarify something you said. When you regained consciousness, you were lying on the carpet. You weren't near the bathroom?*

No. I woke up in the living room area. Someone must have dragged me to the carpet. But then I made my way to the bathroom door. I was just standing there staring at Peter's body and . . . and all the blood.

Serena prompted again: *Tell me more about the money clip.*

I knew it belonged to my father-in-law. I'd seen him pull it out of his pocket many times to tip a maître d', or when he was buying some bigwig a drink. It was sort of buried in the rug. I was lying on top of it when I came to. The imprint of the dollar sign had left an indentation on my arm. The money clip is very distinctive, made of dozens of tiny diamonds.

Franklin described fleeing Peter's apartment without any idea where he was going. He didn't know how long he walked before he decided to go to his father's church. He had a key to the building and stayed there until the next morning when he went out to buy a coffee. Peter's murder, and Franklin's status as the primary suspect, was top news on the TV at the coffee shop. When the story mentioned his gun being found at Peter's apartment, he realized he was being set up.

I never use my gun except at the range. It's for home protection. It's kept in a locked safe in my den.

The tape ended after Franklin described surrendering himself to Charlie, and recounted the gun attack that left him wounded, hospitalized, and arrested.

"That's pretty straightforward," Charlie said.

"I agree. We transported Rogers to Ionia immediately after the video was shot. He's been checked in under an alias. We probably can't keep his identity hidden for long, but he's safe for now."

Charlie nodded. "Can we look at the statements of the hospital shooters now?"

Both shooters admitted to being paid by an intermediary of Canadian businessman Robert Madison. One of them had been involved in the attack on Franklin as he exited the apartment complex on West Grand Boulevard with Charlie, and the other had taken the potshot at Don in Toronto. Both had worked with another man involved in the hospital attack. One of the shooters also admitted knowing about an additional assignment. *I heard a guy talk about taking out some woman. There was like, a hit list.*

"Apparently, all these men know each other and Madison," Wallace said. "The two have given us enough that our prosecutors are willing to make some kind of deal with them. I think they'll be solid witnesses."

"Well, that's encouraging," Don agreed.

"So what do you say, Charlie? Will you assist with the Fairchild interview? We only have two hours with the guy, and I want to make every minute count."

Chapter 27

The butler was back on the job, and Charlie felt heady as he escorted her into Pamela Fairchild's home for what she knew would be the final time. The last couple of days had been frantic. Wallace had discovered, and closed, the leak in his office— another detective in his unit. Wayne County prosecutors had cut deals with two of the hospital attackers for hard evidence against Robert Madison, and Madison had been arrested. Now to get Fairchild.

Extra chairs had been brought into the Fairchild family room. Charlie greeted Detective Wallace, a young attorney with the prosecutor's office, and Don who had arrived before her. A police technician stood against the wall. Wallace and the prosecutor sat in armless straight chairs with their backs to the fireplace. Charlie sat next to Don across from Wallace and the young lawyer. The four outsiders faced each other like cowboys in a seated gunfight.

The distance between the chairs didn't facilitate private conversation, so they made small talk about the snow forecast for next week, the uncomfortable chairs, and the Pistons' disappointing season.

"Let's trade seats," Charlie said in a flash of inspiration.

"You mean you want to sit closer to the fireplace?" Wallace asked.

"No. No. What I'm suggesting is you and I sit together."

Wallace looked puzzled.

"I see what you're doing, Mack," Don said. "You're playing a race card."

"Fairchild has already played the race card by framing his black son-in-law for murder. I'm just doubling down. And, besides, this is going to be fun."

Stan Fairchild entered the room followed by an attorney Charlie had seen in the society pages of the *Free Press*, and *Crain's Detroit Business*. He was a law partner in an extremely expensive firm.

Fairchild was dressed as if this was a shareholders meeting in his corporate board room. He scanned his visitors without making eye contact and sat in one of the armchairs. Charlie couldn't help but admire his expensive gray leather shoes. The lawyer sat on the sofa across from his client.

Wallace cleared his throat and signaled to the police technician, who approached Fairchild and waited.

"Like before," Wallace said. "Our technician will need to fit you with a microphone. May he proceed?"

"Yes," Fairchild said. His voice and movements reeked with annoyance.

The technician attached a tiny black lavalier to Fairchild's gray-and-white silk tie. He asked Fairchild to say a few words while he tested the audio levels on a laptop, which sat on the coffee table. He gave the okay sign to Wallace.

"Are you ready to begin?" Wallace asked.

The lawyer interrupted. "Before we do, I'd like to know why Ms. Mack and Mr. Rutkowski are here?"

Charlie shot Don a 'he knows who we are' look. Don responded with a sophomoric smirk.

"I requested their attendance. They've been working with the department on the Peter Fairchild murder case from the beginning. In fact, it was my understanding, from an earlier conversation with Mrs. Rogers, that it was Mr. Fairchild who suggested bringing in the Mack agency."

Very smart, Wallace, Charlie thought, giving a slight smile to the attorney.

Fairchild's response was an almost imperceptible glint of anger directed at Charlie. It was so slight that probably no one else in the room saw it, but Charlie recoiled as if a finger had been pointed in her face.

"Well it's highly unusual," the attorney said.

"I agree. But I believe this is a highly unusual situation," Wallace countered, "and we're following the parameters your client set for this set of interviews."

The young prosecutor also weighed in on the issue. "There was no mention of who could, or couldn't, be involved in questioning Mr. Fairchild in his interview."

The high-priced attorney knew he had been outsmarted. He nodded to Fairchild and adjusted his posture on the sofa.

"May we begin? Our two hours don't start ticking until we're recording," Wallace said.

"Yes, yes. Let's just get this over with," Fairchild said with a wave of his hand.

Wallace nodded to the tech, who leaned over the mouse and double clicked the record button. Charlie saw the reflection of an illuminated red light.

"This is Detective Maynard Wallace of the Detroit Police Department's Homicide Division. I am with Stanford Fairchild; his attorney, Martin Conway; Wayne County Prosecutor Daniel DePriest; and Charlene Mack and Donald Rutkowski of Mack Private Investigations. I am conducting the last part of a two-part interview with Mr. Fairchild of Palm Beach, Florida, in case number 45767889, an investigation into the death of Mr. Peter Fairchild. It is 10:33 a.m. on Thursday, February 21, 2008."

Wallace began the questioning with statements made in Franklin's hospital deposition.

Fairchild deflected, denied, and dismissed the questions with short answers.

"Despite what Franklin says, I really think the evidence speaks for itself," Fairchild finally said.

"What was your relationship with your son-in-law?" Wallace asked.

"I don't know what you mean."

"How well did the two of you get along?"

"We were cordial."

"Would you say you had a friendship with Mr. Rogers?"

Fairchild gave a quick glance at Charlie, then his attorney.

"Please answer the question," Wallace said.

"No. He wasn't what I'd call a friend. But we spent time together during family affairs, and holidays, and such."

"Were you aware Mr. Rogers kept a handgun in the house?"

"Yes, I was aware that he had a gun for protection."

"Did you have access to that gun?"

"No."

"Do you know who did have access?"

"Well, other than Franklin, I imagine Pamela knew where the gun was kept."

"But you didn't know where it was kept?"

"I believe the gun was kept in a safe."

"Okay. Now I'd like to have your reaction to information we received earlier in the week."

Fairchild looked bored. He crossed one leg over the other and drank water from the crystal goblet on the table next to him. He cleared his throat.

"Now we know you may balk at this next question, and call it attorney-client privilege, but we have filed for an exemption here," Wallace said to Fairchild's attorney. "A deposition by Caesar Sturdivant's attorney indicates that you met with his client the day before your son's murder. Is that true?"

Fairchild's attorney made a note, but said, "You may answer the question, please, Mr. Fairchild."

"I don't know this Sturdivant person, and I've never met with him."

"In a direct conversation with Mr. Rutkowski, a Toronto police

215

detective, and his attorney, Mr. Sturdivant claims you paid him several thousand dollars to assist in the murder of Peter Fairchild. Do you have any comment about that?"

"That's absurd. I am not involved in my son's murder. In fact, I'm aware that you're in possession of a note from Ms. Scanlon implicating Franklin in a horrible accidental shooting and cover-up."

Fairchild's snobbery and finger-pointing angered Charlie, so she fired the next accusation.

"Sturdivant confessed on his death bed that you paid him five thousand dollars in cash to work with Karen Scanlon."

"Why would I possibly do that?" Fairchild raised his voice. "I told you I don't know Sturdivant, and I barely knew the Scanlon woman."

Fairchild lifted his glass for another swallow of water. They were getting to him.

"Your money clip was found at Peter's apartment. Franklin recovered it when he regained consciousness," Charlie pressed.

"What does that prove?" the high-priced attorney interjected. "That clip could have been dropped at any time. Peter might have been the one to drop it, or maybe Mr. Fairchild left it there during a visit."

Fairchild smiled smugly.

"Mr. Fairchild," Wallace said. "Perhaps you're unaware that one of the men arrested in the planned hospital attack against Franklin Rogers says he was hired by a business associate of yours. Robert Madison."

Fairchild's attorney, with a nervous look, jotted a note.

Wallace had been playing with Fairchild the way a cat swipes at a captured mouse. They'd all discussed how satisfying it would be to let Fairchild think his money and power could subvert justice. The plan was to string Fairchild along with questions that no longer mattered. Listen to his answers filled with lies and omissions. Then go in for the kill.

Days before, Robert Madison had laid out the whole plan, naming Fairchild as the architect in a conspiracy to kill his son and later those who could implicate him. Madison had the recorded conversations to prove it. It was Madison who had hired the men who killed Scanlon and faked her suicide, who bribed a Toronto prison guard to deliver a knife to an inmate in Sturdivant's cell block, and who failed in two attempts on Franklin's life.

Wallace, the department, and prosecutors had all the evidence they needed to separate Fairchild from his money, his business, and the reputation he'd spent all his life flaunting in the faces of those he considered lesser. Those people included Franklin and, sadly, his own son.

"Why did you hate your son?" Charlie asked, startling the room.

Fairchild's face shifted from cool boredom to vein-pulsing furious. "How dare you speak to me that way, you . . ."

"Careful, Stan," the attorney said, leaning toward his client.

"How dare *you*, sir," Charlie said. "Admit it. Peter never lived up to your standards. He confided to many people that he could never earn your love."

"That's enough, Ms. Mack," Fairchild's attorney said.

"No. It's not nearly enough. Not when men like your client are so self-important, so egotistical, so manipulative, they believe they have the power of life and death."

Charlie returned her ire to Fairchild. "No matter what Peter did to please you, it was never enough. He wasn't like you. He wasn't hard and efficient and as shrewd as you. You would rather see him dead than be embarrassed by him again. What did he do this time? Did he ask one of your friends for money? Use your name to gain some favor without telling you?"

Fairchild flushed red with rage. He stood, shaking, and his hands tightened into fists. Charlie stood too, and out of the corner of her eye she saw the sudden movement. There was no time to react as Sharon Fairchild slipped through the door with the fleetness of a cheetah and crossed the room to her husband's side. The sound of the shot and the flash were simultaneous. Wallace, Charlie, and Don sprang toward the woman. But they weren't fast enough to

217

grab the gun before a second shot rang out. Charlie grasped Sharon's arm and wrenched the pistol from her shaking hands as Pamela rushed in from the private quarters.

When Sharon's knees buckled, Charlie and Pamela caught her before she crumpled to the floor. Pamela supported her mother— half walking, half carrying her to the couch. The shocked attorney, immobilized during the shooting, stood to make space for the two women.

Don and Wallace grabbed Stan Fairchild, putting pressure on his wounds and finally cutting off a spurting vein in his arm with his tie.

"Ambulance," Wallace shouted to the tech.

"Blanket," Don shouted to the butler.

Holding the gun, Charlie sat in one of the straight chairs. On one side of the stately living room, Peter Fairchild's mother cascaded in grief and sobs. Across from her, Peter's father fought for his life.

Chapter 28

Serena, Charlie, Don, and Judy met with Detective Wallace at police headquarters two days later. The response to the revelations surrounding Peter Fairchild's murder left the city in a swirl of attention from the media, the governor's office, and Detroit's business and civic leaders. The Detroit police were praised by national television networks for their dedication and tenacity in finding the truth in a case of power versus justice.

A statement from the Fairchild family, delivered by their personal attorney, asked for privacy so they could deal with the triple tragedies of Peter's death, Stanford's arrest and injuries, and Sharon's admittance to a nearby respite facility.

"Mrs. Fairchild isn't being charged in the shooting," Wallace announced.

"You think that's right?" Serena asked.

"Yes. And I got that word passed down to me from upstairs. So it doesn't matter if I think it's right or not. Fairchild is recovering from his gunshot wounds, and he's not pressing charges against his wife. We're focusing on bigger issues."

"The brass aren't backing down on Fairchild, are they?" Charlie asked.

"No. Just the opposite. With all the problems we've had in the department the last few years, everyone agrees we should go after Fairchild with all our resources. The chief, the county prosecutor, the mayor's office, even the feds agree. Travers is leading the task force."

"The feds are involved?" Judy asked.

"Yes. The criminal activity in Canada is under federal jurisdiction."

"And my friend, Captain Travers, is coming out of hiding to take control of the investigation. How big of him," Charlie said sarcastically.

"It will be another feather in his cap," Wallace said.

"And Franklin?" Serena asked.

"Your client will be transported back to the city today. He'll be brought here to headquarters. He's still being charged with obstruction of justice, and there's a warrant for evading police hanging over him. But he can do a bond hearing today and be out this afternoon."

"We'll be fighting the obstruction charge," Serena said matter-of-factly.

"Of course you will, counselor," Wallace replied.

"What are the charges against Fairchild?" Don asked.

"So far there are four counts of conspiracy to commit murder, with additional counts if we get valid evidence on the attack on Don in Toronto, and the first attack on Rogers outside of your mother's apartment, Ms. Mack."

"What about obstruction?" Serena asked.

"Yes. Obstruction, bribery, and maybe a few other things."

"When he gets well enough, he'll fight you tooth and nail," Charlie said.

"That's already begun. Fairchild's lawyers are already in full battle gear."

"They'll still be litigating this case five years from now," Serena predicted.

Franklin called Charlie at home asking to meet with her. When she left the house that afternoon it was with the promise that she and Mandy would take a weekend trip to Florida to soak up some sun and relax together. The last-minute plane fares would be expensive, but Charlie was receiving a nice bonus from Serena Carruthers, thanks to the retainer from Pamela Fairchild.

Franklin's mother answered Charlie's ring at the door and gave her a long, warm hug before Franklin escorted Charlie to his father's study. A large desk sat heaped with papers, Bibles, a large monitor, and a computer keyboard. The exes faced each other in two large leather chairs in front of the desk. Charlie had been in this room one other time, when Pastor Rogers consulted with them on the sanctity of marriage.

"I want to thank you for everything, Charlie," Franklin said, smiling. "You found me and saved me."

"There were a lot of people on your side. And now you have Serena. In my opinion, she's the best lawyer you could have to fight the charges against you."

"I agree."

Franklin's arm wound had healed, he was clean-shaven again, and he'd gained back a bit of the weight lost in the stress of being a fugitive and a victim. But he had a sadness that crept into his laugh lines and dulled his eyes. He was still a wounded man.

"How are things with Pamela?"

Franklin shrugged. "I saw her yesterday. We met at Belle Isle and talked in her car for a long time. She's still reeling from the truth about her father and very worried about her mother. There's no happy ending here."

"How *is* Sharon?"

"Depressed. Still recovering at an undisclosed facility. She remembers shooting Stanford, but doesn't remember anything after that. I feel awful for her."

"Does Pamela have any explanation for her father's behavior?"

"Not really." Franklin slid to the edge of his chair and leaned forward. "She's going to leave me, Charlie."

"What?"

"Pamela insists on a separation. She says she needs to focus her energy on her mother's health."

"And her father's defense?" Charlie asked.

221

Franklin nodded. He was crushed with sadness. Like the night they'd met after days of hiding from police. The waves of Franklin's despair touched Charlie over and over as they sat only a few feet from each other.

"She's made a choice," Charlie said.

Franklin reached for Charlie's hand, and their fingers entwined.

"I think I made the wrong choice when I let you go."

"It was more a matter of me letting you go. Remember?"

"I should have fought for us to stay together. To work through our differences."

Charlie released Franklin's hand. "No. It wouldn't have worked. I shouldn't have married you. I apologize for that. I really hadn't accepted myself then. I didn't understand the depth of my feelings for women."

"For Mandy?"

"Yes. For Mandy. I lost myself in the confusion of other people's opinions."

They sat in silence for a few minutes. Two old friends who had loved each other, and let each other go. For all the right reasons.

"What do I do now?" Franklin asked.

"Well, you've come home. Let yourself be taken care of for a while."

Charlie and Mandy dropped Hamm off at Ernestine's apartment before their afternoon flight to Florida. Charlie followed him around the one-bedroom apartment as he sniffed the corners, the carpet, the counters, the patio door. Finally, the two of them sat on the kitchen floor.

"Okay, boy, you're staying with Grandma for a couple of days. You be good now."

"We'll be fine," Ernestine said, laughing. "Your father would be amused to know that I have a forty-pound, four-legged grandson."

"He'll let you know when he's hungry," Mandy said. "Which is all the time. But only morning and evening is good to feed him. All his bowls and food and treats and instructions are in the bag."